DINNER WITH CHURCHILL

A novel

Robin Hawdon

Published by
Llyfrau Cambria Books, Wales, United Kingdom.
Cambria Books is an imprint of
Cambria Publishing Ltd.
Discover our other books at: www.cambriabooks.co.uk

Cover design by Becca Walthall. rebeccawalthall.co.nz
Image credits: Churchill −Yousuf Karsh, Library and Archives Canada, Arch ref. no. R613-566, e010751643. Chamberlain − image is from Alamy. Clouds (background) − image is from FreePik

This story is largely about bravery. It is dedicated to my wife, who is the bravest of the brave.

It is on historical record that, on the evening of October 13th 1939, six weeks after war had been declared on Hitler's Germany, Winston Churchill and Neville Chamberlain, implacable opponents for years over the appeasement issue, met together with their two wives, Clementine and Anne, for a private dinner at Admiralty House, an event which caused ripples throughout Westminster..

Chamberlain was still Prime Minister, but had seen all his efforts to negotiate peace with Hitler shattered. Churchill had been recalled to the cabinet after ten years 'in the wilderness', his dire warnings of the Nazi threat vindicated.

It was the first and only time the four ever met socially alone together. There is no record as to what transpired during that unique evening.

CHAPTER 1

She was a child of the English Lake District. A place where one lives permanently in the shadow of the mountains and the depths of the waters. Such people are doomed to exist with disappointment for the remainder of their lives. Nowhere else on earth compares. Nowhere presents one with such intimate grandeur, such beauty, such ferocity. Nowhere faces one with such jubilation in the joy of the world, and such despair at its cataclysms. Whether one realises it or not, one is on an eternal quest to recapture greatness in life.

At her age of course she never considered such thoughts, not until years later. At the age of sixteen, when virtually all you have known has been the glowering magnificence of the mountains across the lake, and the equal magnificence of the cumulus clouds above, threatening yet more tumultuous rain and wind, you do not analyse your feelings. You simply accept that all such daunting splendour is your due and your inheritance. It is in your bones.

At the age of sixteen all you are interested in is love, and laughter, and the breaking of rules.

Not that Lucy appeared on first encounter to be concerned with any of those things. Few noticed her as they passed by. The villagers knew her well enough, as they knew everyone for miles about in those days, but they never thought of her as anyone other than a familiar teenager amongst all the others who went to the local grammar school, a bus ride away around the lake. If they referred to her at all, it was usually as 'that sweet young baker's daughter', or 'that shy little Armitage girl.'

She wasn't actually little, standing five and a half feet in her stockings, but she gave the appearance of being so, merging into the background as she was so adept at doing. It was only on the hockey pitch or playing basketball in the school gym that she

1

shone, which earned her a modicum of respect amongst her peers, but even they paid her little attention away from those arenas. Like many adolescent teenagers, she was uncertain of her being, unconfident of her personality. The embers of a fire glowed somewhere deep inside her, but they were far from bursting into flame.

Her older brother, Tom, on the other hand, was always noticeable. He stood not far short of six feet, and his broad shoulders, craggy features, and affable smile made him a centre of attention in most companies. Tom had no such inhibitions about putting himself forward, and, on the surface at least, seemed utterly assured of his future and his ambitions. Tom was Lucy's hero, especially as he looked on her as his charge, to be protected against all threats, real and imaginary. The affection between them was one of the guiding lights in Lucy's life.

Another was Tom's best friend, Henry Collins. Henry was almost as impressively built as Tom, and certainly prettier in aspect, with his waving dark hair and wide brown eyes which invited intimacy whenever they engaged with others. It was Henry who first awakened the sexuality in Lucy, for such stirrings came late in young womens' breasts way back in those repressed years between the wars. The stigma of lustful sin, and the hideous threat of unwanted pregnancy was taught in every home and classroom, and thundered from every pulpit in those days. Country lasses especially - who were all too aware of the fecundity amongst the farm animals everywhere about them - were forever wary of the attentions of the opposite sex.

As it was, an early summer evening arrived when the pair found themselves alone together outside the village hall, during a rare birthday party of one of their classmates whose parents had hosted the do. Live music had gladdened the event, and beer and cider had been available in rather unwise quantities. June had been wet and warm, but this evening was pleasantly dry, and the heavens sparkled in their black vault above the peaks. Lucy, as usual a little intimidated by the revelry around her, had wandered out to sit on

2

one of the benches overlooking the lake. She was unaware of Henry's approach until he was sitting beside her.

'Running away from the mob again, Lucy?' he said in his deep voice with its slight Cumberland lilt.

She nodded. Henry, through long acquaintance, was one of the few beings outside her close family with whom she could feel relaxed.

'Bit noisy for me.'

He nodded back at the hall. 'Didn't see you dancing much. None of the lads to your taste?'

She pursed her lips. 'All too familiar, and too tipsy for my liking.'

'Ah, Lucy - when are you going to let your hair down?'

She fingered her straight dark tresses, which were down to her shoulders for the occasion. Thirties Hollywood waves and curls had not yet reached the rural North of England.

'It's down as far as it'll go.'

'You know what I mean.' He put his arm round her in fraternal affection. 'You'd be such a pretty girl if you let yourself.'

'What d'you mean?'

'You know. Open up a bit.'

She was silent. He stared up at the heavens. The half-moon cut a shimmering slice of silver across the black waters of the lake. 'Nice night. Wish it was always like this here.'

'I quite like the rain.'

'In small doses.' He drew back and looked at her. She felt uneasy under his gaze.

'How often you been kissed?' he asked casually.

She blinked her eyelashes at him. 'A few times.' It was a very few actually, but she didn't elaborate.

'That's a shame. Let's make it one more.' And he leant forward and kissed her gently. 'That was nice,' he said, and kissed her again.

3

She didn't resist, although it was such a surprise coming from him. But then he compounded it by slipping a hand into the top of her party dress, and before she was aware of what was happening had cupped her breast in his palm.

She jolted then in surprise, and without thinking slapped him hard on the cheek.

'Wo!' he exclaimed, and withdrew his hand, laughing. 'Sorry. Didn't mean to take you by surprise.'

'Is that what you do every time you kiss a girl?' she asked, eyes flashing.

'Only the ones who have a nice kiss,' he said, nursing his cheek.

'I didn't take you for a seducer, Henry Collins.' She was indignant, but at the same time aware that the feel of his large warm hand on such an intimate part of her had not been unpleasant. 'That's how Amy Little got pregnant.'

He chuckled again. 'Amy Little is a tart. And you don't get pregnant by having your titties touched.'

They were both quiet again. She was assimilating the novel feelings churning inside. What he was thinking she had no idea.

Then he said, 'What d'you think you'll be doing with yourself, Lucy, when you leave school?'

She was taken aback by the question. It would be at least a year before that happened, and in any case it was not often asked of girls then. They were generally expected to seek out an eligible male, get married in good time, and join the production line creating babies - preferably boy babies since the devastation of the male population by the Great War was still in people's minds. The idea of taking a different course was only considered by the minority, and a vaguely suspect minority at that.

'What do you mean, doing with myself?'

'Well, you're a bright girl. You could have a career. A lot of women doing that now. Or are you just thinking of taking over the bakery business?'

She was again silent for several moments. To tell truth she had hardly contemplated the possibility. Although she helped out at the bakery in the early mornings and at weekends, she had always assumed her brother would inherit the business one far-off day when their parents retired from the relentless task of feeding the local population. And as to other possibilities, ambition had not pointed her in any such direction.

'I don't know,' she said. 'Haven't really thought about it.'

'You should do.'

'Why?'

'There are going to be a lot of opportunities for women in the future. Jobs in the cities and all round the empire.'

'The empire?' It was a commonly used term for the vast federation that spanned the globe. She had never considered its potentials, except as spreading pink areas on the geography lessons maps.

'Canada, Australia, South Africa - they're all crying out for qualified people to come and work there. Even India. Think of the adventures.'

'Is that what you're thinking of?'

'Maybe. Not sure yet. There could soon be another war coming. That'll change things.'

'Another war?'

'That's what they're saying.'

She was so ignorant of political affairs. 'Surely not. That would be terrible.'

'It's what the papers are saying. Adolf Hitler's getting too big for his boots. Anyway, that will bring more chances for women. They'll be needed to fill the gaps if the men are off fighting.'

Something opened in Lucy's mind, a small window to a wider horizon. 'Will that really change things?'

'Of course. For everyone.' He brushed a lock of his thick hair back from his eyes. 'Tommy and me are thinking of joining the

5

army actually.'

She turned her head and stared at him. 'Lord, Henry - why would you want to do that?'

He shrugged. 'It's a good career, the army. And if there's a war we'd probably be called up anyway, so it'd be clever to get ahead of the pack.'

'But you...? I mean, why...?' She did not know how to respond. This new scenario was too big to be absorbed.

A voice came from behind. 'What are you two doing, sneaking off from the do?' Her brother Tom appeared, beer glass in hand, and stood beside the bench, his substantial figure outlined against the night.

'Just talking,' replied Henry. 'Discussing how girls get pregnant.'

'Oh, that.' Tom sat next to Lucy on the bench. 'One of the mysteries of the world, that. Don't tell Lucy. She might never recover from the shock.'

She punched him in the chest. 'Don't be a ninny.'

'Well, there could well be a few cases after tonight,' he said, taking a swig from his beer. 'It's getting quite steamy back there. A lot of girlfriend swapping going on.'

'Who?' asked Henry. 'Anyone chasing your Jenny?'

Jenny Conway had been Tom's unofficial girlfriend for six months or so. A pretty, fair-headed girl with green eyes and an infectious laugh, who was in his sixth form class at school and would also be leaving later that year. Lucy could see why Tom was attracted to her, and doubtless the feeling of breasts, and conceivably even more than breasts, was part of the arrangement, but she didn't like to picture such things. She wasn't sure how intelligent Jenny was. She didn't think it would last, but she would never say so to her revered brother.

'Oh, she's flirting with George Smithers,' Tom was saying. 'But then she's always flirting with someone. If you could get pregnant by flirting she'd have triplets by now.'

6

Henry laughed, but Lucy had more serious things on her mind. 'Is it true you're thinking of joining the army, Tommy?'

He glanced at his friend. 'What have you been saying, Henry?'

'Just mentioned it. We were talking careers.'

'Are you serious about it?' she asked.

He stared into his glass. 'Just considering it.'

'Have you told Mum and Dad?'

'No. And don't you either. It'd cause a scene. Haven't made up our minds yet, have we Henry?'

'No.'

'But what...? I mean, what would happen to the bakery?' Tom often helped with deliveries from the shop, unofficially driving its rattling Ford van around the various outlying cafés and hotels.

'What d'you mean, what would happen? It'll go on as always. Mum and Dad and you can handle it. Bring in people from the village at peak times like always.' He threw her a glance. 'I certainly don't intend to end up as a baker.'

'What's wrong with that? Good enough for Dad and his dad.'

'Not for me. Serving buns and pork pies to tourists and the greedy folk of the Lakes for the rest of my life is not my idea of fulfilment.'

'I thought you were going to try for university.'

'Might still. Depends on how things go.'

The sound of music and laughter spilled from the hall behind them.

'Well,' said Henry, rising from the bench. 'Better get back to the fight. See if there's anyone left for me to have a jig with.'

'Go for it,' said Tom. 'Just don't get her pregnant.'

Lucy punched him again, as Henry left and sauntered back towards the party.

7

CHAPTER 2

The bakery was a long low extension to the Armitage home, itself a three bedroomed cottage set on the fringe of the village behind a sheep-dotted field stretching down to the lake shore. The building was probably over two hundred years old - no one knew for certain - and, built as it was of solid granite slabs and slate roof, would likely last for another two hundred. Little had changed during that time, except for the replacement of window frames and oak front door, and the addition of a modern bathroom tacked on at the back. The bakery itself, once just an adjoining animal shed, was the largest room in the whole place. The ovens were ranged along the back wall, shelves along the sides, and a long timber counter splitting the area in two - work space behind, customer space before. Its output was prodigious, ranging from loaves of various shapes and sizes, to buns, scones, Eccles cakes, pies, and even the occasional specially commissioned decorated cake for birthdays and anniversaries. The former were turned out in their daily dozens, the latter were rare, since the nation was just recovering from its post-war austerities, and both money and exotic ingredients were hard to come by.

In winter the shop was a favourite meeting place for folk from far around, since the roaring ovens made it the warmest place in the village. In summer, the opposite prevailed, when customers dashed in and out as hastily as possible to escape the oppressive heat. Lucy's father, Fred Armitage, reigned stolidly over his small domain in all temperatures and all weathers. People said that his amply upholstered form insulated him from such, but his ruddy features betrayed their exposure to decades of fires and vapours, and he carried with him a permanent fragrance of freshly grounded flour.

Her mother too, although built on slighter dimensions, was a regular custodian of the shop counter, and adviser on all things wheaten. The pair knew everyone in the village and beyond. Fred was a gruff, taciturn character who disdained small talk, but his wife Minnie was a petite bundle of congeniality. She was confidante and commiserater to all and sundry, and there was very little of local gossip that she did not know about.

Lucy herself helped at the early morning baking sessions virtually every day before going to school, and assisted with the baking and delivering at weekends. In holiday periods, when the tourists and fell walkers flooded into the legendary neighbourhood, demand for produce was high amongst the local cafés and guest houses, and the bakery was at full stretch. It was a thriving business.

It was two days after the party, early on the Monday morning, that found Lucy in her usual place beside her father, wearing her apron and thick oven gloves, taking the trays of freshly baked loaves to the various shelves as he shovelled them from the brick ovens. She and her mother chatted as they worked, whilst her father rolled, pounded and heaved, and muttered instructions to himself. It was then that Lucy made the error that dogged her for a long time after.

'Did you know Tommy was thinking of joining the army, Ma? What d'you think of that?'

Both parents stopped what they were doing and stared at her.

'What?' growled her father.

'The army?' said her mother. 'When did he tell you that?'

Their looks of dismay warned Lucy, and she remembered too late her brother's instruction to keep it a secret.

'Oh. I shouldn't have said. It was just a vague idea between him and Henry.'

'When did he say that?' demanded Fred. Lucy adored her father, but rather at a distance. She was ever a little in awe of his sharp temper and definitive political views, and their relationship was a delicate one.

'The other night, at the party. I don't think they were serious.'

'They better not be.' Her parents exchanged glances. 'Not the place to be for a bright lad.'

'Isn't it?'

'Not any more. Not just swanning around playing in bands in smart uniforms these days. You're just cannon fodder.' Fred Armitage's two elder brothers had both been killed in the Great War, one at Passchendaele, the other at the Somme. His own parents had never recovered from their grief.

'Is there another war coming then?' Lucy asked, as she arranged a tray load of wholemeal buns along a cooling shelf.

There was no immediate answer. She turned to her mother with raised eyebrows. At that moment the shop door pinged, and old Mrs Tomlinson, the ex-postmistress entered. She was an early riser and invariably one the first customers to arrive.

Minnie Armitage turned to serve her, saying, 'Is there going to be another war, Ada? What do you think?'

The old woman, well into her seventies now, but still alert, said, 'It's what they're sayin'. Can't credit it, can you, God help us. Not after the last lot.' Ada too had lost a son in the trenches. 'But Winston's bin bellerin' again about rearming.'

Fred growled from the ovens. 'He's always bellering about rearming. He's as bad as Hitler. Needs to keep his mouth shut. Pair of warmongers, both of 'em.'

The name of Winston Churchill had provoked fiercely divided opinions across the land for several decades.

Lucy's mother sighed. 'Well, I don't know. I sometimes think the world is mad. The usual, Ada?'

'Small loaf and three of your Eccles cakes, please, Minnie. And get ready to do a million pork pies for the troops.' Ada cackled then, and the atmosphere lightened. She glanced at Lucy, who had been listening to the exchange. 'And what about you, young Lucy? Fancy yourself in nurse's uniform lookin' after all the young men, eh?'

Lucy smiled shyly. 'I hope it doesn't happen.'

'Ay well, that's what we all hope. Meanwhile you just look to your lessons. We need smart young women these days.' And she gathered her purchases and waddled off to her tiny cottage in the high street, which she and previous generations had occupied for most of their lives.

Fred dumped another tray of loaves onto the work surface. 'I need to have a word with that son of mine,' he muttered.

'Don't be cross with him, Dad,' said Lucy, conscience-stricken. 'It wasn't serious. I shouldn't have said anything.'

But, serious or not, it caused a storm later that day. She was back from school and changing out of her uniform up in her small bedroom with its serene views across the lake, when she heard the shouting going on downstairs. She couldn't make out the words, but her father's and brother's voices were clear enough in fierce altercation, with her mother's softer tones intervening spasmodically in an effort to keep the peace.

Lucy herself couped the aftermath before supper, when she came down to the kitchen and found Tom there.

'Thanks, Lucy. Really landed me in it there,' he growled as he threw cutlery onto the table.

'Sorry, Tommy. It just slipped out. I didn't mean to tell them.'

'Caused one hell of a row, and they're not done yet, damn you.'

A tear gathered in the corner of her eye. 'I'm sorry.' She brushed it away, took some dishes from the dresser and helped him set the table. 'Would it be such a bad thing, you joining the army?'

He banged down a jug of water. 'Dad thinks so. You've heard him talk about the last war. But it's not a bad career, especially if you make officer's rank. You have responsibilities, you get to travel around the country. Maybe abroad. There's British soldiers in every corner of the empire.'

'Would you like to go abroad?'

"Course I would. See the world. Who wouldn't?'

11

'There are scary places.'

'Oh, Lucy, don't be so timid. There's more to life than baking buns. And next time keep your blurry mouth shut.'

There was a sullen silence over supper that evening. It extended for several days, occasionally erupting into more arguments. Tom took to staying out of the way as much as possible, and Lucy withdrew into her shell. The seams of the tightly bonded Armitage household were splitting a little.

She did not see Henry Collins again for a couple of days. Then one morning he stopped her as they were passing each other in the school corridor.

'Tommy and me are catching the bus into Keswick on Saturday to go to the cinema. He's bringing Jenny. Why don't you come?'

She hesitated. She loved the cinema, but she was wary of his intentions.

'I'll see,' she said, and went on to her classroom, heart beating a little bit faster.

Later, back home, she said to her brother, 'Henry's asked me if I want to come with you to the cinema on Saturday.'

'Yes,' he said. 'He asked me if I minded.'

'What's the film?'

' "All Quiet On The Western Front." '

'Isn't that a war film?'

'That's why we want to see it. See what it's like being in the army. Supposed to be the best war film ever, but we were all too young to watch it when it came out. They're having a special showing.' He shrugged. 'It's probably not a girlie sort of thing.' He stole a sideways look at her. 'Do you want to come?'

'Maybe. You're bringing Jenny?'

'Yeh. We'd make a foursome.' He added, 'Mum and Dad won't mind if you're with us.'

'I'll see.'

12

She was playing reluctant, but she knew in her heart that she would go. There was a small flutter in the back of her mind for the rest of the week.

When Saturday came, the four of them boarded the bus after lunch, and it wound its way through the country lane, with the glowering heights of Helvellyn on one side and the long, lazy stretch of Thirlmere on the other, to the largest town in the Lakes.

They were lucky to get cinema seats. The Alhambra was one of the earliest picture houses in the country, and the golden age of cinema ensured that it was regularly filled, especially on weekends and rainy days. This was a weekend, and the weather cloudy, but they got into the queue relatively early and were able to get four seats some way back in the stalls. Half of Keswick was crowded in, and the place buzzed with chatter.

It was the era, not only of remarkable film making, but also of newsreels reporting the world's affairs, and of cartoons and short comedy items, all crammed into a single programme. A visit to the cinema was a major entertainment event.

Lucy sat beside Henry with her view of the screen partly obscured by the massed heads in front, and the familiar anticipation bubbling inside her. The fare that day was the usual Gaumont British News - pulsating with stories of the Duke of Windsor on honeymoon with his newly married wife, Mrs Simpson, and with Germany's continued buildup of armaments. It was followed by a Bugs Bunny cartoon, and a Charlie Chaplin short. Finally came the main feature.

Nearly two hours later the foursome came out of the cinema and made their way wordlessly down to their favourite café. They found a corner cubicle and ordered its speciality, 'Sos'n'mash' - pork sausages, mashed potatoes, and gravy that looked like melted chocolate.

Jenny was the first to speak, her green eyes clouded. 'I don't ever want to see a film like that again.'

The boys remained silent. Lucy said, 'It was horrible. Those poor men.'

Certainly the film had portrayed the horrors of war with graphic realism. The indescribable squalor of life in the waterlogged trenches, the pointless slaughter of young manhood marching into the machine guns' hail, the desecration of entire landscapes. It had been almost unendurable to watch. The two boys, almost men themselves, glanced at each other but said nothing.

Lucy looked at her brother. 'Surely you're not going to join up after seeing that?'

He stared down at the table top. 'It's not like that now. They'll never fight wars like that again.'

'How do you know? How else can they fight them?'

'Future wars will be fought with tanks, and artillery, and planes. They'll never do those suicidal full front attacks again. There was too much criticism of High Command after all that.'

'Even so...'

Tom took a deep breath. 'I dunno, Luce. I mean, you more or less have to, don't you? How else do you stop evil people taking over the world?'

'It doesn't mean *you* have to. There's lots you can do to help. Bakers and farmers and... all sorts of people are needed to keep the country going without having to go away and fight.' She looked at Henry, who was also contemplating the wooden table top. 'What do you say, Henry?'

He looked up. 'Someone has to fight.'

'But why you? And why join up now? There isn't even a war yet.'

He shrugged and said nothing.

Jenny chipped in. 'You boys. You just like the idea of fighting. It's the whole stupid manly thing.'

Henry glowered. 'No, it's not. It's much more than that.'

'How? Why? What else is it?'

'It's... well, it's defending your country. It's...'

14

'You shouldn't have to defend it. Countries shouldn't be attacking other countries.'

'Of course not, but... they do.'

Her voice became more strident. 'It's all because of bloody men trying to prove how tough they are. When will they ever stop?'

Lucy looked at her brother. 'Is that what it is, Tommy?'

He stared out of the café window at the busy street outside. 'No, it's not that.'

'What is it then?'

'It's king and country, isn't it? It has to be king and country.'

CHAPTER 3

That summer was one of the hottest on record across the land. Holiday makers flocked to the Lakes. The waters and the hills slumbered in the warmth and absorbed the coachloads, the walkers and the sailers without a murmur. The locals grumbled about the influx of alien intruders, but took their money all the same. The bakery was working at full tilt all summer long.

The two Armitage offspring and Henry Collins all ended their school education that July, and took a few weeks holiday before embarking on adult life. The family strife had continued concerning army signups, but since Hitler's preparations for the invasion of Czechoslovakia had made it evident that war was on the horizon, the parental protests dwindled in the face of the inevitable. The grim headlines on the front pages contrasted with the sunny forecasts within.

Lucy had not seen much of Henry during the last turbulent weeks of exams and school leaving, but remembrance of their brief encounter by the lakeside, and of his brown eyes as he smiled at her, was often in the back of her mind. It was not until they both found themselves sitting together on a hay bale in a large field dotted with tents and pens of bleating animals that they really had the chance to talk again. It was the annual county show, which always attracted crowds from across the region, whether involved with agricultural matters or not.

The pair were watching the junior show jumping competition - mostly young girls on diminutive ponies tackling fences at a suicidal pace, to a chorus of encouraging shouts from doting parents. It was not an activity either of them had ever attempted.

'So, you're away soon for army training?' she said, her face turned up to the August sunshine.

'Mhm. Next month. Off to Catterick.'

'Are you nervous?'

'It's tough training, but I'm looking forward to it.'

'Do you think you'll get to be an officer?'

He shrugged. 'It's easier these days to come up through the ranks. Tommy and I both want to try, but... we'll have to wait and see.'

They were silent for a while as they watched the event. A small girl who looked as if she had just left junior school fell off a Shetland pony to a chorus of squeals from the onlookers. She picked herself up in floods of tears, but was otherwise unhurt. The pony cantered off, happily relieved of its burden.

'What about you, Lucy?' he said. 'Have you decided what to do?'

She loosened the top button of her dress in the warmth. 'I think I want to get away from here now. It's time I saw more than mountains.'

'So, what...?'

'I was thinking of going to a secretarial college. If you have those skills you can work anywhere.'

He grinned. 'Good for you. What do the parents say?'

'I haven't told them yet. They're still upset about Tommy leaving. If I tell them I am too they're going to be distraught.'

'You have to make your own life, Lucy.'

She nodded, and picked a daisy that was growing by her feet. She twirled the small flower in her fingers. 'I'm not sure where to go though. I'm still too young for adult college. I thought maybe next year I could go to Liverpool or Manchester. They must have secretarial schools there.'

'Don't go there, Luce. They're pretty grim places. Set your sights higher.'

'How?'

'Go to London.'

She turned her head and stared at him. 'London? How would I

get there?'

'Same as you get anywhere. Just pack a bag and go.' He put his hand over hers. She felt again its hard strength. 'You've never been to London, have you?'

She shook her head.

'I've been twice. You won't believe it. The buildings, the parks, the river, Buckingham Palace. It's so huge you won't know which way to turn. There's so much to do there, so many people. People from all over the empire, people of every colour and creed. And the money! Hotels and restaurants posher than you can imagine. Shop windows that look like Hollywood film sets. Rolls Royces on every street.'

She laughed. 'Sounds too scarey for me, Henry. How would I cope there?'

'Of course you'd cope. You'd soon get into the swing of things. Start going to the clubs where the poshos go. Probably end up married to a duke.'

She giggled again. 'Yes, sure. I doubt I'd get into college there, let alone a night club.'

He thought for a moment. Then he said, 'You know my sister, Liz, is in London.'

Elizabeth Collins was three years older than Henry, working as a receptionist in a law firm. Lucy only knew her as a distant, confident seeming woman, sporting a sophisticated hair style, who spoke in a king's English voice with little trace of her Cumberland accent.

'So?' she said.

'I'm sure she could show you the ropes. Tell you where to go, how to find digs. Why don't I write to her?'

'It's a bit premature, Henry. I wouldn't be going until next year. And then only if Mum and Dad agree.'

'No, but when the time comes.' He grinned mischievously. 'Then I'd have an excuse to come to London too when I'm on leave. And you'll be old enough for night clubs, and a proper kiss and titty fondle.'

She slapped his arm. 'The sooner you get in the army and learn some discipline the better, Henry Collins.'

They didn't speak much more after that, but it left her with her brain churning.

The year passed in a contrasting succession of unusually fine days and increasingly dark news stories. The nation indulged itself with the pleasures of the jazz age whilst enduring the privations of urgent recruitment and rearmament. It was clear that the relaxation of defence measures after the termination of hostilities twenty years previously had been a mistake. The 'war to end all wars' was proving a delusion. Man's proclivity for murderous confrontation would, it seemed, outlast all experience, however harrowing.

The two boys, along with thousands of others, went off to the huge training camp in Yorkshire to familiarise themselves with the art of slaughter, and the young women adapted to new ideas about employment. There were large gaps left vacant in the trades and professions.

Lucy mourned the absence of Henry as much as her brother, but now she had other matters on her mind. Late one morning in the April of 1938 she was alone with her mother in the shop, arranging the products from the early morning's bakery shift. Her father was off in the van doing the first delivery round.

'Mum, what do you think about me doing a secretarial course?' Lucy tossed the question in casually whilst arranging sausage rolls, still warm, in the counter display case.

Her mother placed her work-worn hands on the bench top and stared. 'Where did that idea come from?'

'I've been thinking about it for a while.'

Minnie Armitage went back to kneading dough, ready for the afternoon's bake, and was silent for a long moment. Lucy began to fear another confrontation similar to that with her brother. But then her mother said as she picked up a rolling pin, 'Well, it would open doors for you, Luce. I never got the chance, but I've always thought you were too clever to be baking bread all your life.'

Lucy turned to her and smiled, a smile of relief. 'How do you think Dad would take it?'

'Oh, you leave that to me. I'd break it to him gently.'

'I'd be leaving you both on your own.'

'Well, it's the modern way, isn't it? Families don't stick together the way they used to. Where are you thinking of going?'

'London.'

Her mother really did stop working then, her eyebrows risen as high as they could reach. 'London?'

'It's where all the best opportunities are. Henry's sister Elizabeth is there, and he says she could help me find somewhere to live. There are dozens of colleges in London.'

'I don't know if we could afford sending you there.'

'There are governments grants. I might even get a free course. I could work evenings. They must have bakeries in London.'

Minnie put a hand on her hip. 'You've worked it all out, haven't you?'

'I've been thinking about it.'

Her mother's eyes beneath the lined forehead were wistful. 'Well, to be sure I don't want you married to a sheep farmer or shovelling bread loaves for the rest of your life. You're worth more than that.'

Things seemed to gather pace at an accelerating rate after that. The preparations for war, the ending of summer, the flurry of college applications, all seemed to be hurtling Lucy on an unstoppable path. Henry's sister Elizabeth provided the required guidance for life in the vast capital, and so it transpired that, five months after the conversation with her mother, Lucy suddenly found herself there for the first time, enrolled in the Mayfair Secretarial College, and sharing a small attic room in a nearby hostel with an intense bespectacled girl from Ipswich, with whom she had nothing in common whatsoever. A change in circumstances could rarely have been more radical.

CHAPTER 4

London had been all that Henry had described. The immensity of its scale - in borders, in buildings, in parks, in population - was something that Lucy had never conceived. For the first few weeks there she had wandered in a daze. She rarely ventured far beyond the hostel, the bus route to the college, situated in the most affluent part of the city's West End, and the classrooms of the college itself. Loneliness and homesickness were her companions.

But gradually she became more bold, and began exploring further afield. At weekends she took solitary bus rides to the various semi-rural suburbs – Chelsea, Hampstead, Wimbledon. She roamed the parks and commons, admired the historic village high streets, treated herself to café teas. Once she took the underground to the East End and Docklands, where she gazed in wonderment at the squalid acres of slums bordering the turgid river Thames. Another time she found herself rambling the profusely flowering acres of Kew Gardens, the world's most illustrious botanical laboratory. The city was ever a revelation and an education.

As for the Mayfair Secretarial College, housed in a large Victorian house fronting a street close to tree-lined Hyde Park, it was there that the education expanded to the myriad aspects of the secretarial profession. Not only the essential shorthand and typing, but the proper layout and headings of countless letter styles, the phraseology of addressing persons of every vocation and social level, the syntax of properly worded official papers, and finally the modes of dress and hairstyle adopted by clerks to the movers and shakers of the British Empire - rocking on its foundations though that mighty edifice may have been. She quickly learnt to lose her Cumberland accent, after initial mockery from her fellow students and raised eyebrows from the imperious staff. Secretaries in the capital were presumed to be the epitome of British formality in every detail.

It was after ten months of the tutelage, with the world now tottering on the cliff edge, when she had almost finished the year long course, that the event happened that altered her life beyond all imagination.

The letter 'S' had broken on her typewriter. Such a negligible incident. Yet how ironic that these can change the course of an existence. How paradoxical that large consequences can ensue from such trivial accidents. For it was that small occurrence which led her, a simple baker's daughter from a village on the edge of nowhere, to finding herself in the thick of global events.

Germany, after months of suspense, had invaded Poland. Prime Minister Neville Chamberlain had informed the nation in his despondent tones that it was at war. The country was urgently preparing for the imagined invasion of Teutonic legions and the onslaught of gargantuan bombing raids. The long college work day had ended, the early autumn evening was closing in, the students had mostly left the building and scurried through the darkened streets to their various burrows, in constant fear of the promised bomb drops. Lucy however had broken the 'S' key on her battered Imperial typewriter with the sheer force of her speed typing, and had stayed behind to try and replace it from the motley collection of spare parts that the college stored in its many cupboards.

As she tinkered ineptly with the machine, the classroom door opened and Deputy Head Mrs Simms put her head in.

'Has everyone else left?' she asked, scanning the room through steel-rimmed spectacles.

Lucy nodded. 'Yes, Mrs Simms.'

'Lucy Armitage, isn't it?'

'Yes.'

'What is your shorthand speed?'

'Um... two hundred.'

'Typing?'

23

'Seventy... about.'

'That's good enough. I've got a job for you. Emergency.'

Lucy frowned. What kind of emergency could there be at six o'clock on a quiet October evening? 'A job?'

'Yes. I don't know how long for, but you will be paid. You have to go to the Admiralty. I'm authorised to put you in a taxi cab. Someone will pay the cabbie at the other end.' She didn't enquire as to whether Lucy had other plans for the evening, she just assumed that if so they would be abandoned.

Lucy stared at the woman. She had never done a 'job' in her life. At eighteen she had never earned so much as a shilling, except for what her father had slipped her from time to time for helping out at the shop. Girls in the pre-war days considered themselves lucky if they could get a job earning half what most men brought in.

'Don't worry.' Mrs Simms was brusque but not unkindly. 'They want a fast typist, but I imagine it will just be typing out naval orders or instructions of some sort. The navy is in the thick of things in the North Sea. It's the only part of the armed forces that's fighting a war at the moment. You'll handle it all right.' She looked Lucy up and down. 'Not exactly dressed for a government secretary, but you'll do. You can tidy your hair in the cab. Get your coat and hat. Come along.'

As Lucy sat in the back of the vibrating taxi cab – the first time she had ever been in such a vehicle – she with difficulty touched up her chignon and make-up in the small mirror she always carried in her handbag, checked that her blouse and work suit were modestly arranged, and practised in her mind the King's English vowels that had almost completely usurped the rural inflexions of her previous life.

The cab navigated an unusually quiet and darkened Trafalgar Square, its lions huge black silhouettes guarding Nelson's sacred monument, drove down Whitehall past the towering headquarters of government institutions, and pulled up outside the entrance to the equally vast Admiralty building. Two naval ratings in battle dress, surely younger even than Lucy herself, were on guard outside the pillared entrance, surrounded by sand bags and barriers posing as defence against invading German hordes. But it was a tall suited official who emerged from the building and met Lucy as she descended from the cab.

'You're a qualified typist?' he demanded in clipped tones as he paid the taxi driver through the cab window.

'Er... well nearly.'

'Right. Well, we must hurry. The old man's getting rather impatient.'

She didn't think to ask who the old man might be. Her mind was in such a turmoil that she did not dare to enquire about anything at all, for fear of being exposed as completely inadequate to the situation. She simply hurried after his long-striding figure into the depths of the huge complex of offices and state rooms.

Up stairs and along corridors they marched, past open doorways where voices muttered, phone bells rang, and papers shuffled, past blacked-out windows and through echoing halls, where the faces of long dead admirals stared down from stuccoed walls. To Lucy it was as if she had been transported to another world, where every opening revealed unfathomable activities.

Eventually they arrived at a lofty chamber humming with voices and illuminated by flickering lights. Charts covered the major expanses of wall, and several large table maps occupied the central space, around which naval officers prowled, and young women in uniform moved coloured pins and model ships, as if conducting some giant board game. Other personnel muttered together in corners or into telephones. The whole had an air of intense and secretive suspense.

'The Map Room,' commented her escort. 'We go this way.' He continued striding through towards a door at the far end. 'He likes to work in more secluded surroundings.'

He opened the door and ushered her in. It was a much smaller office, where stood a heavy mahogany desk, an array of filing cabinets, and another large map laid out on a table spanning half the width of the room.

Three men were present, two in the uniforms of high-ranking naval officers, and one, with his back turned, wearing what seemed of all things to be a form of striped boiler suit. A naval uniformed girl was listening to a telephone, and another was sticking coloured pins into the map. The air was filled with murmured voices and cigar smoke.

Lucy's escort coughed politely and said, 'The typist is here, sir.'

The naval officers looked up, the boiler-suited man turned around, cigar in mouth. Lucy blinked and froze, shocked into paralysis.

He was shorter than she had imagined. His stocky form gave the impression of a solid fixture that hurricanes would find hard to unbalance. His instantly recognisable face had a slightly cherubic aspect. His pale blue eyes stared at her over his oval lenses for fully five seconds before he spoke. Then he took the cigar from his mouth.

'Have you got a note-pad?' No greeting, no introduction. His voice was deep in his throat as if a handful of sand was lodged there. His face showed neither disapproval, cordiality, nor curiosity.

Her brain kicked into action. 'Um... no, sir, I didn't have time to... I didn't know what was...'

'Heavens above – someone give the girl some tools.'

One of the WRNs passed Lucy a pad and pencil. Lucy took them in hand automatically.

'Are you ready? You can sit if you wish. There's a lot to record.'

'Um...' She looked hastily around, and grabbed a wooden chair beside the table.

'Take this down precisely as I speak, and then someone will show you a typewriter where you can type it out. As speedily as possible.'

'Yes, sir.' She hurled her brain into professional mode and opened the note pad.

He strode up and down the worn carpet as he spoke. There was a deliberation and a slight sibilance to his speech, which gave it a sense of casualness, in contrast to its urgent message. 'To the members of the War Cabinet this day October the 2nd, nineteen thirty nine. From the First Lord of the Admiralty. Report on the state of the campaign against German U-boats in the North Sea...'

Lucy scribbled on her note-pad. The words flowed without interruption. A constant stream of facts and figures, sea locations and ship names, weather conditions and wind speeds, battle encounters and casualty figures. The naval officers murmured from time to time in his ear, the girls pointed to map references and pin positions. After twenty minutes Lucy had enough shorthand script to fill six pages of typing. Finally he stopped.

'Signed, Winston Churchill, First Lord.' He puffed on his cigar for a brief moment, staring at the ceiling. 'Yes, that will do. As many carbon copies as you can achieve. Bring them to me as soon as you've done it, and then I'll have more for you.'

'Yes, sir.' She turned to follow her original escort from the room.

The voice growled again. 'You're new, aren't you?'

She turned back. 'Yes, sir. They sent me from the secretarial college.'

He glanced at the escort. 'Has she been through security?'

'I'm afraid there wasn't time, sir,' said the man. 'You needed someone urgently, and the others had all left.'

Churchill glowered at her again for a second. 'Hah. Well, no matter. Welcome to the circle. Do your best.'

'Yes, sir.' She turned again and left.

That was the start.

CHAPTER 5

She soon realised that his peremptory greeting wasn't rudeness, it was simply that his mind was so fixed on the job in hand that he had no time for niceties. His focus was always on some imperative job in hand, whether it was in peace or at war, at home or abroad, in his study or in the maelstrom of Parliament.

That night, and well into the early hours of the morning, she scribbled and typed, scribbled and typed, putting onto the pages the vast outpouring of his phenomenal brain on matters of naval conflict, military strategy, ministerial organisation, governmental policy, global politics, domestic arrangements, social engagements, and shopping requirements. And when she was finally given permission to stagger exhaustedly off to her bed, it was with the first personal comment bestowed for fully six hours.

'Right young miss, that will do for tonight. You've done well. Sorry we've kept you up so long. Get back here tomorrow morning, soon as you can.'

She blinked her tired eyelids. 'Tomorrow, sir?'

'Yes, yes. When you can. The other girls will be in early, but we're short-staffed. Have to fight for good secretaries with every other department.' He was lighting yet another cigar. 'That's all right, isn't it?'

'Um... yes, sir.'

'Good, good.' He glanced around the room. The naval officers had left, and the other two girls were wilting at their posts. 'Ah – seems there's no-one to show you out. You can find your way, can't you? We'll sort out your salary and so forth tomorrow.' The blue eyes peered at her through a haze of cigar smoke. 'What's your name by the way?'

'Lucy, sir. Lucy Armitage.'

'Good, Lucy. Well, you're part of my Secret Circle now, so you'll soon meet everyone and learn the ropes. Don't mind my impatience. Just a lot to get done, that's all.'

'Yes, sir.'

He turned away, and she tottered off to find her way back through the labyrinth, which was still humming with nocturnal activity in its various parts.

She knew so little of the world. She realised that as she floundered her way through the torrent of information and instructions that flowed from his lips that night. Of course she had learned the elementary skills at her little village school, and later the basics of history and geography, science and the arts, at the nearby grammar to which she graduated. But of the infinitely wider landscape of knowledge inhabited by those at the centre of power and business and politics amongst whom she now found herself, she had no experience whatever. This was a universe only hinted at in the books she had read or the newspapers she occasionally glimpsed. This was a cosmos so far removed from that of the hills and valleys, sheep and horses, simple trades and basic life routines in which she had grown up, that indeed it was as if she had been transported through time and space by some Einsteinian trick of science. She realised that, if she was to survive in such an environment, she was going to have to learn fast, and also to keep as low a profile as possible until she had mastered the rules and the methods of its denizens. Her mother had said she wanted her daughter to get on in the world. Well, she was going to be mightily surprised to learn the extent of that progress so far.

She said nothing of her experience to anyone that night. Indeed she hardly saw anyone that night. When she awoke late the next morning her room mate had already left for the college without waking her. Maybe she had heard her arrive back in the early hours and, eschewing any curiosity, left her to sleep on. In any case, by the time Lucy had roused herself, bathed and dressed in the sparse hostel bathroom, and found the right bus to take her back to the

Admiralty, it was already mid-morning and the place was humming with even more activity than the previous night.

Lucy had already gleaned from all her typings during those hours that the war, now only a month old, was still confined on land to the eastern regions of Poland and Czechoslovakia - in the air to nowhere especially as far as Britain was concerned - and at sea to the North Atlantic, where things were not going well, with numbers of ships being sunk every night by packs of marauding German submarines. And of course it was with the sea that she and her famous employer were mostly concerned.

When she got to the Admiralty for the second time, she was not greeted as before by any welcoming official, but had to wait at the entrance until someone was summoned who could grant her access. Two even younger looking ratings were on guard on either side. They studiously stared out front as she glanced at them, wondering how fearful they were of their possible involvement in the growing conflict.

Then a neatly dressed girl, not much older than herself, arrived and beckoned her inside. She had blonde wavy hair, bright lipstick, and humorous eyes, and introduced herself as Mary, one of Churchill's personal staff. As they walked she commiserated that Lucy had first to go through some security procedures before she could be admitted back into the centre of activities.

'Very tedious, but we all have to go through it,' she said in a cheerful voice. 'But with any luck, you'll be interviewed by a dishy officer.'

She led the new recruit through the corridors to another brightly lit office, where sat a number of other girls intently tapping at typewriters. An older woman stood to one side talking with a naval officer. It was to them that Mary led the new recruit.

'This is Lucy Armitage, Mrs Hamblin.'

The woman, a striking female with bobbed hair and immaculate black suit, turned and held out a hand.

'I am Grace Hamblin,' she said. 'The Churchills' principal

30

secretary. I gather you were rather thrown in at the deep end last night.'

Lucy nodded. There was a trace of sympathy in the other's smile. 'Well, you'll get used to it. We're all in the deep end of things here.' She turned to the officer. 'Now this is Lieutenant Commander Thompson. He has a few questions for you concerning security and so forth, and then I will take you along to Mr Churchill and we'll see what he has for you this morning.' The smile tilted. 'I should warn you that it may not always be secretarial matters. Everyone is expected to perform whatever is necessary around here, to keep the ball rolling. You may be asked to read the newspaper headlines to Mr Churchill, carry domestic messages to Mrs Churchill, search the library for obscure books, make his dentist appointments, shop for his paints or his cigars, bring him a change of shirt, or feed the cat. You must be prepared for anything, is that all right?'

'Yes, miss.'

'And you may call me Mrs Hamblin.' She had the air of someone long accustomed to the exigencies of her position, and wholly confident of handling them. 'Off you go then with the Commander.' She turned to the other girl. 'Thank you, Mary. Back to your typing now. What are you working on?'

'The book, Mrs Hamblin.'

Grace sighed and glanced at the officer. 'As if fighting a war isn't enough, he has to write the entire history of Britain at the same time. I do wish he'd get his priorities right.'

The man smiled, and beckoned for Lucy to follow him.

They went into a small adjoining office and sat on opposites sides of a table. The Lieutenant Commander lit a pipe and pulled out a file. He was indeed quite 'dishy', as Mary had promised, but considerably older than Lucy. She felt intimidated as he went through various standard questions about her family background and education, but whether that was by his uniform or his precise military bearing and diction, she wasn't sure. He then asked about

31

her acquaintances and pursuits, on which matters she had very little to say. She felt ashamed at the paucity of her life experience to date.

He sat back, puffing on the pipe. She had the impression it was all very much a formality. Then he said in a more friendly manner, 'Well, that's all fine, Lucy. Welcome to the Admiralty. You will be employed as part of Churchill's governmental staff rather than by the Royal Navy itself.' He tapped the file. 'Your salary will be two pounds ten shillings a week for the first probationary month, rising to three pounds if everything is satisfactory. Is that understood?'

Lucy nodded. It was riches beyond measure.

He laid down the pipe and took further papers from the file. 'Now there is one other thing we must do. Working for Mr Churchill you will of course be privy to a large amount of information which is top secret. Information which would be extremely useful to the enemy. It goes without saying that you are strictly bound by the Official Secrets Act and the Naval Discipline Act.' He pushed the papers across the desk. They were official looking documents headed with the royal crest. 'I must ask you to sign both these forms. You needn't necessarily read such long-winded epistles, but what they mean is that you are promising not to divulge any information, however trivial, to anyone outside these walls. Not to your mother, your postman, your sweetheart, or your pet canary. On pain of life imprisonment or even, in the case of military secrets, capital punishment. Do you understand?'

The weight of such gigantic responsibility descended on Lucy's narrow shoulders like an invisible mantle. Her voice was a whisper. 'Yes.'

He smiled then, showing even white teeth. Perhaps his smile was more than just a friendly reassurance, but the virginal Lucy was in no state to respond.

He rose and smoothed his immaculate trousers. 'By the way I am the Flag Lieutenant to the Admiralty. I organise the First Lord's official activities.' She nodded. 'I'll take you back to Grace now. She will be your main supervisor. She's been with the Churchills

32

for some years, and she runs everything to do with their personal and working lives.'

Indeed she did. It transpired that, as well as organising the Churchills' considerable staffing requirements, Grace Hamblin handled most of their domestic and financial affairs, and also acted as Mrs Churchill's personal secretary. There was very little about their lives that Grace didn't have a hand in. As she now demonstrated to Lucy.

'Mr Churchill is working in their private apartment this morning, Lucy,' she said. It's in Admiralty House, above the Map Room where you were yesterday. He and Mrs Churchill moved there from their country home a couple of weeks ago, immediately after he was called to office. He divides his time between the Map Room and the apartment, where all his personal files and papers are. I'm going to take you there now, and we'll see what he needs. A couple of the other girls are on duty there also, but you can be sure he will keep you all busy.' The dry smile again. 'He keeps everyone around him busy.'

She led Lucy through the connecting passages to Admiralty House, and up wide staircases to the apartment serving as the Churchills' wartime London home. Thick carpets, embroidered drapes, antique furniture, vast paintings, and the smell of ancient existences and modern imperial wealth. To Lucy, who had never seen anything grander than the local vicarage, it seemed she had entered a palace of the imagination.

The familiar sound of brisk typing came from somewhere within the apartment. As they passed through the main chandelier-hung reception room a woman entered from the other side. She wore a dark close-fitting dress that emphasised her slender frame, and she walked with that upright grace that the upper classes adopt so easily.

'Ah, Mrs Churchill,' said Grace Hamblin. 'Let me introduce you to our latest member of the team. This is Lucy Armitage. She joined us last night.'

Clementine Churchill smiled and held out an elegant hand. Her

33

face had that sculpted aristocratic air that results from generations of privileged breeding. It looked both tired and alert at once.

'Welcome aboard, Lucy,' she said. 'Are you prepared for a war fought on many fronts?'

Not for the first time Lucy was lost for a response.

The other smiled. 'Never mind. You'll get used to us. Just do your best and don't let my husband bully you. It's not intended.'

That was what everyone kept saying. Lucy prayed they were right, as she followed Grace through to the outer room. Grace knocked, and they entered. This was a much more intimate place than the official offices. The furnishings were homely, the walls hung with small paintings which Lucy later learnt were mostly his own, the large desk littered with books, ink wells, whisky bottles, pill boxes, and other nick-nacks.

He was wearing a conventional dark suit this time, and a less conventional bow-tie, as he stood, feet apart, cigar in one hand, glass of something presumably alcoholic in the other, dictating to the girl Mary, who had met Lucy at the Admiralty entrance earlier. A budgerigar twittered in a cage in one corner, and a brown poodle sat nearby, eyes fixed on its master as though also mesmerised by his words.

Grace paused with Lucy at her side, waiting for the flow to stop. He had glanced up at their entrance, but there was no halting his oration.

'...at this point the march of invention brought a new factor upon the scene. Iron was dug and forged. Men armed with iron entered Britain from the Continent and killed the men of bronze. At this point we can plainly recognise across the vanished millenniums a fellow-being. A biped capable of slaying another with iron is evidently to modern eyes a man and a brother.'

He stopped. 'Type that out, Mary. It's for insert into the preface. Might have to review it later.'

'Yes, sir,' said Mary.

'And check those dates. Unsure I've got them all right.' He

34

dismissed her with a wave of the cigar. 'I must return to less illustrious, but more urgent matters now.'

Mary left with her notepad, giving Lucy a quick smile as she passed. The dog wagged its tail hopefully. Grace stepped forward.

'I've brought Lucy now, Winston. She worked with you last night.'

'Yes, yes.' The voice was as gravelled as always. He stood staring up at the ceiling, as so often when in thought. His compact, slightly portly form had that same air of immobility that Lucy had observed earlier. 'Not going well, ladies. Not going well,' he murmured.

Lucy was uncertain to what he was referring, but Grace wasn't. 'The Atlantic?' she asked.

'Submarines,' he said. 'Not ready for them. Should have foreseen it. Going to be a problem.' He sipped at his glass, which Lucy, unfamiliar with alcohol, guessed must contain either whisky or brandy. 'Sunk the *Athenia* and one of our aircraft carriers already, and they're targeting the merchant fleet. We're sitting ducks.'

'I'm sure you'll work out what to do,' said Grace with evidently long familiarity. 'I must get back. I'll leave you with Lucy.'

He grunted, waved the cigar and went towards a wide side-table littered with papers, files and maps. Grace departed, leaving Lucy feeling abandoned and wholly overawed. The First Lord showed her no sign as he smoothed out a large scale map of the North Sea and bent over it.

'Bases. That's the secret. Get to their bases.' He muttered further, then looked up as if recognising her presence for the first time. 'Where are you from, young miss?'

'Cumberland, sir.'

'Ah. Fine county. You don't sound like a northern lass.'

'Well, they make us lose our accents at the secretarial college, sir.'

35

'Do they indeed?' He frowned. 'Pity to deny one's heritage. Whereabouts in Cumberland?'

'Near Thirlmere. My father's a baker.'

'Is he now? Make good cakes, does he?'

'I think so, sir. But it's mostly bread and buns.'

'Of course. Fuel for the nation.' He stared into space for a moment. 'Thirlmere. Beautiful spot. Did you know that the lake was of prime importance to Manchester's factories and the Industrial Revolution?' He nodded to himself. 'Huge battles over turning it into a reservoir, and if they'd been lost this might not be the great country it is now.'

'Yes, sir. They taught us that at school.'

He smiled then. A beguiling smile. 'Good. I'm glad our history education is up to scratch.' He sipped at his glass. Its pale liquid was floating with ice cubes. He turned back to the map. 'What does one do about the sly menace of the U-boat, Lucy?'

Lucy had heard the naval term only the night before. 'I don't know, sir.'

'Mm.' His lower lip protruded as if to orally skewer the problem. It was a characteristic she was to become familiar with. 'There are ways. There is always a way. One just has to discover it.'

She did not think to respond. He was merely giving voice to his thoughts.

He jabbed his finger onto the map. 'The North Atlantic. Supplies. That's where this war will be won or lost. Doesn't matter how big an army or air force you have, without supplies you're impotent.' He looked up. 'Yes, that reminds me. Now Lucy, take a letter to the Minister of Supplies. At least I think that's where it should go to. Subject – Operational dress for naval ratings.'

'Naval who, sir?'

'Ratings, girl, ratings!' His bark was impatient. 'Don't you know what a rating is?'

'Sorry, no sir.'

'Ordinary seaman, for heaven's sake. Carry on.' He paced. 'Dear Sirs, the current regular sweater and duffle coat for sailors manning the North Sea routes is inadequate for temperatures and weather conditions in those regions. I suggest an extra woollen vest be added to standard issue, and...'

It continued. She had already realised that his attention could switch from one topic to another at the flick of a brain cell. She also knew not to take his irate outbursts seriously. They would be forgotten within minutes. Her own brain went into automatic pilot mode as she recorded his words. She was beginning to get the hang of his rhythms and inflexions now, and she had little difficulty in keeping up with him. She also learned that it was best to delay requests for clarification until he had finished that particular dispatch, and then produce them all at once. That did not interrupt his flow of thought.

What did interrupt his flow of thought though, was a knock and the entrance of an elderly man in dark butler's uniform. He had a slow upright gait and a dour expression. He bore an envelope on a silver platter.

'Pardon me for interrupting, sir, but there's an urgent message from the War Office. I thought you would wish to see it.'

Churchill grunted and took the envelope. As he opened it and read the contents the butler looked Lucy up and down.

'New, are you, miss?' He had the trace of a Scottish accent.

'Yes. As of yesterday.'

A slow reflective nod of the head.

Churchill waved the paper irritably. 'Why do they keep sending the navy's damage reports, Inches? As if we don't know ourselves here what's happening.'

'I don't know, sir. In the interests of efficiency perhaps.'

'In the interests of damned bureaucracy.'

The man called Inches glanced at Lucy apologetically. He had the air of someone long resigned to his employer's idiosyncrasies. Churchill picked up the look. 'Oh, don't mind my swearing, young miss. There'll be much of that around this place.' He peered at the butler. 'You all right, Inches? Looking a bit peaky.'

'I'm fine, sir. Just didn't sleep too well last night.'

'Why not?'

The other hesitated. 'Oh, just worry. The blackout curtains are not too good in the apartment. I keep listening for the sirens.'

Churchill chuckled and waved a hand. 'Don't worry, David. The bombers won't arrive for a bit yet. Adolf is too preoccupied elsewhere. Time enough for the curtains.'

'If you say so, sir.'

Churchill turned to Lucy. 'By the way, er... Lucy, isn't it? This is Mr Inches, my butler. Been with the family a long time, haven't you Inches?'

'Indeed, sir. Seventeen years.'

'Is it really? Good heavens! Anyway, Lucy, there is very little about us – good or bad – that Inches doesn't know. So if you ever need advice on anything, go to him.'

Inches said, 'Or to Mrs Hamblin, sir.'

'Yes, yes, of course. To Grace Hamblin for professional matters. And to Inches for domestic matters.'

Lucy wondered what domestic matters might possibly involve her, but said nothing. Inches nodded to her, turned, and equally slowly left the room. Churchill stood for a moment, cigar in mouth, staring at the message in his hand. Then he shook his head and tossed it onto the table amongst all the other papers there.

'Madness,' he muttered. 'Utter madness.'

What was the madness, Lucy could not divine. The dog was wagging its tail. Presumably it felt the same way. Churchill glanced at it. 'Yes, Rufus,' he growled. 'Why don't we learn from you canines. The world would be a better place.'

The dog's tail wagged faster.

'That's Rufus,' its master said to Lucy. 'One of the family. You'll need to make friends. Might have to attend to some of Rufus's many needs sometimes.'

She remembered Grace Hamblin's words about the breadth of her duties. That was all right. She liked dogs.

'Which reminds me,' he was continuing. 'Make a note to get in a stock of Rufus's tins. They could run short if Hitler has anything to do with it.' He threw her an impudent smile. 'We may go short, but Rufus can't.'

'Yes, sir.'

'Now, where were we...? Ah, yes. Placing of weapons on the new K Class destroyers...'

That wasn't where they'd been, but Lucy knew better than to correct him. She scribbled on her pad. The morning passed faster than a clap of thunder.

CHAPTER 6

Bloomsbury hostel
October 3rd. About 10 o'clock pm.

Dear Mum and Dad,

I'm writing this in my bedroom late at night. I can hardly keep my eyes open I'm so tired, but I just had to write to you.

You will never believe this, but your Lucy is now working at the Admiralty for Winston Churchill!!

There was an emergency call out for shorthand typists and I was sent by taxi to the Admiralty not knowing what to expect. Then who should I find myself taking dictation from but the great man himself! I had to work for him all that evening and the next day, and it looks as though I will be doing so for the foreseeable future (as long as I can keep up - the pace is furious).

He is the most extraordinary man. Rather frightening is some ways, but so brilliant, and has an astonishing memory and command of facts. Everyone around him is terrified of his quick temper, but they adore him really and will do anything for him. His wife is nice too, though I've hardly met her. He's always surrounded by secretaries and staff and pets as well, and he keeps everyone busy.

I have made a nice friend, another secretary called Mary, who has been here for some time and shows me the ropes. The Admiralty is HUGE and swarming with high ranking naval people, and everyone is incredibly focussed on the war effort. I'm not allowed to tell you anything about it but we are in good hands. If anyone can beat the Boche, as they call the Germans, it is the British.

I must go to bed now. Do write and tell me how you are. Have you heard from Tommy?

Lots of love, Lucy.

P.S. I am being paid two pounds ten shillings a week!

CHAPTER 7

For several days she endured the torrent of work thrown at her, along with her fellow employees, by their boss. Thrown under the most diverse circumstances that any secretaries could surely have ever experienced. The girls took dictation in offices, in parliamentary corridors, in male washrooms, in his ministerial car, running beside him in parks and on pavements, at the kitchen table as he personally prepared Rufus's dinner, in his bedroom as his valet dressed him, even, astoundingly, sitting outside his bathroom as he wallowed, cigar in mouth, in his bath, glistening pink body glimpsed through the half open doorway. There was no activity, it seemed, that precluded the simultaneous continuity of the business in hand.

During their brief moments of respite the girls would exchange stories of their experiences, and giggle at the eccentric ways of their employer. They had all seen him in the most intimate of situations – breakfasting in bed, performing ablutions in the bathroom, changing shirts in his closet, or swearing angrily at his staff in the War Room. Not one of them, exhausted and intimidated though they may have been, would have exchanged their post for any other.

On the fourth day of her employment Lucy was sharing a lunch table in the communal Admiralty dining hall with Mary, her first-met fellow secretary. Mary had worked in several government departments, and could contrast the experiences with the current one. Churchill, she said, worked in ways which no other employer did, and created an atmosphere that existed nowhere else.

'It's no wonder they didn't want him in the Cabinet,' she murmured confidentially across their shepherd's pie and peas. 'None of the other ministers would get a word in edgeways. None of them would know how to argue with him.'

'So why is he in now?' queried Lucy. Her knowledge of the political scene was elementary.

'They had to let him in. He's the only one who saw what Hitler was up to. He's been hammering away at ministers for years about standing up to the monster, but none of them wanted to hear. Now he's been proved right they couldn't keep him out any longer.' Mary had an air of assured and eager sensuality about her that Lucy envied.

'But why the Admiralty?' asked Lucy. 'Does he know about ships and things?'

Mary looked at her with raised eyebrows. 'Don't you know your history? He's done it before. He was First Lord of the Admiralty during the Great War.'

'Oh.' Lucy's shame at her ignorance multiplied.

'He's been Home Secretary, First Lord, Chancellor of Exchequer - God knows what. All in his thirties.' She leaned forward even more conspiratorially, her prominent bust almost dipping into her shepherd's pie. 'They're saying he'll be the next Prime Minister. Chamberlain can't stay there for long after all he's done.'

Lucy felt too embarrassed to ask what terrible deeds the current PM might have perpetrated. She toyed with her food, silently resolving to instruct herself better on British parliamentary history.

Mary gave a discreet hiss, and she looked up. Her companion was surreptitiously pointing her knife off to one side.

'Don't look now, but I think you might have an admirer.'

Lucy obeyed the instruction, and shielded her eyes. 'What? Who?'

'He's over there.' Mary glanced sideways. 'He's not looking now. You can take a peek.'

Lucy glanced in the direction. A youngish man in a pale grey suit was sitting alone two tables away.

Mary's voice was a whisper. 'He's an American, attached to

their embassy. He comes here sometimes, working with our people on dispatches and diplomatic exchanges.'

'What do you mean, admirer?'

'He's been looking over here quite a lot. He's quite a dish, isn't he?'

'Perhaps he's looking at you.'

'No. We've said hello a couple of times. He's not interested in me. I told him I already have a boyfriend.'

'What...? I mean, what makes you think he's interested in me?'

'Why wouldn't he be? He's been trying to catch your eye for some time.'

Lucy reddened at the thought. She was still so inexperienced in sexual matters. She had encountered various approaches from youths who hung around the girls at the secretarial college like wasps, and she had begun to realise that she had something they desired, whether it was due to her trim figure, her wide brown eyes, or her frank expression. But her innocence had been an insurmountable barrier. Sex was an issue that had barely surfaced in her life, apart from Henry's clumsy approach. However here in London, surrounded by far more worldly and sophisticated males, whether in uniform or city suits, things were evidently going to be different.

She stole another glance in his direction. It was true, he was rather nice looking. He had that short-haired, clean-cut American air, and the pale colour of his tailored suit emphasised his faintly exotic nature.

He looked up, and caught her eye before she could look away. He smiled, an open white-toothed smile that no British man would ever venture before a stranger. She blushed further.

'Told you.' Mary's voice was an amused hiss.

Something akin to panic rose in Lucy's breast. 'I must get back to the Map Room. I'm next on duty,' she said. She drank the last of her lemon squash, pushed aside the remains of the unappetising lunch, and rose.

'What shall I tell him?' asked Mary, still seated.

'Tell him? Don't tell him anything.'

'I bet he asks about you. He's not shy in coming forward.'

Lucy was bewildered. 'I don't... I... There's no need to tell him anything. I just work here.'

Mary sat back. 'Well, all right. But why turn down an opportunity? He's American. He's probably well off. He'd take you to good restaurants. Give you a nice time.'

'Well, I...' Lucy shook her head. This was a scenario she had no idea how to deal with. 'I'll see you later.'

She was forced to pass by his table as she left, but she studiously avoided his look as she did so, praying that her cheeks weren't too obviously flushed.

Churchill was as usual talking in the Map Room. He was surrounded by navy personnel as he bent over one of the charts. His voice rumbled on, and the WRNs manipulated ship models and coloured pins. Whether anyone had eaten lunch that day wasn't clear.

Lucy knew better than to interrupt. When he was ready to dictate something he would simply call 'Miss' over his shoulder, and expect the nearest secretary to be ready with pencil and paper on the instant.

This time however the command did not come. She stood to one side for ten minutes as he queried and commanded, cigar in mouth, unlit and merely chewed. Eventually he straightened up, took the cigar out, and muttered. 'That's enough. Time for my nap. I'll see you all in half an hour.'

The group broke up. He turned, and saw Lucy waiting patiently.

'Ah! Lucy, m'dear. Don't need you now, but my wife does. Grace is off duty today. Trot along to Admiralty House, will you, and see Mrs Churchill. She's got letters and things.'

'Yes, sir.'

'And while you're there, clean out the budgerigar's cage, will you? Fearful mess. Hasn't been done for days.'

One of the WRNs hastily smothered a snigger.

Lucy repeated, 'Yes, sir.'

He waved her away with the cigar, and strode off to some sanctum elsewhere. Lucy headed with her notepad to the residential apartment.

She entered via the connecting passage and stairways, and paused at the front door to the private apartment. There was no bell or knocker, so she timidly knocked with her knuckle and pushed open the door. As she entered, the butler was crossing the wide entrance hall with an armful of polished shoes.

'Ah, Miss Lucy,' he said. 'The master isn't here. He's down in the Map Room.'

'I know, Mr Inches. I've just come from there. He says Mrs Churchill needs a secretary.'

He stopped, looking flustered. His face seemed tired. Lucy had no idea how old he was, but guessed in his seventies.

'Ah, yes... of course. Grace is off today. I, er...' He looked around vaguely. 'I think you'll find Mrs Churchill in the study.'

'Right, thank you,' said Lucy, and started towards that place.

He stopped her. 'How are you fitting in here? Getting on all right, are you?'

'Yes, thank you, Mr Inches. I'm finding it all quite exciting really.'

'Exciting?' His watery eyes showed a flash of amusement. 'Yes, well I suppose you could call it that. Not finding the work too daunting then?'

'No.'

He nodded. 'Good, good. One or two girls have done so.'

'Have they?'

'Oh yes. Left us fairly smartly. Couldn't stand the pace.' An expensive looking female shoe fell to the ground. Lucy stooped to pick it up, and handed it back. 'Thank you. Well, must get on. You'll er... you'll find the missus rather easier to work for, I fancy.'

He went bandy-legged on his way. Lucy walked to the study door and knocked.

'Come in.' Clementine Churchill's low voice was unmistakable.

Lucy entered. The 'study' was more like a library, with book shelves on three sides and a reading table in the centre, lit by a brass chandelier hanging from the stuccoed ceiling. Clementine Churchill was seated there, writing with an old fashioned quill pen. A large cat was rubbing against her leg, purring. Its mistress looked up.

'Yes?'

It was only the second or third time Lucy had met the lady of the house. They had exchanged no more than a few words. 'Mr Churchill said you were in need of a typist, ma'am.'

'Oh yes, of course. Thank you.' Clementine's face softened into a smile. 'It's good of you to come.'

Lucy relaxed a little, though why her coming should have been considered a charitable action she wasn't sure.

'It's Lucy, isn't it?'

'Yes, ma'am.'

'Do call me Clementine. We're all on first names here.'

'Yes, ma'am. Er... Clementine.'

Clementine pushed the cat aside with her leg and rose from the desk. Lucy realised that she must be several inches taller than her husband.

'How are you getting on here, Lucy?' The handsome face looked concerned.

Why was everyone so solicitous about her welfare? Lucy replied, 'Fine, thank you.'

'That's good. We do rely so much on our secretaries. Such an awful lot to get done always, and it can be quite demanding.'

46

'I'm quite enjoying myself actually,' Lucy replied. 'It's exciting to be...' She tailed off.

The head tilted. 'To be what?'

'Well...' How to describe it? 'Involved with everything.'

Clementine nodded. 'Yes. Yes, I suppose we are all involved, aren't we? Traumatic times. But if we are to win through, then we must all do our bit.'

'Yes, ma'am.'

The grey eyes were steady on Lucy's. 'You're from the North, aren't you?'

'Cumberland, ma'am. The Lakes.' The Christian name salutation was not coming easily.

'A long way away. Are you homesick?'

'It's all right. My mum writes quite often.'

A nod. 'Large family?'

'One brother. He's in the army.'

'Ah. Well, safer than the navy at present.' She glanced back at the table. 'Well, I've been writing some personal letters, but there are one or two which I think should be typed up more formally. Would you mind taking dictation on those?'

'No, of course not.'

Clementine sat at the table again. The cat tried to jump onto her lap, but she pushed it away. 'Not now, Nelson, not now.' She put her fingers to her forehead. 'I think we'd better start with the most difficult. You need to type this on official Admiralty notepaper.'

'Yes, ma'am.' Lucy opened her notepad.

The faintly greying head stooped as its owner pondered. 'Difficult this,' she murmured. 'Not sure how to phrase it.' She looked back up at Lucy. 'It's to the Prime Minister. You'd better just address it to him at Number Ten Downing Street.'

Lucy was getting used to daunting surprises. She scribbled on the pad.

'Dear Prime Minister... No. Make that, Dear Neville.' Longish pause. 'Winston and I do hope that you are bearing up well under the huge...' Hesitation. 'No – under the very great strain you must be enduring at this turbulent time. I can assure you that we, and indeed the nation, have every confidence in your ability to steer us all through such stormy waters and bring us to ultimate victory.' Another pause. 'Yes... yes. New paragraph, continue – In the meantime we would like to invite you and Anne to dinner at Admiralty House next Friday, October 13th...' Clementine broke off. 'Oh dear. I've just realised that's an unlucky day, isn't it - Friday the 13th?' She frowned. 'Still, it's the only day we're free, and his secretary says he is too. Let's just hope they aren't superstitious.' She waved an elegant hand. 'Continue. Just a casual evening with only the four of us dining. We feel it is high time we got to know you and Annie a little better after so long, and after all that has happened in the turmoil of Westminster, and we thought that an intimate dinner here, away from the... the hullabaloo of Downing Street, would be conducive to a relaxed and friendly occasion. Do please let us know if that will be acceptable.' She looked up at Lucy again. 'Signed Clementine Churchill. Did you get all that?'

'Yes, ma'am... Clementine.'

'Did it sound all right, do you think?'

Lucy faltered. 'Oh yes, I'm sure. It sounded very, er... polite and hospitable.'

'Good.' Reflection shadowed the other's face again. 'It's difficult, you see, Lucy. We've never met those two socially on their own before. And after all that's passed between Neville and my husband over the years... well, it's a delicate situation.'

Lucy had little idea as to why it was delicate, except for a vague awareness that there had been much historical dissent within the upper echelons of power concerning the growing Nazi menace. She said nothing, but gave a little smile which she hoped showed sympathy.

Clementine sighed. 'Relaxed and friendly, I called it. I hope I'm

48

right. My husband has insisted we make the invitation, but it will be me who has to keep the peace.'

'Keep the peace?'

A wan smile. 'Well, they haven't been the best of friends over the years. At least, not in Parliament. We just have to hope that things will be more tranquil around the dinner table.' She ran a hand through her carefully arranged hair. 'That reminds me. We have a dozen people for dinner tonight. I must go and talk to Inches and the cook. We'll leave the other letters for now. That's the most urgent. Type it up, and bring it to me to check will you, Lucy.'

'Yes, ma'am.' Lucy hesitated. 'Um... Mr Churchill said something about the budgerigar's cage.'

Clementine laughed, a low infectious chuckle. 'Oh good heavens, don't worry about that. The maids will do it.' She lifted an ironic eyebrow. 'I sometimes think he cares more about his pets than he does his family. But don't tell him I said that.'

She walked ahead out of the room, with the cat running beside her. Lucy followed to go to her desk.

CHAPTER 8

The American was in the dining hall again two days later. He was already seated at the same table when Lucy entered. There were only a couple of dozen others lunching at that time, and the hall was relatively empty.

Lucy was on her own this time, and she hesitated on seeing him there. She averted her eyes, and went quickly to the serving counter. She picked a chicken salad from the fare on offer, and was contemplating a lemon tart when his voice spoke beside her.

'Better make the most of it. They'll be rationing stuff soon, and there won't be so much choice.'

She knew from the smooth transatlantic accent who it was. She feigned casualness as she turned. He was helping himself to a bottle from the drinks cabinet. He was quite tall. His short-cut hair was a pale brown, and his eyes inevitably were blue.

'Rationing?' she said.

'Sure. The way the war at sea is going, Britain soon won't be able to import stuff in the usual way.'

'Oh.'

His teeth shone through a slightly tilted smile. 'So, Mr Churchill has allowed you time off for some lunch.'

'Um... yes. How did you know I worked for him?'

'Mary told me. I asked about you.'

'Oh.' She hesitated. 'Why?'

'Why not? You're a pretty girl.' That American candour again.

She blushed and picked up her tray.

He went on. 'You'll be lonely on your own. Come and sit with me.'

She could find no reason to refuse. They both sat at his table –

she with her chicken salad, he with a bottled beer and a slice of Cheddar cheese and crackers. A couple of girls at another table noticed, and whispered together.

'I'm Daniel by the way,' he said, opening the beer with an expert twist.

'Lucy.'

He shook hands across the table. 'Where are you from?'

'Cumberland.'

He nodded. 'The Lake District. I've never been. Hear it's beautiful.'

'Yes.'

He nodded again, a slow reflective nod. 'So much history in your country.'

'Well, yes. Old countries do have a lot of history.'

He acknowledged the jibe. 'I guess so.'

She relaxed a little. 'Which part of America are you from?'

'New England. Near Boston. Can't you tell?'

'How could I?'

'The smart-ass accent. It's a giveaway to most people.'

'I'm not familiar with American accents. What are you doing over here?'

'There's quite a few of us here. A lot more coming. I'm attached to our embassy. Cipher clerk.'

'Cipher clerk? What's that?'

'I decipher and compose messages that are in code. Everything that's important has to be coded now. In case the Boche get hold of it.'

'But does America send important messages?'

He sat back with a quizzical look. 'My God, I thought you were secretary to Churchill. Don't you know what goes on between our countries?'

She flustered. 'Yes, of course, but... I mean, America isn't in the

51

war.'

'Not yet. But believe me, we probably soon will be. And in any case we're doing all we can to help you guys. If Hitler overruns Europe it'll be our door he's knocking on next.'

'So that's why you're here?'

'Sure. Hell of a lot of communications going between London and Washington, I can tell you.' He glanced sideways, and lent forward confidentially. 'I had to decode a direct message from the White House to Downing Street only this morning.'

Lucy said nothing. Every day seemed to add to the momentous circumstances in which she found herself.

He was sitting back, studying her with a smile. Again she flustered under his candid gaze. The girls at the other table were watching.

'You don't look old enough to be a highly qualified secretary,' he said.

'I came straight from secretarial college. It was an emergency.'

'Emergency?'

'There's a shortage of typists apparently. Anyway, I came as a temp, and I seem to have been taken on permanently.'

'You must be up to the job then. Word is the old man is demanding.'

'He is quite.'

'Scary, working for him, is it?'

'It was at first. But I'm getting used to it. He's not unkind. Just impatient.'

He nodded, still smiling.

'I wish you wouldn't look at me like that,' she said.

'Like what?'

'As if I'm a cream cake you fancy.'

The smile broadened. 'Good description.'

She reddened again. She'd walked into that.

'Tell you what, Lucy' he said. 'Why don't I take you out to dinner one evening, and we'll have something better than cream cakes.'

She hesitated, a forkful of salad poised in mid-air. 'I don't know you.'

'Of course you don't know me. The whole point of a date is to get to know me.'

'Well, I...'

'And for me to get to know you.'

'Why do you want to get to know me?'

'I've told you. You're a pretty girl. And it's lonely for a Yank here in London. I want some friendly female company.'

Her instincts were a turmoil. 'I'm not sure if...'

'If what?'

'If it's allowed.'

He waved a hand. 'Sure it's allowed. No one's going to arrest us for having dinner together.'

'Where would we go?' She had rarely been out to a smart restaurant, certainly not in London.

'Oh, I'll find somewhere nice. Where are you living?'

She wondered whether she was permitted to divulge such information. 'I... I'm in a hostel in Bloomsbury. But I have to leave it soon if I'm not going back to the college.'

'Where will you go?'

'I don't know. I have to look for a room somewhere. I haven't had time so far.'

He nodded and was quiet.

'Where are you living?' she asked, more to break the silence than from curiosity..

'The embassy's putting me up in a rather seedy hotel. But I'll have to find somewhere too if I'm to be here for long. Thank God, they pay the rent. London's expensive.'

'Don't you know how long you'll be here?'

'No idea. Depends how the war goes. So far there's not much happening except at sea. But this phoney war won't go on for ever. If London's attacked, they may say I've got to stay on.'

'Do you think it will be attacked?'

'Oh sure. Hitler's boasted his bombers will obliterate London sooner or later.' A dry smile. 'Let's just hope it's later.'

She toyed with her chicken and was quiet.

He downed the rest of his beer. 'Tell you what. How are you fixed tomorrow night?'

'Um... I'm on duty in the morning, so...'

'So you'll be free for the evening. Great. Why don't I pick you up from your hostel, and we'll go somewhere nice in the West End?'

Again, she couldn't think of a reason to say no.

The girls were still whispering.

Mary clapped her hands when Lucy told her.

'There! I told you. You've bagged him!'

Lucy frowned. 'Bagged?'

'He's a catch. He's good looking, he's bright, he's obviously well-off. What more could you want?' She whispered. 'Bet you he takes you dancing afterwards.'

'Dancing?'

'Of course. Americans love dancing. There are plenty of places still open in the West End.'

'I'm not very good at dancing.' The modest social affairs she had known at home had scarcely involved the art of sophisticated ballroom steps.

'He'll teach you.' Mary lowered her voice again. 'Just don't get too tiddly. And don't let him up to your room afterwards.'

Panic rose in Lucy's breast. 'He wouldn't... I mean, he

wouldn't...'

'Oh, he might. The Yanks think that English girls are easy meat. Just be careful, that's all.'

Wow, thought Lucy. It seemed she was having to leave her adolescence behind very quickly. She worked that afternoon with only half her mind on the job.

CHAPTER 9

He took her to an Italian restaurant in Chelsea.

Her own experience of Italian food was of a rare visit to a bistro-style establishment in Keswick, where they did a medley of pasta dishes, smothered in tomato sauce and guaranteed to add pounds. This was different. Low lighting, red velvet upholstery, white table cloths, and effusive aproned waiters. The scents wafting from the kitchen were enticing.

'You can always tell a good restaurant from the smells,' said Daniel as he seated her opposite him. 'I'm afraid I only go to French or Italian restaurants in London. Not too keen on English cooking unless it's the Savoy Grill, and I can't afford to go there too often.'

She said nothing, merely avoided the bedroom eyes of the young Italian waiter as he flamboyantly unfurled her linen table napkin, and laid the expansive menu before her.

'Do you have champagne by the glass?' asked Daniel as the lad did the same for him.

'No champagne, signor. But we have very nice Asti Spumante.'

'Not too sweet, is it?'

'No signor, is good.'

'Okay – we'll try a couple of glasses.'

'Si signor.'

'Is that all right with you?' he asked across the glow of the table candle.

'Yes.' She had no idea what Asti Spumante was.

As the waiter left, Daniel studied the menu. 'If you want a meat dish I'd recommend the veal. Safer bet than the other meats.'

She had never eaten veal. She knew it came from cows, but didn't know how it differed from ordinary roast beef. 'All right.'

He smiled at her. 'And if you want to be adventurous, how about some calamari to start?'

'Calamari?'

He leant back. 'Don't know what that is?'

'No.'

'Boy, I'm going to have fun educating you. It's baby squid.'

He watched amused as she contemplated the idea. 'I've never had that.'

'Well, it's high time you tried it. Mediterranean speciality. Probably a lot of garlic but, hey, what's some garlic between friends.'

She abandoned herself to his expertise.

He glanced around the room. Several other well-dressed diners were present. 'Wouldn't think there was a war on, would you?'

'No.'

'I fear things will be a bit different in a month or two.'

'You think Hitler will invade?' Whitehall was vibrating with such speculation.

'Not immediately, no. But he will probably start with a bombing campaign. And your air force is ill prepared to counter that.'

'We're building lots more fighters, aren't we?'

He threw her an amused glance. 'Picked up that in the Admiralty War Room, did you?'

'Well, it's common knowledge.'

'They've left it late in the day. Just like the ship building. There's a lot of catching up to do.'

'And there's the barrage balloons.'

'Not much use against high-flying bombers.'

'Oh.' This foreigner appeared to be better informed than her about the war preparations.

He sat back. 'Let's not talk about the war. Too depressing. Tell me about you.'

She noticed again that he had an unusual tic. One side of his mouth tilted in a half smile whenever he asked a question. It was if

57

he was apologising for the impertinence. 'Tell what?' she said.

'About your family. Your life up there in chilly Cumberland.'

'Oh, it can be quite hot in summer.' She threw him a challenging glance. 'We often go bathing in the lakes.'

'Now you're talking. That's my kinda fun.'

She relaxed a little, and told him more about her upbringing. He seemed intrigued about her provincial lifestyle, and the intricacies of English baking methods.

The waiter appeared with two wide-brimmed glasses, their yellow liquid almost audibly fizzing.

Daniel clinked his glass against hers. 'Cheers, as you say here.'

'Cheers.' The drink was novel, and not unpleasant to her taste.

He thought differently, and wrinkled his nose. 'Syrup,' he said. 'Never mind. They'll catch up with France one day.'

A much older waiter arrived and took their orders with weary Italian familiarity. Daniel rattled off the dishes in an authentic sounding accent.

When the old boy had left, the blue eyes gazed at her over the champagne glass, and the mouth tilted. 'And what about boyfriends?'

'Boyfriends?'

'Back home. Have you got a sweetheart?'

'No. Not really.'

'Why not? The country lads not to your taste?'

'I don't... I've just been too busy. And I've been in London for a year now.'

'So what about London guys? Don't tell me you haven't had offers?'

She felt slightly irritated at his persistence. 'I just... I haven't had time to...'

'Wow.' He sat back again and swirled the liquid in his glass. 'You really are an innocent English rose, aren't you?'

58

'I suppose so.'

'How old are you?'

'Twenty,' she lied.

'Well I'm twenty seven, so I have a head start on you.'

It was time to deflect the talk. She gazed at him directly. 'So is your job at the embassy very important?'

'Pretty, I guess. I'm involved with creating new codes as well as translating them.'

'Does that mean you have a mathematical brain?'

'Not so much mathematical as inventive. Lateral thinking.'

'What's that?'

'Thinking outside the box. You assume that the enemy will be thinking along conventional lines, so you have to find unconventional ones.'

'Ah.' She allowed herself a mischievous smile. 'Well, you're certainly unconventional.'

'By British standards maybe.'

She sipped her drink. It *was* a bit sweet. 'Are we very conventional?'

'In some ways. That's what a long history does to you. Establishes conventions. In other ways you're quite unconventional. That's why you've had such an impact on the world.'

'Ah.' She was again perplexed. 'How are we unconventional?'

'An island race aloof from the historical centres of civilisation. The creators of the industrial revolution. Sufferers of a lousy climate, which sends you exploring across the globe. It all adds up.'

She couldn't amalgamate those factors. 'Wow!'

'Look at your boss. The most unconventional guy that's ever lived.'

She laughed. 'Yes. Probably.'

The tic again. He watched her across his glass. 'What's it like working for him?'

'Unconventional.'

'What's he working on at the moment?'

'He's always working on a dozen things at once.'

'No, but specifically. On the North Atlantic situation.'

'Well, he...' She stopped. The words of Commander Thompson came to mind. '...no information, however trivial, to anyone outside these walls. Not to your mother, your postman, your sweetheart, or your pet canary.' She played with her napkin. 'I'm not supposed to talk about it.'

He chuckled. 'Oh, come on. We're on the same side here.'

'Yes, but... I signed a form. Secrets Act.' She smiled demurely. 'I could get shot.'

'My God! Even the secretaries?'

'Of course. We hear everything.'

'I bet you do.' He leaned forward and dropped his voice. 'So have you heard who's going to be the next Prime Minister?'

'Why would we change this one?'

'Oh, hey. Everyone knows his time is up after the Munich fiasco. And he's not a well man.'

'Well, I haven't heard anything.'

'I don't believe you. You said it. You secretaries hear everything.'

She was searching for an evasive answer when she was saved by the arrival of their first course. The assortment of small cephalopods stared at her balefully from a pool of garlic juice.

'Ugh!'

He laughed again. 'Don't be such a wimp. It's delicious.' As if to encourage her he speared one and put it whole into his mouth. 'Yes! That is good.'

She cut a small segment, closed her eyes and did the same. Once she had got over the rubbery texture, she admitted the taste was intriguing, if not immediately seductive.

'See,' he said. 'There's a whole world of delights out there.'

Over the rest of the meal he chatted on about his own erratic family life in New England, his college days, his time in Washington. He didn't refer to her work again. She tried to assess her feelings about him. Attractive certainly, congenial company, intriguing background. But there was something else. Something she couldn't put a finger on. A hidden dimension that she couldn't evaluate. She put it down to his coming from such a different culture from hers. America was after all another universe to Great Britain, much shared heritage though they may have had.

The dinner passed for her in a medley of unfamiliar food flavours, wine tastes, and easy conversation. She was aware that she was getting rather more tiddly than was wise, but she kept a cool head. 'Whatever you do, don't let him up to your room.' Mary's words were imprinted on her mind. She drank a cup of black coffee to finish.

He didn't take her dancing. After he paid the bill, he took her back to her hostel in a taxi. When it pulled up outside, he leaned across her and opened the door. 'I hope you enjoyed the evening,' he said.

'Yes, I did. Very much.' She meant it.

'Would it be too forward of me to ask an English rose for a kiss?'

She shook her head. He kissed her gently. His lips felt cool. Or was it that hers were hot? She had been kissed a number of times before, but it had never meant much.

He pulled back. 'We must do this again.'

'Mm,' she said, and got out. 'Thank you for a lovely evening. Good night.'

'Good night.'

She watched the cab drive off, then turned and went in just as it was starting to rain. Distant Big Ben was chiming eleven o'clock.

CHAPTER 10

'Monstrous! Utterly monstrous!' Churchill was in his silk dressing gown, striding back and forth in his study in Admiralty House, the lower lip jutting. Lucy was sitting at one end of the desk, pencil poised over her notepad. Rufus the dog was on the floor by her side. Both were nervously waiting for the tirade to end.

'If there is anything more duplicitous than a German tyrant, it's a Russian tyrant. Fascist or Bolshevist, they're both the same species of crocodile.'

He stopped pacing and stood, chewing the end of his cigar. 'However we need to capture this particular crocodile.' He raised a finger. 'Right, take this down.'

Lucy raised her pencil.

To Lord Halifax, Foreign Office. Dear Foreign Secretary. We must realise that this shameful invasion of Poland by Russia, in the wake of Germany's own annexation, is nothing more than a purely opportunistic venture on Stalin's behalf. We must recognise that this is as callous and acquisitive an action as is Adolf's. However we have to approach the situation with ingenuity for our own purposes. I would urge you, now that you and the cabinet have finally understood the urgency of the situation that confronts us...

He rumbled on, and Lucy scribbled on her pad, awed again at the immensity of world events around her. When he finished, he stood as usual staring upwards for a few moments.

'Yes, that will do. Type it up, Miss Lucy, and send it straight over to the Foreign Office.'

'Um... do you want me to deliver it, sir?'

'Heavens no, dear! I have far more important things for you to do than delivering messages. Send one of the messenger boys from the War Room. Then return here. And meanwhile, call in one of the other girls.'

'Yes, sir.' She hurried off to obey.

On the way through to the main Admiralty building she passed Lieutenant Commander Thompson, himself heading for Churchill's lair.

'Ah, Lucy,' he said, stopping in his stride. 'How are you getting on?'

'Fine, thank you, sir.'

'Good.' He smiled. 'Keeping you busy, is he?'

'Very busy, sir.'

'I've no doubt.' He hesitated, looking at her with his head on one side. 'I hope he's leaving you time for some private life.'

'Private life, sir?'

'Yes. Managing to get out a bit, I trust. Have a bit of fun away from all this shenanigans.'

'Oh, er... yes sir.'

'Good. We all need a bit of relief from time to time.' He smiled again and continued on his way.

Lucy did the same, puzzling as to why he should concern himself about her social well-being. She found Mary hovering in the Map Room downstairs.

'He wants you, Mary,' Lucy said. She waved her pad. 'I've got to type this up.'

Mary sighed. 'I knew it was too good to last. I thought I might have a quiet morning.'

'Quiet morning? Is there such a thing here?'

Mary grinned. 'Course not. What is he wearing?'

'Wearing? Um – his dressing gown.'

The other sighed again. 'That means either that he's been up all night, or that he's been too busy since breakfast to get dressed. Either way he won't be in the best of moods.'

'He's not,' said Lucy. She raised the notepad again. 'He's

ranting about Russia's invasion of Poland.'

'Oh well... it'll make a change from submarines.' Mary was about to go, then stopped. 'How did you get on last night?'

'Get on?'

'With Mr dishy Yank? Did he take you somewhere nice?'

'Yes. An Italian restaurant. And made me eat squid.'

Mary laughed. 'And afterwards?'

'Kissed me, and dropped me off at the hostel.'

'Nice kiss?'

'Quite.'

'Well, perhaps it'll be dancing next time.' And she hurried off.

When Lucy got back to the hostel that evening, as usual weary after the day's intense activity, there was a note waiting for her in the mail rack. It was hand-written in a languid foreign looking script.

I enjoyed last night. I hope you did too. I've got tickets to an Oscar Wilde play tomorrow night. 'An Ideal Husband'. Would you like to join me? I'll assume the answer is yes, and unless I get a message here to the contrary, I'll pick you up again at the hostel at 7.00 pm. That is presuming you can escape your tyrannical employer's clutches by then.

Daniel Mountview (US Embassy).

Strange. She hadn't known his surname until then. She stood in the hostel hallway staring at the note for several moments, before going up to bed.

She slept the sleep of the innocent, and rose next morning in time for her official eight o'clock start back at the Admiralty. As she rode the bus to Whitehall, she gazed at the passing traffic and the grandiose buildings of central London, thronged with people going about their business. There was little sign during the daytime that the nation was at war. She knew that men were dying in their hundreds out on the cold waters of the North Atlantic, and she wondered whether all those ordinary citizens knew also. She wondered also how many hundreds themselves might be dying in the months to come. Herself perhaps included. Ah well, she would at least have been to an Oscar Wilde play before it happened.

She got to her destination and walked smartly - everyone at the Admiralty walked smartly - to the main administration office to get her orders. Grace Hamblin was already there, immaculate as always, organising the secretaries and clerks on duty.

'Ah, Lucy,' she said. 'The Commander wishes to see you before you start work. You'll find him in the other office.'

Lucy frowned. 'What about?'

'I don't know, my dear. Why don't you go and find out?'

Lucy went through to the small office where the officer had originally interviewed her. He was seated behind the desk in his uniform, and another man stood beside it. This one was dressed in a city suit. He was probably in his mid-forties, with lean features and a bland, impassive expression. He carried a thin file in one hand.

'Come in, Lucy', said Lieutenant Commander Thompson. 'Take a seat.' He gave her an encouraging smile, and indicated a chair on the opposite side of the desk. She sat and waited. 'This is Agent Kenneth Miles from MI5. We just wanted a chat with you about... um, well, certain matters.' It was rare for him to be so unexplicit.

Lucy's heart weighed in her chest. An agent from MI5? Certain matters? Had she already breached the severe conditions of the Official Secrets Act?

The other man was wandering up and down beside the desk, one hand to his forehead as if uncertain how to begin. Then he stopped, and sat in an armchair to one side.

'We believe you went out a couple of evenings ago with a man named Daniel Mountview from the American Embassy.' Both his face and his voice were curiously inexpressive. 'Is that so, Miss Armitage?'

Her panic increased. 'Er... yes, sir.'

Thompson threw her a reassuring smile. 'Don't worry, Lucy. You haven't done anything wrong.'

The panic lifted, but the perplexity remained.

Miles went on. 'You went to a restaurant in Soho. Terazza Mario, yes?'

'Yes.' Silence as they both looked at her. 'How... how did you know?'

'You were followed,' said the Commander. 'You were followed for a reason. Agent Miles will explain.'

The other man's expression still didn't change. He was sitting upright in the chair with the file in front of him. He twiddled a pencil between his fingers.

'May I ask, Miss Armitage, how this dinner date came about?' He had a soft, high-pitched voice which contrasted with his appearance.

Lucy stared back at him. 'He invited me.'

'Yes. But how did you know him in the first place?'

'I met him here at lunch. He introduced himself, and we chatted briefly. Then later, he was there again and we... I sat at his table.' It sounded thoroughly forward of her. 'I mean, he asked me to sit with him, and then... we talked, and he invited me to dinner.'

The man nodded. 'What did you talk about?'

'Um... I can't remember. Nothing important. He told me that he worked at the embassy, decoding messages and so on.'

'Did he ask about your work?'

She reflected. 'He asked what it was like working for Mr Churchill.'

'And what did you say?'

'I said he kept us all very busy.'

66

'Did he ask about the detailed nature of the work you were doing?'

'Um... he knew I was a secretary. A typist. That was all.'

'Nothing specific?'

'Not really. I...' She tried to remember. 'He asked what was happening in the North Atlantic. He asked who I... who people thought the next Prime Minister might be.'

'And what did you tell him?'

'Nothing. I just said I wasn't supposed to talk about my work.'

He nodded. The Commander said, 'Good girl. Well done.'

She relaxed a little more.

The MI5 man continued. 'And after dinner he took you back to your lodgings?'

'Yes. In a taxi.'

'Yes. We followed you.'

She blinked. Had they witnessed the kiss?

'And are you going to see him again?'

She hesitated. 'Well, he's asked me to go to the theatre with him tonight.'

The man stared for a second. 'This was when you said good night after the dinner?'

'No. He left a note last night at my lodgings.' She fished in her shoulder bag and held it out. He read it thoughtfully, then handed it to the Commander. Lucy waited.

Miles folded his hands. 'Let me explain, Miss Armitage.' His lack of expression was beginning to irritate her. Was this how intelligence agents were trained to behave? 'We suspect that this man, Daniel Mountview, is acting as a foreign agent. We think he's working for the Soviets.'

She stared back. Her brain could not assimilate what he was saying.

He watched her for a moment, then went on. 'We believe he is trying to wean his way into your affections because, as one of the First Lord's secretaries, you have much crucial information on the progress of the war, and of the British defence preparations. We suspect he will continue to press his attentions, and eventually try to seduce you into divulging some of this information.'

He stopped, and waited.

Her bewilderment increased. 'But why...? He's American. Why would he...?'

'He has Marxist sympathies. As a student he was a member of the Communist party. For perfectly respectable reasons. The party at that time championed many socially righteous causes. It was against racial segregation for instance, and for workers' rights.' The man's expression if anything congealed further. 'It was also against the democratic capitalist philosophy of the western world. Mountview has since renounced his communism, but we believe that he still espouses the cause, and considers that Russia presents the strongest bulwark against fascism. And against - let's say - the aberrations of western society.'

She tried to make sense of it. 'But Russia has... Russia is fighting with Hitler.'

'On Hitler's side. Not exactly *with* Hitler.' Miles looked at Thompson. The Commander took up the conversation.

'It's complicated, Lucy. Stalin is playing a devious game. He has been negotiating with both us and with Hitler at the same time. For the moment he has sided with Germany because he believes he will win more territory by allying himself with the Nazi advance in the Balkans. However, if the tide turns, and it appears that we and France and our allies are capable of mounting an effective defence against Hitler, then he might well change sides and join our effort.' He raised a cynical eyebrow. 'All very duplicitous. But then Stalin is a duplicitous man. As your boss well knows.'

'And you think that Daniel... that Mr Mountview is passing information to Russia?'

Miles spoke. 'We do. He's in a key position at his embassy. He

68

has access to a lot of the messages passing between America and the allies.'

'Yes. He told me he had decoded messages from the White House.'

'There you are.'

She didn't know whether to be disappointed or appalled. 'So... so do you want me to turn down his invitation?'

'Not necessarily.'

She frowned. 'I don't understand.'

Miles shifted his position. 'May I ask, do you find this man attractive?'

She reddened slightly. 'I... well, he's quite good looking.'

'But do you like his company?'

'Yes. He's intelligent. He's much more sophisticated than me.'

Miles glanced back at Thompson. 'Well then, we'd quite like it if you continued your association.'

'Why?'

'It may be that we can exploit the situation to our own advantage. We'd all have to be clever about it – you included – but we might be able to fool him into sending false information to the enemy. Which could hamper their efforts, if you take my meaning.'

'Oh.'

Thompson sat back at the desk. 'How good are you at amateur dramatics, Lucy?'

'I don't know. I've never done any.'

'Well, it would be quite a simple role to play. The naïve secretary who unwittingly gives away a few apparently innocuous facts about naval tactics or government policies. Which nevertheless could lead an inquisitive mind to deduce various scenarios. Misleading scenarios.'

'Oh. I see.'

'Do you think you'd be up for that?'

'So it would mean... that I'd have to keep seeing him?'

Miles spoke. 'It would be quite useful for us if you did establish an ongoing relationship.' A brief twist of the lips. 'There would be no danger for you in it, provided you were subtle in your exchanges. But it could lead to a valuable method of confusing the enemy in his preparations.' His eyelids drooped. 'What gets to the Russians invariably gets to the Germans also.'

'I see.' She was quiet.

'You need only take it as far as you wished,' said Thompson. 'We aren't saying that you should become his mistress or anything. That side of things would be entirely up to you.'

She reddened further, but said nothing.

Miles rose from his chair. 'We'll leave you to think about it. We realise that it's quite a big demand for a young girl, but it could be of immense benefit to the war effort.'

She looked up at him. He seemed even more alien from that angle. 'You're quite sure? I mean, you're certain that he's a spy?'

'Pretty certain. We know that he's been communicating with Russia by various means. We're not sure how much information he's already passed, but we're working on it.'

Thompson rose, went to the door and opened it for her. 'Have a think, Lucy, and we'll talk again tomorrow. Meanwhile I suggest you go and enjoy the play.'

'What if... what if he asks me things tonight?'

'You can tell him ordinary stuff. Things he'll probably know already.' Thompson smiled. 'You're a bright girl. You'll know what's crucial information and what isn't'

At the door she stopped. 'Does Mr Churchill know about this?'

'Of course.'

'Oh.'

Thompson gave a wry smile. 'Don't worry. Knowing him, he'll enjoy the development.'

CHAPTER 11

Churchill did seem to enjoy the development.

When Lucy's turn came to attend to his wishes that morning, he was busy in the Map Room, pouring over one of the large table maps with the usual contingent of naval officers and WRNS in attendance. She stood to one side, awaiting his next command.

He straightened up from his scrutiny, and reached for his whisky glass with its heavy load of ice.

'A mighty challenge, gentlemen. A mighty challenge.' He took a sip. 'We need time, we need assistance.

'But where from?' asked one of the senior officers at his side.

'It's available from only one direction at this time.'

'America is never going to break neutrality so soon,' said another.

The lower lip protruded. 'Not overtly perhaps. But there are other ways.' He fished for his cigar case. 'Politics is the art of getting your opponent to surrender to your requests, whilst thinking it was his idea.'

Laughter around the table. He turned. 'I need to write a letter. Who's on duty?'

Lucy stepped forward. 'Yes, sir.'

'Ah, Lucy! Right. Er...' He hesitated. 'Better keep this discreet. Let's go into my sanctum.'

He waved to Commander Thompson, who was nearby. 'You come too, Tommy.'

He led the way to the small office at the back. Once inside, he closed the door on the three of them.

'No need for the whole world to know what's going on.' He waved to the desk. 'You sit here, Lucy dear, and have your notepad

71

ready.' The pale eyes glinted at her. 'I gather you've been enlisted into the ranks of the Secret Service.'

'Um... sort of, sir.'

'Never thought that would be part of your duties, eh?'

'No, sir.'

'Well, that's what war does to you. Sends you down paths you had never contemplated before.' He waved his cigar at Thompson. 'I'm writing to President Roosevelt again. We're going to have to discuss how much of this she can divulge to her American friend.'

'Yes, sir,' replied Thompson.

'Right.' Churchill began his pacing. 'This is thorny. To President Roosevelt. Dear Mr President...' Lucy began her shorthand. 'I know that you have been corresponding with my Prime Minister on this matter, but I thought I would just add my reflections. You will understand well the trials we are experiencing in the North Sea. The vital convoys commuting between our two nations are being severely assailed by the furtive activities of the German U Boat packs. Many tons of shipping, much needed cargoes, many brave lives are being lost. We have accelerated our ship building programme to the limits of our present capacity, and ditto for the air force. However these will inevitably take time to complete, and meanwhile we are in desperate need of reinforcements.' He paused in thought, mumbling to himself. Then continued. 'Of course I understand well the political problems you have in overtly assisting us in our war efforts, but as you and I understand, there are many ways of expediting such assistance, through trading, loan, or exchange arrangements, which would not seemingly contravene the conditions of your neutrality status. If by such means we could, ah... take possession of some of your large fleet of semi-obsolete destroyers and small warships, and also of whatever aircraft you could see your way to releasing, then this would be of immense help in our present predicament. And I might suggest also, of insurance against far greater commitment in the future.' He stopped again, head in the air. Then in the lighter tone he used for one of his quips, 'You may be familiar with the popular

72

British proverb, 'A stitch in time saves nine'. This could indeed be a case of ships in time saves ninety nine.' He grunted with pleasure at his invention. 'I do hope you can see your way to helping us in this hour of greatest need.'

He was lighting the cigar as he spoke. 'New paragraph. 'I am sending this by coded message for obvious reasons. I suggest you reply by the same way. We all have to conduct our affairs with perspicacity in these problematic circumstances. Exclamation mark.'

He puffed on the cigar for a few moments. Lucy waited. He nodded. 'Yes. Type that up, Lucy, then give it to the Commander. He will have it sent via our covert system.'

'Yes, sir.' She rose.

'Just a moment.' She stopped.

He peered at her over his spectacles. 'This, er... contact of yours. When are you seeing him again?'

'Tonight, sir. He's taking me to the theatre.'

He raised his eyebrows. 'Is he indeed? A whodunnit perhaps?'

'No, sir. An Oscar Wilde play.'

'Which one?'

'It's called 'An Ideal Husband,' I think.

His eyes lit up. 'Ah, very apposite. Full of deceit and subterfuge. Well, that will be fun. At least you'll get some pleasure from your cloak-and-dagger adventures.' He turned to the Commander. 'How should we deal with this, Tommy? What should she tell the man?'

Thompson replied, 'He already knows you are communicating with the President, Winston. There's no harm in her letting slip that it's ongoing. What the agent mustn't know is the extent that Roosevelt is sympathetic to the cause.'

'No...' Churchill puffed some more. 'Tell you what, Lucy. If the subject comes up – don't force it – but if it does arise, what you can indicate is that we aren't getting much joy from America in our need for assistance. The political situation over there is too sensitive. The President can't afford to antagonise his opponents in the government. And so on. Do you understand?'

'Yes, sir, I think so.'

'Just hint that we don't hope for much backing from our American friends. No need to go into details, but that will all help to lull the enemy into a false sense of security.' He twinkled at Thompson. 'As if they haven't got plenty of that already, eh Tommy?'

The other grinned. Lucy went to the door.

'Enjoy your evening, 'said Churchill. 'Tell us about "An Ideal Husband" tomorrow.'

'Yes, sir.'

'Just don't let it seduce you into thinking he might make one for you.'

She gave him a small smile, and left.

CHAPTER 12

Dear Mum,

I hope you are well. I hope Dad is too, and the bakery is thriving.

I am well, but very busy and quite tired at night. Mr Churchill keeps everyone around him on their toes, and the whole place is always buzzing. The war effort is going well. I'm not allowed to tell you much of what we do, but he and all the government are working extremely hard at bringing our armed forces up to scratch and developing our defences in case Mr Hitler decides to invade. I am having to type endless letters and reports to people all around Britain and the world. I also have to type stuff for Mrs Churchill sometimes. She is a kind and thoughtful lady. She and Mr Churchill sometimes have arguments, but you can see that they love each other very much.

I have met a nice man, who works at the American Embassy. He's very clever and cultured, and is taking me to the theatre tonight to see a play by Oscar Wilde! So you see, my education is improving on the professional, political, and artistic sides all at once.

Must go now. So much to do.

Give my love to Dad. And lots to you.

Lucy.

The play was intriguing. She had never been able to afford theatre tickets during her year at the college. Occasional cinema visits had been the extent of her cultural life. And as for Oscar Wilde, her only previous experience had been a home town amateur production of "The Importance Of Being Ernest", which she consider a rather frivolous piece. This was a weightier story, and far better performed, and she was enthralled throughout. In fact the

75

entire experience, from the exotic architecture of the theatre itself, to the animated chatter of the London audience, to the radiance of the production and cast, was a revelation to her inexperienced self.

Daniel appeared to enjoy her enjoyment as much as he did the play. However, her own appreciation was tempered with the completely new dimension to their relationship. She was now utterly confused as to her feelings towards him.

'I watched you during that,' he said as they walked down Shaftesbury Avenue afterwards. 'You were engrossed. Did it ring bells?'

'Bells? You mean with my own home life?'

'Yes.'

'Good heavens, no. I come from a very ordinary family. I told you, we make bread.'

'That doesn't preclude you from complex relationships.'

'Nothing like the play.' She threw him a quick smile. 'I sometimes wish we were a little more complex.'

'Complexity is disturbing. My family were complex and very dysfunctional. It was not a good environment to grow up in.'

'Dysfunctional?'

'Oh, yeh. Affairs, breakups, rows upstairs and down. Highly confusing for a kid, I can tell you.'

She risked a quick glance behind her as they walked to see if they were being followed, but couldn't see anything suspicious. He took her to dinner at the Lyons Corner House near Leicester Square. It was where all the theatre people went after the shows, he said.

Sure enough, when they entered the huge room with its low lighting and scattered discreet tables, she recognised several well-known cinema faces already dining.

'Wow! Who'd have thought that stars ate at Lyons?' she exclaimed.

He grinned. 'It's one of the few places that stay open late. Even stars have to eat.'

They had prawn cocktails and roast beef. She drank more red wine than she was used to. The evening glowed. They chatted easily. Her ambivalence faded to the background.

Over the apple pie dessert he said, 'I got wind today that your boss has been communicating directly with my President.'

She was back to reality. 'How...? How did you hear that?'

He toyed casually with his fork. 'Oh, everything has to be coded, as you know. And it gets sent via the embassy's lines. We don't all get to know the content of everything, but we hear who's talking to who.'

'Oh.'

'Has he been dictating to you?'

'Sometimes.'

'I guess it's all about getting the US to assist with the war effort. Your PM's been banging on about it for a while.'

'Yes.'

'So is it having any effect, d'you think?'

She didn't respond directly. 'You mean, on America helping with...?'

'With the convoys in the Atlantic. With the air defences. All that kinda stuff. You guys certainly need some backup there.'

She glanced about her. The other tables weren't close, and their occupants were engrossed with their own concerns. 'Well, I... from what I gather we're not getting much joy from your side. America is neutral, isn't it?'

He also kept his voice low. 'Sure. But we know that Roosevelt is as worried about Hitler as you are. He doesn't want him to succeed any more than Britain does.'

'Well, no, but his hands are tied, aren't they? By his parliament.'

'We don't have a parliament. We have a senate and a congress. But yes, it amounts to the same thing. The majority there want to keep the US out of the war.'

'So there's not much he can do.'

'Well, there are ways round it.'

'How?'

His gaze was straight. 'You tell me. What's your government suggesting?'

Her brain worked. How was she to fulfil her task? 'Not much. Anyway, I'm not supposed to talk about it.'

He grinned. 'Oh, come on. It's not a state secret, is it?'

'Well, yes it is. Why do you want to know anyway?'

He shrugged. 'I'm curious. Everyone wants to know the outcome of this war, don't they? Is it going to be over soon? Or is it going to be a long business like the last one?'

She put down her spoon. The pie helping was too much after such a dinner. 'I hope not. That lasted four years.'

'Yep. And millions of deaths. So the sooner our... your side can stop Hitler, the better.'

'We have to stop Stalin as well, don't we?'

He hesitated, his glass halfway to his mouth. 'Well, now... What does Churchill say about that?'

'Just that he... he doesn't trust him either.'

He nodded. 'Sure. He's a wily guy. But you know, the communists might be the clue to stopping the Nazis.'

'How?'

'They have a pact at the moment, but Stalin's as suspicious of Hitler's intentions as is everyone else. He is right to be. Hitler has his eyes on Russia's empire, along with all the rest.'

'You think Stalin may change sides?'

He shrugged again. 'Who knows? The winds are blowing in all directions. He'll go with the one that suits his purposes best.' He watched her over his wine glass as he sipped. 'It would be good for us if he did, huh?'

'I suppose so.'

He put down the glass and pointed his fork. 'I tell you, Hitler won't stop until he's conquered the world. Neither did Napoleon. And Napoleon's ambition came to grief in Russia. Everyone's ambitions come to grief in Russia. We need Russia.'

Her history was hazy on such matters. She said nothing.

He was going on. 'But anyway, papa Stalin isn't going to do anything unless he thinks your side is going win. He's only interested in the winners. Which is why he's waiting to see if the Yanks are going to join the party.'

'Oh. I see.'

'What do you think?'

'About what?'

'About that. What does Winston say about having Stalin onside?'

'I don't know. I haven't taken any dictation about that.'

'But he is hoping that America will?'

'Will what?'

'Get onside, for Christ's sake!'

She was carrying her innocence too far. 'He... he doesn't think there's much chance.'

'Really?'

'No. He thinks your President's hands are tied. He thinks we'll probably have to go it alone.'

He nodded, poured more wine, and sat back. He didn't pursue the matter, for which she was grateful.

He took her home again in a taxi. The kiss was longer this time, and he placed his hand over her breast. She didn't resist. He was attractive, the wine was working, her hormones were stirring.'

'Can I come up?' he murmured in her ear.

'No. I share with a room-mate.'

'It's time you got your own place.'

79

'I know.'

'Well, perhaps next time we'll go to mine.'

She felt half thrill, half terror.

He kissed her again, and opened the cab door. 'I don't know when I'm free again. I'll see you next week. I'll leave you a note.'

She nodded and got out. She had no idea of the time, but it was way past midnight.

CHAPTER 13

Dear Tommy,

I do so hope you are well, and the army is looking after you. We are all so proud of all the new skills you've learned, and of your promotion. Mum sent me a photo of you in uniform. I must say, you look extremely dashing. Do you have any girls in your unit???

As mum has told you, I'm working for Mr Churchill now. Of course I can't say what it involves, but I'm learning so much about the war effort, and also about how politics and governments function. We ordinary folk could never imagine the immense scale of the work that goes on here. There are hundreds of people working in the Admiralty alone, and everyone has their own special role and duties. The war still does not seem to have started here in London, but when one realises what is going on at sea, and in other parts of Europe, one can see that this is going to be a terrible conflict.

Oh, Tommy, I do hope you keep safe and well. I know you can't say too much about what you are doing either, but do write and tell me how you are. And how Henry is.

Much love, your sister Lucy.

P.S. I'm seeing a very nice American man who works at their embassy. He is opening my eyes to the world also. What a cloistered life we've led!

CHAPTER 14

'So how was the evening?'

Lucy was sitting opposite the desk, and Lieutenant Commander Thompson was behind it. He was smoking his pipe. The same MI5 man, Kenneth Miles, sat in the armchair to one side. It was Friday. She was not at her best after the late night. She was hoping to have at least part of the weekend off.

'It was nice, sir. The play was wonderful.'

'And after?'

'He took me to a Lyons Corner House for dinner.' There was no response from the men. 'Didn't you follow us?'

'No. We thought it best to leave you alone. There are always risks when people are followed.'

Miles spoke. 'How was the dinner?'

'Very nice. I'd never been there before.'

He nodded. 'It's a useful place. Open twenty four hours every day. You'd be surprised what goes on there.'

'So what did you talk about?' Thompson puffed on his pipe. In her slightly hungover state, Lucy did not appreciate the smell.

'Well, he did ask some more about my work. He knew that Mr Churchill had written to President Roosevelt yesterday.'

The two men sat up.

'He knew that already?' said Thompson, his pipe forgotten.

'Yes.'

'Had he read it?'

'No. Someone else coded it. He just knew a message had been sent through the embassy.'

'What did he say about it?'

'He guessed what it might be about.'

'What *exactly* did he say?' demanded Miles.

'Well, he... he presumed that it was to do with the government's request for aid from America. Ships and planes and so on.'

'And what did you tell him?'

'What Mr Churchill told me to say. That, yes, we wanted help from President Roosevelt, but that people didn't think there was much hope.'

Silence. She wilted under the intensity of the two pairs of eyes.

Thompson nodded. 'Good, Lucy. Well done.'

'Did you tell him anything else?' asked Miles.

'Not really. We talked about whether Russia might change sides.'

'Did he think it likely?'

'He thought it was possible. He said Stalin was hedging his bets.'

Miles's face was as expressionless as always. 'What happened afterwards?' he said. 'After the dinner?'

'He took me home in a taxi.'

'Did he come in with you?'

She shook her head. 'I'm staying in a hostel. They don't allow visitors after dark.'

'Will you see him again?'

She hesitated. 'I don't know. Perhaps. He said he'd leave me a note again.'

'You're not meeting this weekend?'

She recoiled under the barrage of questions. 'No. He said he didn't know when he'd be free next.'

Thompson's voice was gentle. 'Would you like to see him again?'

She looked down. 'I wouldn't mind. He's very interesting.'

'And attractive?'

'Yes. Quite.' Had they asked how much on a score from one to ten, she couldn't have answered. 'However, I...'

'What?'

'I'm quite frightened. I'm not...'

'You're not ready for the Mata Hari role?'

'No.'

Miles took over. His high voice was expressionless. 'You needn't fear. He's a political animal, not a hostile one. How much do you know about his background?'

'He told me about his career.'

'And his family?'

'He said his family was...'

'What?'

'He'd had a difficult childhood.'

'Yes. His father was rarely there. His mother married three times. One of them was abusive. But there is no evidence that he could be the same.'

Thompson was back puffing on his pipe. 'Well, it's up to you, Lucy. But it would be useful to us to know what he's up to. And maybe we can feed him more misleading information.'

She nodded. Her mind was a tumult. She was in a situation unprecedented in so many ways.

He sensed her dilemma. 'Don't worry about it. Take your time. We don't want you to do anything you're unhappy with.'

'Yes, sir.'

She got up and went to the door.

'One other thing,' said Miles. 'Did he say anything about the dinner here tonight?'

She turned. 'Dinner?'

'The Churchills have invited the Chamberlains to dinner at Admiralty House. Did he mention it?'

Of course! She had forgotten the letter that Clementine had dictated over a week ago.

'Oh. No.'

Miles showed the vestige of a frown. 'That's odd. Most people know about it. Those two are sworn enemies. It's caused quite a few ripples.'

'He said nothing about it.'

Thompson said, 'The dinner's probably just a case of Winston building bridges. Mountview may not necessarily know about it.'

'Yes,' said Miles. To Lucy, 'Well anyway, don't turn down another dinner invitation yourself.'

She and a couple of the other girls spent the rest of the morning typing up the various supply needs that daily flooded in from the ships at sea and in port. A constant flow of requests for armaments, ammunitions, spare parts, provisions, personnel, technical assistance, etc, etc. These had then to be forwarded to the Ministry of Supply or relevant departments. It was tedious work. She was relieved when the lunch break came.

It was a fine day outside, so she took her break out in nearby St James's Park, with a sandwich and an orange juice from the dining hall. She sat on a bench watching the bird life around the lake, and the assortment of other citizens enjoying the sunshine. She reflected on her time in this extraordinary job. Such a brief period, and yet so much happening. She wondered whether it had changed her. There was no question that it had expanded her own horizons and ambitions beyond anything that might have happened had she remained in her cloistered existence in Cumberland. Or that might have happened had she not broken the 'S' key on her typewriter. The whims of fate. She turned her face to the sun, and tried to rest her mind for the next half hour.

When she returned to her place of work, Grace Hamblin was as usual directing the girls to various jobs. She sent Lucy back to the apartment in Admiralty House.

'Winston is working upstairs this afternoon, Lucy. You'd better get up there. He's in full flood. He's already sent out reams of dictation on the state of the air force - although what that has to do with his responsibility as First Lord of the Admiralty, I've no idea.' She hesitated. 'Be warned. He's more ruffled than usual because of this dinner engagement tonight'. '

'Yes, Mrs Hamblin.'

'And you should call me Grace now.' She smiled. 'It looks as though you're a permanent fixture within the Secret Circle.'

Lucy felt as though she had been promoted. She smiled back, and left for the Churchill residence.

As she climbed to the first floor and passed the kitchen quarters, she was aware of intense activity within. The clattering of pans and utensils, the chatter of voices. Prominent among them that of Mrs Landemare, the Churchill's long-time cook brought from Chartwell. Preparing for the dinner, thought Lucy. As the MI5 man had said, it was causing ripples everywhere.

She knocked gently on the door of Churchill's study, and went in. Far from being ruffled, he was asleep on the chaise longue in the corner of the room. Rufus lay on the floor beside him, also dozing. Winston, as she now thought of him, was in one of his boiler suits, half a cigar and a half-full glass of iced whisky on the table beside him. His prominent belly rose and fell with his soft snoring.

The girls were all used to his frequent catnaps, and knew not to intrude. They rarely lasted long, and his vitality when he woke up was redoubled. Lucy quietly retreated, prepared for the onslaught that she knew would shortly follow.

She sat on a sofa in the lounge next door and gazed at the oil paintings, the heavy chandeliers, the curious furniture featuring carved dolphins at the corners. Here in this tranquil sanctum it was hard to believe that the world outside was embarked on yet another calamitous conflict. Why was man so wedded to the self-destruction of war, she wondered? What were the primitive instincts which drove him so frequently to confront other members of his species in do-or-die contests? She reflected that, if women were in charge of political affairs, such insanity would surely not prevail.

Her reverie was interrupted by the entrance of Clementine Churchill from the far side.

'Oh, Lucy,' exclaimed the lady. 'Is he asleep?'

'Yes, ma'am... Clementine. I'm waiting for him to wake up.'

Clementine nodded. 'Right. Well, perhaps it's as well. We have a bit of a crisis on.'

'A crisis?'

'For tonight.' She paced up and down. 'You know that Mr and Mrs Chamberlain are coming to dinner?'

'Yes. I typed the invitation for you.'

'So you did. Well, the maid who was going to assist Inches at table this evening has called in sick. She's got the flu or something. The other one is away on compassionate leave. The poor thing's lost a brother at sea. So Inches has no one to help him, and he doesn't think he can manage all the serving and clearing by himself. I wonder whether...' She paused reflectively. 'Just a moment. We'd better bring him in on this conversation.'

She went to a bell rope hanging in one corner, and tugged at it. The two women waited, Clementine staring out of the window, Lucy wondering what was coming next.

Inches knocked and entered, wearing his habitual worried face.

'Yes, ma'am?'

'Oh, David. About our little staffing problem. If we can't find an immediate replacement I was wondering whether Lucy here might step into the breach. What do you think?'

Inches contemplated Lucy for a few seconds. 'Have you any experience of waiting at table, miss?' he asked.

'Um... not really.'

'Well, you're a baker's daughter, aren't you, Lucy?' said

87

Clementine. 'You must have served teas and so forth at home.'

'With respect, ma'am – not quite the same thing,' said Inches. 'Serving tea to vicars and school children is not on a par with serving Prime Ministers.'

'No, but she's a sharp girl. You can instruct her. It's any port in a storm, isn't it?'

Inches looked dubiously at Lucy again. She was aware of his reputation as a stickler for perfection.

'Well, I don't... there's not much time. What do you feel about it, Miss Lucy?'

Lucy was sitting frozen in uncertainty. 'I don't know. I... What would I have to do?'

'Well, you'd have to help me in bringing the dishes from the kitchen, having them ready on the serving table, and then serving them at the right time and in the right manner around the dinner table. You'd also have to assist with the wine pouring, with the drinks and the canapés beforehand, and with the coffee and drinks afterwards. There's quite a lot to do.'

'It's mostly common sense,' said Clementine. 'There are a few points of etiquette which you probably know already, or if not, Inches will show you. I'm sure you could do it.' She smiled engagingly. 'Just think of it, Lucy. You'll be able to boast to your grand-children that you once served a Prime Minister at dinner.'

Lucy was far from thinking about boasts to grand-children. 'What would I wear? I haven't...'

'Oh, that's no problem,' said Clementine. 'You just need an apron and cap over your blouse and skirt. We can find you those.'

'Well, I...' Lucy hesitated, completely uncertain how to respond.

Inches settled it for her. 'Yes, I think it's possible. You could do it. You'd just have to take directions from me.' He glanced at his mistress. 'She can't be any worse than Jill, ma'am. That girl is not the most competent, if I may say so.'

Clementine gave a small sigh of relief. 'That's it then. You are free this evening, aren't you, Lucy?'

'Yes.' No smart theatre or dinner dates tonight, that was certain.

'Right, well off you go with Inches and learn the ropes. I will square it with my husband. I'm sure you'll do it brilliantly.' She turned to the butler. 'You will instruct her how to deal with any situations that may arise later in the evening, won't you, David? You know what I'm talking about.'

'Yes, ma'am. Don't worry. We'll handle things together.'

The pair left the room - he determined, she apprehensive.

'What situations?' she asked, as they headed for the kitchen.

Inches pulled a lugubrious face. 'Ah, well, it's just that when the boss is in his cups, as he frequently is late on in the evening, things can get lively. It will be our job to try and curtail the intake of alcohol as much as possible.'

'Lively? What do you mean?' She had not seen Winston in a social situation.

Inches seemed to realise that she was in need of further information, and stopped walking. 'Well, he can get even more loquacious than usual, and sometimes more... let's say, bellicose than usual. And as this is such a unique occasion, Lucy, we don't want anything untoward to happen.' He heaved a great sigh, and sat heavily on an antique sofa at the side of the passageway.

'Are you all right?' she asked.

'Oh, it's just... I don't want this stress. I'm too old.' Inches fingered his collar. 'There's not many situations I can't deal with – I've seen it all – but this... well, this is just too bloody unnerving – pardon my language.'

'Will it really be so difficult?' she said, still standing.

'Oh, it might be. Believe me, it might be.' He blew out his cheeks. 'It's not just... I mean I'm used to distinguished company. I've handled statesmen, aristocracy, royalty even... and some are best not commented on, let me tell you. But this is different.'

'Why?' She was becoming more apprehensive, rather than less.

'This is an occasion... well, how does one describe it? – quite beyond the scope of *my* imagination.' His Edinburgh accent had become more pronounced with his emotion.

'Really?'

'Well, look at the picture. Here we all are, six weeks into what we laughably call a war... six weeks with the boss back in cabinet, causing mayhem naturally – after no less than ten years kept out of it – shameful in itself, I have to say – and tonight, for reasons known only to himself, he's asked the Prime Minister and his missus to dinner!'

'What's wrong with that?'

'Do you know nothing of their past together?'

'Not much, no.'

'Well, let me tell you it hasn't been exactly friendly. In fact it's been quite the opposite.'

'Oh. Why?'

'Good heavens, girl, don't you know your politics? Don't you read the papers?'

'Not very often.' Once again she cursed her ineptitude.

'Well, you should know that the two of them have been sworn enemies for years. Over many things, but mostly over the appeasement business. The Prime Minister and most of his cabinet have been trying every which way to negotiate with Hitler, with the aim of avoiding war. Winston on the other hand has been warning them constantly that the tyrant was not to be trusted, and we should be preparing for hostilities. Well, for that reason he's been extremely unpopular, not only with the government, but around the country as well. People don't want hear unpleasant truths. That's the reason he's been excluded from office for so long.'

'Oh. I see.'

Inches shook his head. 'It hasn't been pretty, I can tell you. All those years of antagonism. All the snarling and clawing at each other – in public and in parliament. All the insults and the recriminations. And now this...' He took a deep breath. 'An intimate dinner together as if they were old friends.' He waved a hand aimlessly in the air. 'Two of the... no, count the women, and it's *four* of the toughest personalities you're ever likely to encounter – who've never...' He raised a gnarled finger, '...and this is the extraordinary thing – never before actually met all together on their own – now having an intimate dinner as if they were old friends.' His eyes lifted to the ceiling. 'With oysters and Irish Stew of all things, on the menu.' His hands waved in a hopeless gesture. This wasn't the unflappable butler she was used to. 'What's it about? What's the purpose, I ask you? And more to the point, what's it going to lead to?'

'Lead to?'

'Yes. One war out there, and another one in here?' He pointed the finger at her. 'With you and me in the middle. Is it any wonder I'm nervous?'

'Well, surely they're on the same side now?'

'Yes, Lucy, but there's still a lot of choppy water between them. The boss is trying to push the PM further than he wants to go. And furthermore he knows his time is probably up.'

'Whose time?'

'Chamberlain's!' Resentment showed in his tone. 'He's botched the whole deal. Hitler's run rings round him. Winston's been proved right all along. And now a lot of people think he should be Prime Minister instead.'

'Oh, yes.'

'So you see, it doesn't make for a very amicable situation – oysters and Irish stew notwithstanding. And as I said, the old man can get extremely... bombastic when he's had a bit to drink. You've never seen him like that. I have. On many an occasion.'

Lucy's reservations were increasing. 'His drinks are usually only weak ones, aren't they?'

'Ah, yes, during the day. The night's another matter. He'll start on the champagne or the whisky – take your pick – he'll go onto the wine, and it's a brave man who'll stop him consuming a bottle or two – and then there's the port or the brandy to come. I don't know how his liver stands it. He's got the constitution of a rhinoceros.' The finger wagged more. 'It's up to you and me to try and limit his consumption as much as we're able.'

'Right.' She didn't know how she was supposed to do that.

He relaxed somewhat. 'Of course it's easier for me down at Chartwell. He's got a dozen staff running around after him there – not that he can afford them – but up here in London...' He tailed off. 'Ah well...' Inches heaved himself to his feet, and went on in a lighter tone. 'I have to admit, however, that you might say I'm privileged. How many would give their right arm to have witnessed what I've witnessed, eh? It's history in the making. As it usually is with my boss. And I've been there to see it. Yes, I suppose I'm a privileged man.'

'Yes, Mr Inches, you are.'

His lower lip jutted as though he'd learnt it from his employer. 'But it's very stressful!'

He led the way on to the kitchen.

Lucy spent the next two hours being instructed in the various procedures of serving a formal dinner. There was so much protocol attached to what, for her, had always been a pretty simple business. She learned where to stand, when to come forward, when to step back, where to place things, how to hold dishes, how to present cutlery, how to serve vegetables, how to cut cheese, how to pour drinks, when to clear away – the rituals of upper class dining were endless. She could only imagine what her mother might have to say about it all.

'Good,' said Inches eventually. 'I think she'll manage, don't you, Georgina?'

Mrs Landemare was a stout down-to-earth woman, who had served the Churchills for many years, and whose culinary skills were legendary. She had aided the instruction and now she nodded, her double chin wobbling. 'You'll do very well, dear. Just remember, whatever happens, stay calm and sail on as though it never did.'

Lucy felt scarcely reassured.

Inches looked at his pocket watch. 'Nearly four o'clock. The Chamberlains are due at seven. I suggest that you are here by six, Lucy, to prepare. Go and take a rest now, and we'll see you later.'

CHAPTER 15

'The Lieutenant Commander will meet them at the entrance, and conduct them up to the apartment. I will greet them at the door, with you standing over there. I will take their hats and coats and hand them to you. You place them in the hall closet, whilst I conduct them through to Mr and Mrs Churchill in the drawing room. Is that clear?'

Inches, equilibrium recovered, was speaking to her as they stood in the wide vestibule to the First Lord's apartment.

Lucy, clad in white maid's apron and small mob-cap, and feeling somewhat ridiculous, nodded. 'Yes.'

'You may then follow through to the drawing room, and stand by the drinks table until it's time to fetch Mrs Landemare's canapés. I will pour the drinks for everyone and hand them round. When I give you the signal, you and I will fetch the canapés, which will be waiting in the kitchen freshly made. You will hand them round with the miniature napkins. I will let you know when to offer them again. We don't want everyone to eat so much early on that they don't want the cook's Irish Stew.'

Lucy had been through it all already, but she said, 'I understand. Um...?

'Yes?'

'Isn't Irish Stew an odd dish to serve Prime Ministers?'

He threw her a wry glance. 'It was Mr Churchill's choice. It's one of his favourite dishes. He has always liked plain cooking.'

'I see.'

'Besides, Mrs Landemare does a superb Irish Stew.' He looked at his pocket watch. 'Fifteen minutes to go. Let's go and do a last minute check of the dining room.'

They found Clementine already doing the same thing. She was wearing a pale blue evening dress with lace trimmings, which emphasised her lean figure. The large dining table was set with just four elaborately laid places in the centre, but was adorned with flowers and candelabras.

Clementine looked up as they entered. 'It all looks very nice, David.'

'Thank you, ma'am.'

She surveyed Lucy's outfit. 'And so do you, Lucy. I think you'll find this evening an experience.'

Of that Lucy had little doubt.

Clementine was not smiling. She wandered, wringing her hands. 'Oh dear, I do hope it all goes to plan.'

'I'm sure it will, ma'am,' said Inches.

'As if our dinner parties ever go to plan.' She stopped and turned to Lucy again. 'You will be hearing a lot of confidential talk tonight, Lucy. A lot of things about the war, about the government, about important political matters. Sometimes the discussion may get a bit heated.' She smiled wanly. 'Even politicians get emotional over matters that deeply concern them. But we must trust you to be extremely discreet about anything you overhear. You must not divulge anything to anyone – however small. Do you understand?'

Lucy, in her maid's outfit, almost felt obliged to bob. 'Of course, Clementine.'

'And for the purposes of the evening you should refer to me as 'Mrs Churchill' or 'ma'am'. And to Winston as 'sir'.

'Yes... ma'am.'

Clementine sighed. 'It's at moments like this that I wish we were back at Chartwell.'

Inches was adjusting the blackout curtains on one of the windows. 'The price of office, ma'am.'

'I suppose it is.' She fingered the pearl necklace at her throat. 'One shouldn't complain. After all this time waiting for it.'

At that moment the man in office himself entered at the far end, wearing evening dinner suit and black bow tie. He had on his metal framed glasses and was carrying a file.

'Aha!' he exclaimed, peering over the spectacles. 'The reception committee is gathering. Good, good.' He recognised Lucy, and his eyebrows raised. 'Lucy? Is that you?'

'Yes, sir.'

'Good heavens! Are we running out of maid servants as well as war materials?'

Clementine moved forwards. 'We had a small staff crisis, dearest. We didn't want to bother you with it. Lucy has bravely stepped up to the mark, and will be helping Inches with everything.'

'Well, well. Is there no end to your talents, Lucy? Thank you. I'm sure Inches is extremely relieved to have you on side.'

'Yes indeed, sir,' said Inches.

Churchill gazed at the table, fingering his bow tie, which was crooked. 'All looks very smart. How's the dinner coming along?'

'Splendidly, sir. Mrs Landemare has everything well organised.'

'The oysters? What are the oysters like?'

'A good crop. Fresh from Whitstable this morning.'

'Splendid. We'll have the Pol Roger with those.' He always lit up at the mention of food. 'And what's to follow?'

'You should know, dear,' said Clementine. 'You ordered it.'

'Oh, yes of course! Irish Stew – my favourite!'

'Let's hope it's theirs,' she murmured drily. 'And please remember he's still the boss. Don't bully him.'

The lower lip protruded. 'Bully? Chamberlain?'

She took the spectacles from his nose, folded them, and slipped them into his top pocket. 'Even him. I understand your frustration, my darling, but others do find it intimidating.' She straightened his bow tie. 'Especially Prime Ministers.'

He brushed her hand away. 'It's a Prime Minister's concern to recognise frustrations. Almost his first concern. However I think... I hope... he's finally seen the writing on the wall.'

'Of course, how could he not?'

He glowered. 'The issue is whether we read the same message in it.'

They stood close together, she with her hands on his lapels. 'So is that what this evening is? A lesson in hieroglyphics?'

'No...'

'What then?'

'I tend to naval metaphors these days. Call it a sea trial. He needs me to power the ship, as much as we all need him to steer it.'

She stepped back and opened her hands in a gesture. 'After twenty years at sea together, you should know each other's methods.'

'Relatively calm waters though, puss. When a hurricane's in the offing you discover men's true colours.'

Something rang in Lucy's head. Her father's words from another era.

'It's when you're in the middle of a storm that you find out who your friends are. None of your family have helped us, - but who'd have guessed it – my bloody minded old Uncle George comes up trumps in our hour of need.'

'Yes, Fred, well I've never liked him much, but I must admit he's saved our bacon this time. Especially when he's hard up hisself. Will you ever be able to pay him back?'

'Of course, luv. Soon as the business is going. May take some time, but I'm not going to be beholden to anyone.'

'I'll remember that next time I let you into the savings jar.'

Inches coughed. 'If you don't need me, ma'am, I should get back to the kitchen.'

'Yes, of course, David.'

He turned to Lucy. 'You stay with Mr and Mrs Churchill, Lucy, and let me know if there's anything they need.'

Lucy nodded, and he left the room.

Churchill had put his glasses back on, and was studying a paper from the file.

'Farcical!' he exclaimed in his rasping growl. 'How can we fight this war with half the number of troops we fought the last one with?'

'The last one killed most of them.' Clementine was surveying the table again. 'Anyway it's not yet your concern, pug.' She turned. 'Are you quite ready?

'Eh?'

'They'll be here any moment. Unlike you he's a stickler for punctuality.'

Lucy watched them from the side. The bond of long-standing affection between the two was palpable, despite his preoccupation with the file. Clementine took it gently from his hands. 'Let me have that. Time for papers tomorrow.'

He allowed it to go. 'I never cease to wonder at man's capacity for self-delusion,' he muttered.

She placed the file on a side table. 'You're not always innocent of that, you know. Why don't you concentrate on your bit of the war?'

'I feel lonely. At the moment mine's the only department fighting one.'

'Yes, well just remember, we don't want you fighting it here this evening.'

He chuckled then, and glanced at Lucy. 'Course I won't. I'm just a harmless teddy bear, aren't I, Lucy?'

She smiled. 'One might say that, sir.'

98

He finally put away his spectacles, and gestured to the door. 'How's Inches?' he asked her. 'He seemed nervous.'

'A little, sir,' replied Lucy. 'He's concerned that the evening goes well.'

'So'm I,' added Clementine.

'Why all the fuss?' he demanded. 'It's a small dinner party. We've handled far bigger occasions with aplomb.'

Clementine's tone was dry. 'Bigger, but scarcely more bizarre.'

'Bizarre? Nonsense. They're normal amiable people.'

Her eyebrows rose. 'Amiable is not the first epithet I'd use for Neville.'

His head waved in an ironic movement. 'Oh... there are many sides to him. He might surprise you.'

She straightened one of the silver serving spoons on the table. 'Yes, well... I do wish....'

'What?' Pause. 'What?'

'I've told you. I wish I knew what the purpose of this dinner...'

'What?'

She turned and looked at him directly. 'Don't you see enough of him in cabinet, Winston?'

He pouted, a child's pout. 'Cabinet, pussy cat, is a boxing ring. Parliament's a gladiatorial arena. I need him by the fireside with his defenses down.' The pout increased. 'I need a whisky. Let's go to the other room.'

He stalked off to the drawing room. Clementine murmured into Lucy's ear. 'Pour him a whisky, but with lots of ice.' And she followed him, with Lucy bringing up the rear.

In the next room, the lights were brighter, a coal fire burned in the grate, and the scene was generally more hospitable than in the formal dining room. Lucy went to the drinks table, laden with many bottles, and did as she was instructed. Churchill was lighting a cigar as he paced up and down.

'After all, I'm the one who should be apprehensive,' he declared.

Clementine sat on a sofa. 'Why?'

He waved the cigar. 'Well... he does that to me. Beware the quiet opponent.'

She raised an eyebrow. 'So this is an ambush – is that a good idea?'

'It's nothing of the sort.' He stopped pacing. 'I realise you... everyone believes we're....'

'Yes?'

'The world assumes mutual loathing between us, Clemmie, because we've roared at each other so often across the jungle...'

'You roar,' she interjected drily. 'He just growls.'

He shrugged. 'Maybe, but his growls are usually worth hearing – even when he's growling in the wrong direction. We will no doubt be recorded as staunch enemies, but I have...' He searched for his words, '...immense respect for the man.'

She shook her head. 'Your capacity for forgiveness will never cease to amaze me.'

'Well...' He growled himself. 'Forgive and forget...'

She flashed with anger in a way Lucy had never seen before. 'Ten years! Forget?'

Churchill made a placatory gesture. Lucy brought him the drink she had mixed. He regarded it critically, then went on. 'I tell you, Clementine – I have worked with and against him for twenty years. People don't understand him.'

'Oh...'

'Under that arid exterior lies a remarkable mind – even though it's not always easy to fathom.' He raised his finger. 'You know the great irony?'

'What?

'It galls me to state it, but without this war history could well

100

have declared him one of our finest Prime Ministers. The war is his tragedy.'

Lucy pondered the dichotomy. It had never occurred to her that circumstances might so dictate a politician's legacy.

'The war is all our tragedies,' said Clementine.

'Yes, well it's brought me office but it's a bitter reward.' He took a swig at the whisky, then threw a disgruntled look at Lucy. 'That's a very weak one.'

'I told her to make you a weak one,' said his wife. 'There's a long evening ahead.'

He grunted, and continued his theme. 'I do understand the pacifist sentiment, believe me.'

'That's nice to know,' she responded.

'Just a pity it's not universal.' He circled the glass, making the ice cubes clink. 'It's the problem the gods set us...'

'What is?'

'How do we.... how do nations for that matter – coexist with those who are temperamentally at odds with themselves?'

'Yes, well...'

'I don't mean conflict of opinions – those you can hammer at until you're both too weary to bother any more.'

'Mmm,' she murmured with meaning.

'I mean a deep fundamental divergence in spirit. As we appear to have with the Germans.'

'Is it so fundamental with him?'

'I still don't know, you see. I fear so. I need to know.'

'And my part in this voyage of discovery?' she asked.

'Thaw him out. You're wonderful at that.' He pointed his cigar at her. 'Get under his shirt – if not his trousers.'

She grimaced with distaste. 'Oh please....'

Lucy wondered whether she had heard aright. They both appeared to have forgotten her presence. But she had already understood that those accustomed to the attendance of servants ignored their presence as a matter of habit.

He was going on. 'Shouldn't think his trousers are pregnable in any case.' The lower lip protruded. 'Annie too. I suspect she's not one of my fans. Delve.'

'I don't think she's a fan of politics generally,' said Clementine.

'But he dotes on her. She may despise politics, but she must know where his soul lies. In the end that's what politics hangs by.'

'Really?'

'Ah puss...' He threw her a rueful glance. 'Don't sink to the electorate's level.'

'Your disdain for the voters will bite you one day,' she said quietly.

'I don't disdain them. We are their servants. But all too often they are like rabbits who only think of the next meal.'

Lucy wasn't sure she understood all that was being said, but she was enthralled. Such talk was far beyond her experience.

Churchill was rumbling on. 'No, Clemmie - we're on the brink of the greatest tempest in history, and we have to rely on that peculiar man to captain us through it. History often turns on one man's decision, and I...'

There was a knock, and he stopped. Inches put his head in.

'They've arrived in the courtyard, sir.'

'Ah, right.'.

'Lucy and I should go to greet them.'

'Yes, yes.' Churchill went to put out his cigar. 'Run along, Lucy, and say good evening to the Prime Minister of Great Britain.'

Lucy followed Inches to the entrance hall.

CHAPTER 16

If it had not been for their formal, old-fashioned dress – he in dinner suit and wing collar, she in a pretty, but slightly prim floral cocktail dress – they would have been an insignificant couple. Had she passed them in the street Lucy probably wouldn't have recognised them. They were both a touch less than medium height. He, frail looking, moustached, gaunt of feature. She, comely, buxom, with a somewhat austere expression. They stood in the hallway as Inches took their coats, and handed them to Lucy.

'Thank you,' said Chamberlain. 'The coats are a little damp. We walked from Downing Street and there's a bit of a drizzle.'

'We'll have them dried for you, sir,' replied Inches in his most formal butler's voice. He nodded to Lucy. She wasn't sure how she was supposed to do that, but for now she went to hang them in the closet.

'This way, sir, madam.' Inches led the way with stately bandy-legged gait to the drawing room.

The small group entered. Lucy was not party to the initial greetings as she was preoccupied with the coats, but she entered a few moments later. The Prime Minister was looking round the room, his greying hair glinting in the light from the chandeliers.

'I can't remember ever having been up here,' he was saying in his light, accentless voice. 'Rather grander than our quarters in Downing Street.'

'Confirming that the British have always valued their sailors above their politicians,' said Winston. He was standing, feet apart, neither cigar nor glass for once in hand.

Chamberlain threw him an amused glance. 'Oh, they value everyone above their politicians.'

Winston grinned. 'Hah! True.' He stepped forward and clasped

Anne Chamberlain's hand. 'Annie – it's good to see you.'

She smiled, a slightly forced smile. 'Winston.'

'You look lovely. What will you drink?'

She hesitated. 'Sherry, please. Dry.'

Winston nodded at Inches, who went to the drinks table. Lucy stood beside it, awaiting her orders.

'Drink, Prime Minister?' said the host.

'Let's not be formal – Neville, please. A weak whisky.'

'Ah,' said Winston, 'we're good at those.'

Chamberlain nodded back towards the hallway. 'A lot of activity downstairs.'

'Yes,' rasped the reply. 'Night is the time for predators. Especially at sea.'

'Are you down there much?'

'He's always down there,' interjected Clementine. 'I'm thinking of siting the war room in my divorce petition.'

He gave a wry smile. 'Silly question.' He glanced round again. 'Some magnificent paintings in this place. What an inheritance. They do show up the shallowness of some modern daubs.'

'Indeed,' said Winston. 'Is it the truth of all the arts, do you suppose?'

'Ah. Too deep for me. Do you still paint?'

Clementine answered for him. 'Oh yes, he does. Well... did.'

'I have a love affair with the spectrum,' said Winston. 'One might say it was my salvation during, um...' He tailed off.

There was an awkward pause, which Lucy could not interpret.

Chamberlain broke it with a cough 'Rather good you are too, they tell me.'

'A competent amateur,' said Winston. He pointed to two small water colours hanging on the wall, one above the other, between much grander traditional oil paintings. 'Those two are mine.'

Lucy had not noticed them before. She was reminded of her

mother.

'If I'd had my life over again, Lucy, I'd have been a painter. Wonderful thing to be a painter if you've got the talent. I was quite good when I was your age. People said I could 'ave made a go of it. But I needed to go to art school to become a proper artist, and my parents thought it was a silly idea.' Sigh. 'We didn't 'ave the money anyway. So I made cakes instead.'

Chamberlain had moved over and was peering at the water colours. 'Is there anything you don't do well, Winston?'

The reply was brisk. 'Ski, make money, and make friends in Parliament.'

His guest turned from the paintings. 'Ah, you have plenty of those, I think.' There appeared to be a dry humour beneath the solemn exterior.

'Well, they're very good at concealing themselves when the flack's about.'

The tone again was waggish. 'And you do tend to attract a lot of that.'

Clementine raised her hands. 'Gentlemen – you're not on the floor now.'

The PM raised his own hands in apology. 'Forgive us. No shop talk tonight.'

Anne spoke with a dry inflection. '*That* will be a hard resolution to keep.'

'Anne won't have any politics in the boudoir or the ballroom,' said her husband.

Clementine raised her eyebrows. 'Good rule, Anne. How do you impose that?'

'He lets me be boss in the boudoir, and we're rarely seen in ballrooms.'

'What an exemplary life you lead,' said Winston, moving to pick up his whisky glass. 'In great contrast to ours, I fear.'

'Well, it's true we don't find much fun in casinos, Winston.'

He threw her a quick look. 'Ouch. You know where to aim your rapier, Anne.'

Clementine's comment was equally dry. 'Yes. If it wasn't for gambling casinos, and stock market casinos – at both of which my husband has a genius for picking wrong numbers – we'd have no money worries at all.'

'Woah – assault on all sides!' he exclaimed. 'Help me, Neville.'

'Ah, no. I can only handle one war at a time.'

Winston gave one of his grunts, and spoke more somberly. 'Well, anyway... no casinos or ballrooms for anyone now. Not for a long time I fancy.'

'No.'

'No,' repeated Anne.

To Lucy, the talk of money worries was intriguing. How could this high-living family, with their big country house and their champagne lifestyle have money worries? She knew what it was like to have *real* money worries. She had been barely a teenager when the Great Depression struck.

'Come on, Jim, you must think of something. I 'aven't even got anything proper for supper, there's the rent overdue, the kids shoes falling apart, the coal's running out – and all the rest.'

'I know, luv, I know. I'm trying. It's just there's no jobs. I don't know where else to look. Everyone's in the same boat.'

'Well it's a ruddy leaky boat if you ask me. You need to plug the holes with summat, or the whole thing's going to sink.'

Inches came forward with the drinks on a silver tray. Winston waited until they each had a glass in hand, then raised his in a flamboyant gesture. 'To an emphatic victory!'

'To a *swift* victory,' responded Chamberlain more soberly.

106

'To an honorable victory,' said Clementine.

'Oh dear,' said Anne. 'That doesn't leave me anything.'

Winston turned to her. 'Then just to victory, Anne.'

'Yes.' She lifted her sherry glass. 'To victory.'

Inches turned to Lucy and murmured, 'We'll fetch the canapés.' The pair slipped from the room.

'Victory, huh!' On the way to the kitchen, the butler was muttering. 'Easy to drink to. Not so easy to achieve.' Lucy almost had to run to keep up with him. 'Hard to credit, but we've gone into this war with a third the number of soldiers Germany has.' He waved a hand at her as he marched. 'That's supposed to be secret, but in my job you hear a lot of things you're not meant to.' He rumbled on, 'Half the number of tanks and guns, half the number of aircraft. Half the number of pikestaffs too, I shouldn't wonder.' His thumb jerked back towards the drawing room. 'And he's been telling them. Hammering away about rearming, year in, year out, to anyone who cared to listen. And all that time they were calling him a crank, a warmonger, a loose cannon, a bull-in-a-china-shop - and anything else they could think of.' He shook his head in disgust. 'With Adolf calmly marching into country after country, and no-one lifting a finger.' They approached the kitchen area. 'So now we're finally at war with the bugger, they're all lauding the old man as the only person who can save us from the mess! Huh - politicians! Any wonder they don't get respect.'

He flung open the kitchen door and marched in. The large kitchen, its walls hung with copper pans and iron tureens, was clattering with activity. The cooking range bubbled and steamed from all its rings and plates, the huge central table sagged beneath the weight of dishes, Mrs Landemare and her two kitchen maids were bustling around with intense deliberation. It seemed a lot of effort for a dinner for four, thought Lucy. Her mother would be much amused.

'Canapés,' demanded the butler at the doorway.

The cook pointed an imperious finger. 'Over there, David, over there.' She continued with her preparations as Inches went to the side table where two large porcelain dishes rested. He handed one to Lucy. It contained what looked like delicate pieces of toast, bearing slices of smoked salmon and prawns on a bed of creamed mayonnaise. His own dish held some sort of miniature puff pastries enclosing she knew not what. Her own taste buds stirred. She realised she was quite hungry. In all the tension of preparations she hadn't thought to eat anything beforehand.

'Everything going to schedule, Mrs Landemare?' asked Inches, dish in hand.

'Of course it is!' she retorted sharply. 'Why wouldn't it be?'

The kitchen maids sniggered.

'Sorry I asked,' he said, pulled a face to Lucy, and turned to the door. The pair marched back to the drawing room with their loads.

'Even she's uptight today,' he muttered as they went. 'Used to plenty of trained help down at Chartwell, and fresh produce from the gardens. Does dinner for twenty without blinking. You wouldn't think dinner for four would create such a kerfuffle, would you? Ah, well... back to the fray.'

CHAPTER 17

As they entered, the group were still standing, drinks in hand. An awkward stillness prevailed. Inches whispered in her ear, 'I'll check the drinks, you offer round the dishes. Your fishy one first.'

As she obeyed, Chamberlain broke the silence by clearing his throat. 'Well, so here we all are...' Then he tailed off.

'Indeed,' replied Winston.

'This is pleasant.'

'Yes,' said Clementine.

'What are we celebrating?'

Winston raised his chin. 'Eh?'

'Tonight.'

'Do we have to be celebrating anything?'

Chamberlain looked at him with meaning. 'If not, then you want to pin me to the wall over something.'

The eyes of the two women went to Winston. 'Must an innocent dinner invitation herald ulterior motives?' he said cheerfully.

Chamberlain turned to Clementine. 'Since your husband joined the cabinet, Clementine, I've been bombarded with missives and memos, directives and petitions - enough to bury my entire staff.'

'Only to the waist,' muttered Winston.

Clementine looked amused. 'I sympathise.'

'If Hitler had been subjected to such an onslaught,' said Chamberlain, 'he'd have thrown in his hand already.'

'Oh, I sent him a few,' said Winston, and took a long swig at his whisky.

'Yes, well... I've no doubt.'

Winston held out his glass for Inches to fill. 'I'm merely trying to make up for lost time, Prime Minister.'

The other looked awkward. 'Yes... well... yes.'

Winston raised a finger, as so often when emphasising a point. 'The facts are....'

Anne interjected to Clementine before he could continue. 'You must miss Chartwell, having to be here.'

'Well, Chartwell's a different world.' said Clementine. 'Peace and greenery and countryside. Everything that politics isn't.'

Yes, thought Lucy, peace and greenery. A part of her was longing for those things, such a fundamental part of her past life. But then she was trapped in this intense urban existence as much as were these people.

Clementine was indicating the chairs. 'Please sit down, people.'

They sat, except for Churchill who stood, legs astride, holding the floor. 'The facts are, we have weeks only... a few months at most. Once he's swallowed Poland, devoured Scandinavia, this thing commences for real.'

'Perhaps,' said Chamberlain.

'Oh yes. Mind you...'

'Sit down, dear,' said Clementine in her school governess voice.

He ignored her, and continued. 'Mind you, this lull could be his undoing.'

Chamberlain cocked his head. 'How so?'

'We need to remember, Neville, how the taste of war galvanises the British working man.'

'You think so?'

'Yes, yes. Allow him a comfortable peaceful existence and he's the most cussed, pig-headed, union minded bugger on the planet...'

'Oh,' Anne exclaimed gently.

'Neville knows, Anne - his family's employed enough of them. However, face that man with a war, and suddenly he's all fire and patriotism and his productivity goes up ten-fold. Germans don't work like that. Adolf doesn't know what he's up against.'

'Well, I pray you're right,' Chamberlain had a sombre face.

Lucy circled the group with the canapés. Anne gave her a brief smile as she helped herself. Chamberlain barely noticed her presence. Winston took two, before sitting down. Lucy returned to the drinks table, wishing she dared to take one herself. But that would be an appalling breach of her position.

Anne was speaking. 'We walked here tonight. The Whitehall way. Strange to see London so quiet, so dark.'

'All those magnificent buildings,' added her husband. 'The symbols of empire. All in darkness.'

'As he wants,' growled Winston. 'In pursuit of his own empire.'

Chamberlain contemplated his glass. 'Ours was on the whole constructively ruled, you know. Peacefully relinquished. Despite the critics, we haven't judged things too badly.'

'Apart from relinquishing India,' commented Winston.

'Now, Winston – old ground.'

'Nevertheless...'

'I'm sure you don't wish to revive charges of racism.'

The response was sharp. 'I was never a racist! I'm an evolutionist. It's accidents of history that the white races have advanced the quickest. India owes us a lot, and many of them acknowledge it.'

It was another topic Lucy knew little about.

Chamberlain turned to Clementine. 'Never knows when he's beaten, does he?'

'No,' she said.

He went on before Winston could protest, 'When I was in my twenties my father sent me out to the Bahamas. A wild scheme to create sisal plantations. Turned out I didn't stand a chance in that climate. But I saw the effects of British rule.'

'Ah.' Winston was nodding.

'A small island on the far side of the world. Backward people. But there was order. There was law. There was basic education.'

'Yes, yes – good.'

'Yet now here... the supposed apex of civilisation, and we have anarchy.'

Winston gazed upwards and quoted, 'In this seat of peace tumultuous wars shall kin with kin confound...'

Lucy listened to the chatter with half a mind. The other half was contemplating the extraordinary situation in which she had found herself. What was it her mother had said?

It's a right opportunity for you, love. You can learn shorthand and typing and all that stuff. You could end up working for some big company.

Could any of her friends or family at home have seen her now they would scarcely have believed it - waiting on these people, listening to their talk. Talk involving the history of nations and the lives of millions, whilst she served them smoked salmon and prawn titbits. Was this a dream?

Chamberlain was speaking again. No, it was no dream.

'I often conjecture what would have transpired if I had made a success out there. Would I now be a wealthy plantation owner, living a life of idle pleasure far from the turmoils of Europe?'

'Destiny will not be eluded so easily,' proclaimed his host.

Anne smiled at him, a tolerant smile. 'You're a great believer in destiny, aren't you, Winston.'

'I'm a believer in the fulfilment of a man's character, whatever that may be,' he responded.

'Positive *or* negative?'

'Certainly. Which is why Hitler's vision of his destiny is so transparent.'

Chamberlain looked dubious. 'Ah... well...'

'You still don't think so?'

'I...'

'You still think he can be diverted?'

The other was evidently disconcerted. 'I think he...'

Awkwardness again clouded the atmosphere.

'What do those high-ups in the government actually talk about?' her mother had written in her last letter. *'Do they talk serious stuff, or do they just make jokes about us poor ignorant folk out in the sticks?'*

'Very serious stuff, Mum,' she had responded. *'Stuff that you and I would never have thought about. But that's their job, isn't it?'*

Clementine had come to the rescue. 'Prime Minister...'

'Neville,' he corrected her.

'Neville. Excuse my husband's persistence...'

'I'm used to it,' he said. 'His stock in trade.'

She was speaking with intensity. 'I think the burning question for everyone... I don't think this counts as politics... you've met the man several times now....'

'Three times.'

'What...? I mean...' She searched for words.

'What do you make of him?' demanded Winston. *'As* a man?'

Chamberlain hesitated, blank faced.

'You catch him at a disadvantage,' said Anne.

Clementine looked contrite. 'We're being tactless.'

'No.' Chamberlain's distress was evident. 'It's a question that should be asked.'

'My dear...' his wife put a hand on his arm.

'It's all right, Anne,' he said. He turned back to Clementine. 'I thought... I used to think I knew how to judge men. But now I... I've lost faith in my... You see, I thought Hitler was - whilst ruthless, yes - at least someone one could do business with. Someone whose methods one could comprehend. But he...' He

113

shook his head again. 'The world is not the place I thought it was.

'He's still shaken,' said Anne.

'Inevitably,' replied Clementine sympathetically.

Winston had been listening silently. Now he growled, 'Yon Cassius has a lean and hungry look...'

Chamberlain threw him a sharp glance. 'You're entitled to crow, Winston.'

Winston came back equally brusquely. 'I'm not crowing! Give me credit please.'

The other retreated. 'All right, I...'

More placatory - 'But I do... I blame myself for not finding the way to... Had we been closer, Neville, you and I, perhaps...'

'Well...'

No one seemed able to complete their sentences.

Winston's hand was waving. 'I tried... I have tried. As you say, I never mastered the arts of diplomacy.' He faced the other directly. 'However the fact is we *have* to travel together now.'

Chamberlain nodded. 'Yes.'

'We have to be agreed on what is the route. On what is the challenge.'

'I think we know that now.'

'No. No, I'm not sure we do, Prime Minister.'

'Darling, please.' Clementine held up an admonitory hand.

But he would not be stopped. 'Not all of us appreciate the nature of this beast crouching in our path. It is so far beyond what we have experienced in this fortunate land that we have no true conception of such alien mentalities.' His voice had taken on a low implacable tone that Lucy had not heard before. 'You least of all, Neville.'

Anne appealed to him. 'Winston...'

'I'm not casting blame, Anne,' he growled, inclining to her. 'Your husband has too good a soul for this world. But now he has to understand.' He turned back to her spouse. 'You, Neville, have to learn the ultimate cynicism and turn demon too.'

'We agreed no politics, remember,' she admonished.

His tone was fiercer again. 'This isn't politics, this is life at its starkest! This is the unknown street in the dark. This is the bear pit. We have to explore our blackest selves in order to comprehend what the monsters are about.'

The atmosphere was vibrating with tension. Lucy stood frozen, the dish in her hands. She glanced at Inches. He was focused intently on his master as though ready to leap in to restrain him.

'Do we have to become monsters also?' said Chamberlain.

'Yes! That's what you... what everyone in the nation must now realise.' The stubby finger waved. 'You cannot fight devils with an angel's reasoning.'

Clementine's voice cut through the air like a knife. 'It's too early in the evening for melodrama, dear. Diplomacy. Sit down and stop pontificating!'

He glanced at her, hesitated, then grumbled,'Bully. She's the monster in this household.'

He deflated like a punctured tyre, and sat.

CHAPTER 18

There was quiet in the room for several seconds. The butler proffered the bottles round, at the same time waving Lucy forwards with her canapés to reinforce the diversion. Churchill was the only one who took up the offers.

Then Chamberlain spoke in a steady voice. 'I'll tell you something extraordinary, Winston. When I came back from Munich with what everyone believed... well, some believed... was a genuine promise of peace from the monster...'

'You didn't believe it?' The query came from Clementine.

'I had my doubts, Clementine' he replied. 'But I thought that if I made enough song and dance about it to the world, it would at least stay his hand. More fool me. Anyway as I say, when I got back I received forty thousand letters of congratulation. Forty thousand - can you imagine it?'

'Twelve thousand more came to me,' said Anne.

'We were showered with gifts, flowers, ecstatic messages from all corners of the earth. Each one a testament to the relief of the ordinary citizen that war, as they thought, had been averted.'

'That man is a godsend! That man has saved us!' Her father was listening to the Prime Minister on the radio. 'You see what a bit of diplomacy, a bit of intelligence can do. You don't have to go to war, if you just sit down together and talk things through. It doesn't matter how long it takes, just talk things through.'

Chamberlain's gaze was directed at Churchill. 'So how do we now turn those citizens into monsters?'

Winston responded instantly. 'How did Hitler? He has three million men under arms, and the rest of Germany cheering them on. How did he cast the spell that transformed a civilised people into barbarians?'

Chamberlain's face was dark. 'It's something I will never comprehend.'

'As I said, you are too virtuous,' said Winston, rattling the ice in his glass. 'The human breed is but three steps out of the jungle – that's the reason.'

'Speak for yourself, dear,' said Clementine coolly.

'I don't like such cynicism,' said Anne. Her coolness towards Winston was evident.

'Realism, Anne, realism.'

'How depressing!'

Clementine continued her valiant attempt to normalise the conversation. 'How do you find Number Ten, Anne?'

'Number Ten? Well, hardly my idea of home. But one can't swim against the tide. And London is... let's say, stimulating after Birmingham.'

'It will be his target.' Winston sat, immovable as stone.

Chamberlain looked up. 'London?'

'He is a hunter. He knows that if he has the heart he has the creature.'

Clementine sat back, resigned to defeat.

'So, on that theory should we go for Berlin?' asked Chamberlain.

'Certainly. Once the air force is up to strength.'

Anne exclaimed, 'It can't be right.'

'What?'

'Targeting civilians.'

His lower lip protruded. 'Civilians chose him as their leader. The populace backs him. They all share the blame.'

'Is that what they call collective responsibility?' she answered drily.

'Absolutely,' he replied. 'Gullibility is no excuse for criminality.'

117

Chamberlain expostulated. 'Germans aren't all criminals. We could still win this contest by reaching *out* to the populace.'

The voice rasped, 'With propaganda?'

'Well, I would rather drop leaflets than bombs.'

'Leaflets...' Winston cocked an ironical eyebrow. 'Well, that would revolutionise the art of warfare.'

'The pen is mightier than the sword, Winston.'

His host mumbled into his glass. 'I've never yet seen the pen that can stop a tank in its tracks.'

'Right, kids,' said her father, 'I want you take these leaflets and deliver them round the village. Tommy, you take the far side – High Street and Church Lane - and your sister can take this side – Keswick Road and River Lane. Every house. We're telling them that the village has a new bakery. Fresh bread every morning, and your mother's biscuits and cakes to order.' He had sighed, his weathered face lined with the years of worry. 'And if that doesn't bring in the customers, then bugger the lot of 'em, and we'll emigrate to Australia.'

Inches came discreetly to Clementine, and murmured in her ear. 'Should I give the cook a time for the first course, ma'am?'

'Tell her twenty minutes, David.'

He nodded and turned towards the door.

'And make sure the blackout's tight in the dining room, Inches,' growled Churchill. 'We don't want the enemy drowning us in leaflets.'

'Yes, sir.' Inches waved to Lucy to offer the canapés again.

As she handed round the vol-au-vents, Chamberlain was saying, 'You may mock, Winston, but...'

Anne intervened. 'How appalling that one man can dictate whether we leave our curtains open or closed. I cannot *understand* how we can be at war again so soon after the last one!'

'Man's inhumanity to man...' rumbled Winston.

'Well, if women were in charge I'm sure things would be

118

different.' It was the echo of Lucy's own thoughts.

'Women – ah,' he said.

Her voice was challenging. 'I'm married to a Prime Minister, yet it baffles me that the men we choose to lead us can't resolve things rationally round a table.'

'Hear, hear!' exclaimed Clementine.

Winston glanced at Chamberlain. 'This isn't politics. This sounds a philosophical boudoir issue, Neville.'

'A frequent one,' responded the other drily.

'So, Anne, if women led nations, would wars never happen?'

'Ah, but you see, Winston,' she said, 'women aren't interested in running nations – which is a hopeless task. We prefer to run families, which is not.'

His eyes twinkled now as he chewed on a mouthful of vol-au-vent. His mood could turn on a sixpence. 'Don't let the women's liberation movement hear that.'

'Oh, I've no time for them. They miss the real issue.'

He looked interested. So was Lucy, reminded again of her mother.

'I wish I was in charge of that mob down in Westminster. I'd sort things out smartly, I can tell you. Can't see the wood from the trees, that lot. So busy fighting their political battles, and dreaming up new bureaucratic complications, they don't realise that if it's just left to ordinary folk to run their lives the country'd get along fine. Trouble with politicians is, they think they have to organise everything for everybody because nobody's capable of doing it theirselves.'

'So what is the real issue, Anne?' Winston asked.

Anne sipped delicately at her sherry. 'I'll tell you something. You'll laugh at me, but I'm serious. I say I find London stimulating, but I'm never happier than when I'm working in my garden in Birmingham. Why? Because plants are so much more congenial than humans.'

'Congenial?' asked Clementine with a frown.

'Willful, eccentric, poetic... yet so civilised. They nurture each other, propagate each other, coexist in quiet harmony. So much to teach us.'

'Romantic, Anne,' muttered Winston. 'But it took humans to cultivate your garden.'

She raised a finger. 'With the plants' consent. One of my favorites is an Arabian Jasmin.' She threw him a dry smile. 'You'll like this, Winston. It's said that in the seventeenth century it seduced its owner, the lecherous and warlike Duke of Tuscany, by producing such a magical perfume that he abandoned all his amours and all his battles to stay close to it, and thus let his kingdom wither away. Perhaps, instead of bombing Berlin, you might secretly plant one in Hitler's garden - what do you think?'

Winston smacked his free hand on his thigh, and roared with laughter. 'Yes! War by herbal assault. Get onto it first thing, Neville.'

Chamberlain smiled tolerantly.

Winston warmed to the theme. 'Yes, if we could all find subjects to explore so passionately, then like the Duke of Tuscany we'd have no taste for fighting. Eh? With your background, Neville, you could compose theses on the wonders of engineering. Clementine could give public lectures on the science of raising problematic children – of which we have four. My butler could write manuals on how to run large households on small budgets.'

'Yes, indeed,' said Clementine with feeling.

He carried on, 'So then, Neville, here's the question. What might be Adolf's saving obsession?'

'Ah.'

'You tried to negotiate. Would any subject have diverted him from his manic path?

'Model soldiers perhaps.'

'No. He'd soon get bored and revert to real ones.'

120

'Cookery,' said Anne brightly. 'They say he's a vegetarian and a teetotaler. The poor man can never have learned to enjoy a good dinner.'

'That's it!' exclaimed Winston. 'We should have sent him gastronomic volumes years ago, and diverted his interest. Instead of over-running nations he'd now be playing havoc with their cuisines.'

Chamberlain muttered. 'He could certainly do something to improve his own nation's – it's horrible.' He looked up at Churchill. 'And you?'

Winston was feeling in the pockets of his dinner suit. 'Ah well... I'd write elegies on the mystical properties of the Havana cigar – for which I have a great yearning at this moment. Inches...' He looked around. 'Where's Inches?'

'Gone to the kitchen,' said his wife.

'I'll get it myself.' He rose and came to the side table, where Lucy was replacing the canapé dish. He grabbed a vol-au-vent and put it whole into his mouth, winking at her. Then he fished in the cigar box for a cigar. 'So now, Lucy,' he said through a mouthful of pastry, 'have you got a question for Mister Chamberlain?'

She froze, taken aback.

'Now's your chance,' he said. 'Liberated woman to Prime Minister. Give him a challenge.'

She felt her cheeks flush. 'No... no, sir.'

'Well, I will.' He whirled around, cigar at the ready like a weapon. 'Here's the *serious* question, Neville. How are we going to tackle the undermanning in the forces?'

The focus off her, Lucy inwardly sighed with relief. Chamberlain waved it away, and took out a cigarette case. 'It's others' problem, Winston, not yours.'

'But what are they doing about it? Bugger all as far as I can see.'

'Conscription's in hand. What more can we do?'

'Expand it. Too many exemptions.'

'We still need people to run the vital services.'

Winston circled the carpet as Inches returned from the kitchen. 'Women may not start wars, but they can play their part in them. Eh, Anne? Women can run the factories, bring in the harvests, police the streets...'

Anne recoiled. 'I can't quite see myself in a police woman's uniform.'

'Oh, yes,' he replied with a mischievous glint. 'I see you as a draconian Chief Constable running Scotland Yard.'

She returned the glance. 'Hardly flattering.'

He turned back to Chamberlain. 'But it's the men we need to get into military uniform, Neville.'

'Sensitive topic, Winston,' answered the other. 'For the Cabinet room, not this one.'

'Thank you, Neville,' said Clementine.

Winston waved the cigar at Inches. 'Inches, I need a light, and so does the Prime Minister.'

'Yes, sir.' Inches picked up a table lighter.

'Oh Tommy, Tommy, you're only twenty years old. You've your whole life ahead of you. Why d'you want to wear a ruddy uniform?'

'There's a war coming, Mum, the country needs soldiers.'

'There's plenty of others to do the soldiering. 'Ave you any idea what you're letting yourself in for? It ain't all flag waving and bugle blowing, you know. It's muck and blood and death and misery. Ask your father. He went through it in the last one.'

'I know, Mum, but it's something I've got to do. All my friends are doing it. And anyway, it's better than baking bread.'

'Is it? That's about feeding people, not killing them.'

CHAPTER 19

'It's so rare we get a social occasion together, Annie and I,' Chamberlain was saying pointedly, as Winston puffed on his butler's proferred light.

'Hm...,' murmured Winston to Inches over the flame. 'I hope Adolf's taking time off for social occasions.'

'What was that, dear?' said Clementine.

'Just talking to Inches.' He came and sat in his chair. Inches went to add more coal to the fire.

Chamberlain drew on his cigarette as he watched the butler poking the flames. Then he lifted his chin and said. 'However, that said, I'm reminded of something. Winston...'

'What?'

'I'd like to take back with me your new figures on the fleet refurbishment costs.'

Winston frowned. 'What? Tonight?'

'I need to look them over before the budgetary meeting tomorrow.'

'Well, they er...'

'I apologise if it's inconvenient. Do you have them to hand?'

Winston looked decidedly put out. 'They're down in the Map Room somewhere. I could find them if, er...'

'Could I trouble you now? Rather than risk leaving it until we're going.'

The other looked suspicious. 'Now? Is this a diversion?'

Chamberlain's expression was innocent. 'I'd just hate to depart without them.'

Winston's lip jutted, but he heaved himself back out of his chair.

'Very well, I'll er... I'll fetch them.'

'Sorry to be such a nuisance.'

His host muttered as he left, 'Scarcely bed-time reading.'

There was a moment's silence in the room. Lucy looked at Inches for guidance but he remained still, as though waiting for something new to arise.

Chamberlain smiled at Clementine. 'Apologies.'

'Not at all...'

He looked ill at ease. 'I, um...'

Anne intervened. 'How are all the children, Clementine?'

'The children? Oh... endearing and infuriating as ever. Just as they seem to be getting their lives in order, they always manage to produce another crisis.' She gave a small laugh.

'Yes, well children are a worry, even when they're no longer children.'

'Yes.'

'Especially when it is they who will bear the brunt of this war.'

Lucy knew little about the Churchill offspring. She wondered what crises they had produced.

Chamberlain was playing with his glass. He had drunk little. 'Forgive me, Clementine,' he said. 'I hope that little ploy of mine wasn't too obvious.'

'Ploy?'

'To divert Winston for a moment.' He threw her a small smile. 'I've no doubt he has his own reasons for wanting tonight's get-together. But so have I.'

'You have?'

'Annie knows my problem. I, er... This is very sensitive, but I... I would like your advice.'

Clementine gestured. 'Please. Ask me anything.'

He ran his thumb through his moustache. 'You see, Clementine, your husband poses me a huge dilemma.'

'Oh?'

'Not just me. The cabinet as a whole. He would pose it to whomever was Prime Minister. The problem - which I'm sure you are familiar with - is that he is so much more loquacious than everyone else, that, er...'

'No-one else can get a word in,' she finished.

He nodded. 'Yes, to be blunt. It's the reason, you see, that none of them would tolerate him in office until now.'

'Hm.'

'It's the reason – *one* reason Baldwin, and now myself, have had to resist his very legitimate claims for so long. People... ministers... civil servants... are all afraid that they'd be steam-rollered over every issue.'

He rose from the sofa and paced the carpet, cigarette in hand. 'The fact is, you see... his opinions on any topic are so definitive, his thought processes are so sweeping, his oratory is so overwhelming, that it's a serious problem for anyone in the same room as him to ever determine what their own thoughts *are*.'

'I sympathise,' she said drily.

He stopped and faced her directly. 'Now I don't want to seem disloyal over this. I don't wish to put you in a difficult situation. But I would sincerely welcome your views as to how... how I should handle him. You see, although I have huge respect for his phenomenal abilities, I have never yet discovered the way to harness them. I may theoretically be in charge... I may be chairman of the proceedings, as it were, but, like King Canute, once the tide is in full flow I simply have no idea how to stop it.'

He waved a hand hopelessly, and took a cigarette puff.

'Yes... well, I do understand,' said Clementine. 'It's a common problem.'

'I apologise for bringing it to you, but I'm rather at my wits end.'

She sipped from her glass as she thought. Then she said, 'The answer's quite simple really, Neville.'

'It is?'

'Give him more to do.'

'More?' He sat again.

'It all stems from frustration, you see. He has such energy, such a wealth of ideas, that when it's not utilised he's like a pressure cooker about to blow. I know from long experience that you'll never beat him in an argument.' Her eyes twinkled. 'And he won't hear your side of it in any case. '

'True,' he said with feeling.

'The thing to do is distract him with tasks, with challenges. Once he's got his teeth into a project, then he has no interest in anyone else's, and they can get on in peace. You just have to make sure it's a big enough one.'

'But good heavens – he's in charge of the navy!' he exclaimed. 'You can't get much bigger than that.'

'Give him more,' she said. 'Exploit the energy. Deluge him with jobs. You'll never overstretch him.'

He pulled a rueful face. 'The trouble is, I fear it'll never be enough. Not until he has everyone else's job.'

'Including Neville's,' added Anne.

'Ah, well. That may be. I'm afraid I can't answer that...' Clementine lifted her glass towards him. 'But, Neville, you need have no fear. Until that moment comes - if it should - you'll always have his loyalty.'

'Will he?' said Anne.

'Winston doesn't do treachery, Anne.'

Chamberlain nodded. 'That I believe.'

'I do think you'll find it's better having him inside the cage roaring with you, than prowling outside roaring *at* you.'

There was a pause. Chamberlain drew thoughtfully on his cigarette. Lucy was thinking how ironic it was that her employer presented the same problem to everyone – from secretaries to Prime Ministers.

Then Anne asked, 'And Winston's reason?'

'Sorry?' said Clementine.

'For tonight?'

The other gave a wry smile. 'Ah, well... I haven't quite discerned that myself. It's never anything frivolous, but...'

At that moment the man himself returned, puffing from the climb, a bunch of papers in hand.

'You'll have to ask him,' she said.

'Ask me what?'

'Later, dear.'

'Hm,' he grunted, and waved the papers. 'Here they are.'

Chamberlain took them. 'Thank you.

'They're very comprehensive, Prime Minister. You may find the overall figure somewhat alarming, but the point is...'

'Yes, Winston, I'll study them later tonight. Thank you so much.'

Pause. Winston's chin jutted. 'So what have I missed?'

'Nothing,' answered Clementine. 'We were just discussing the children.'

'Ah. Unfathomable subject.'

'And also how you use your unfathomable energies,' said Chamberlain.

'Ah... well...' He picked up his glass, and descended into his chair. 'It's force of habit.'

'Habit?'

'When I was a child myself I had little to do but expend energy... about the place.' His expression was distant.

'Sorry?' asked Chamberlain, puzzled.

'I was largely on my own, you see. No family. I hardly saw my parents...' His cheeks flushed, and he suddenly seemed almost on the point of tears. Clementine reached out a hand, but he didn't take it.

'People think that Winston had a privileged upbringing,' she said. 'They don't know how hard it was. Little family life, sadistic school life. It's not all fun amongst the aristocracy.'

There was a silence. Winston was blinking into his glass.

Chamberlain said, 'You must have found it hard, Winston.'

The other looked up. 'My childhood?'

'No. These last years. Being without office for so long.' He stroked his moustache again, as he often did when searching for words. 'If circumstances had been...'

Clementine spoke. 'He filled his time. Created his garden, wrote his books, painted his pictures...'

'Of course. Even so...'

'And I built things,' said Winston, rallying.

'Ah – your famous wall.'

'I helped build a cottage in the grounds for Inches to live in.'

Inches straightened at the mention of his name. 'Very comfortable it is too, sir.'

Winston's voice took on its rhetorical tone. He seemed, as always, more at ease dealing with metaphysical matters than personal ones. 'There's something far more satisfying about laying down bricks than laying down laws. There's little doubt about their place or their function, and once set, they can't then be manipulated for the wrong purposes.'

Anne laughed. 'Like my flowers.'

Chamberlain gazed at Winston over his glass. 'And of course, whilst laying them, you still managed to keep in touch.'

'In touch?'

'With political developments.'

'Ah.'

'Extraordinary how well informed you always were, Winston. We were constantly astonished at your sources of information.'

Winston blew smoke from his cigar. He had regained his

equilibrium. 'I was fortunate. Many people believed as I did, and confided in me.'

'There were times, I have to say,' added the other, 'when you seemed to have more up to date information than did the government.'

There was amusement in the host's pale eyes. 'Yes, well... being out of government has its advantages. People will pass on things to a bystander that they'd never dream of telling to ministers.'

'Such as the progress of the German war machine.'

The lightness faded. 'You had those messages, Neville.'

'Yes, but...'

'But sometimes when there are ugly discords in the air we choose not to hear.'

'We heard. We just...' Chamberlain looked down. 'I have to admit, I've always had an aversion to expending vast sums on armaments.'

Anne spoke. 'When one thinks of the schools that money could have built, the hospitals, the amenities...'

'It's one of the great criteria of government, Anne,' declaimed Winston. 'You must protect what you create. The more valuable the structures, the more essential the defences.' The cigar waved. 'It's the lesson the Romans forgot. The Greeks, the Egyptians... With greatness comes complacency.'

Chamberlain responded. 'Not complacency in our case, Winston. Reluctance if you like.'

'Same thing, but worse. You can't plead ignorance as an excuse.' There was another flush of emotion. He glowered at the burning end of his cigar. 'That's what I... I could never...'

'Sorry,' said Chamberlain. 'I shouldn't have...'

'Hieroglyphics...'

'What?'

It was a mumble. 'On the wall. One man sees an omen, another sees a balance sheet.'

Clementine came to the rescue. 'He did get despondent sometimes.' She added wryly, 'The whole household had to tread warily then.'

His voice was gruff. 'I wasn't that bad.'

'Well, woe betide anyone who crossed you. Isn't that right, Inches?'

'Oh yes, ma'am.'

'Traitor!' muttered Winston.

'Well, sir, I have had to duck for cover a few times.'

There was a ripple of laughter round the room. The tension lightened.

'Ay lor, lass, I 'ave to watch myself when your mother's got a bee in her bonnet over something. The pans can fly then, I can tell you! She likes to say I'm the boss of the family, but when it's something she cares about, there's no arguing with her. Take your life in your hands if you stand up to her then.'

Chamberlain raised a jocular glance to Inches. 'Tell us more, Mr Inches. I've never seen your master lose his temper completely. Is it a terrifying prospect?'

Inches looked at Winston. The latter waved a dismissive hand. 'Tell him, Inches. I'm used to being humiliated.'

'Well, sir,' Inches replied to the guest, 'it wasn't surprising. Your see, he had all this information at his finger-tips – day after day, reports, documents, statistics, flooding in from everywhere...'

'From where?'

'Well, from civil servants, top dogs of the army and navy, scientists, diplomats... I mean, he had the whole picture of the Nazi strategy laid out in his study for anyone who cared to see it. I had to make sure it was all dusted, so I and the staff saw it. But few else did.' He sniffed. 'They didn't want to. Too unpalatable probably.' He stopped, eyes blinking as if he had gone too far.

The room was quiet. Chamberlain's face was a mask. Churchill had risen again, and was walking backwards and forwards, glass in

130

one hand, cigar in the other.

'Stop prowling, Winnie darling,' admonished his wife.

'Eh?'

'Why don't you take Neville down to the war room, and show him the scene now?'

He stopped. 'What? Now?'

'You may not have seen it at night, Neville...'

'No, I...'

'If anything it's more hectic than in the day. A lot has happened today, hasn't it, dear?'

Winston looked more cheerful. 'Three more merchantmen down, but several U-boats tracked. These new sonic things are a godsend.' He raised his eyebrows to Chamberlain. 'I could show you if, er...'

Chamberlain replied without conviction. 'Yes, I'd like to see.'

'Good,' said Clementine. 'Then Annie and I can talk women's talk for a while.'

'Ah, that's what they want!' declared Winston. 'Why didn't you say so? Come on then, Neville - we might catch some action.'

'I hope not,' murmured his guest, but followed all the same.

Inches held open the door for the two men, then turned to Clementine, 'I'll just check we're ready for the first course, ma'am.'

'Thank you, Inches.'

He followed them out.

CHAPTER 20

Lucy stood waiting for requirements from the two women left in the room. Her legs were beginning to ache. Her role as innocent wallflower so far had been a source of equal awkwardness and fascination. She wondered what Daniel Mountview would have made of the conversation had he been present. Was there anything in the general talk and the considerable differences which he would have found especially interesting? Was there anything which would have been useful to an enemy? Probably not, unless it was that the Minister for the Navy was confirmed as an implacable critic of all that Germany stood for.

As the door closed behind Inches, Clementine rose and came with her glass to sit beside the Prime Minister's wife on the sofa.

'Diversionary tactics at sea and at home' she said.

Anne looked uneasy. 'For a specific reason?'

'Just to talk. I think it will be up to you and me to avert serious fisticuffs tonight.'

Her guest looked taken aback. 'Will it come to that?'

'Oh, just metaphorically. But when he's in the ring my husband doesn't understand the concept of simple sparring.'

'Even at dinner parties?'

'They're the worst.' Clementine sipped her sherry, 'Was it hard to persuade Neville to come tonight?'

Anne hesitated. 'He was rather... apprehensive. He's been mauled by Winston so often in public. He has something of a complex about him I'm afraid.'

Clementine's tone was reassuring. 'It's never malicious, you know.'

'I know.'

'It's just that his convictions are so...' she tailed off.

'Yes.'

'Tell me, how is Neville holding up?'

'Holding up?'

'Under the strain.'

Anne's expression was distant. 'All right, I think. He doesn't tell me much.'

'He carries a great burden.' The tone was sympathetic.

A slow nod. 'Too great. He's seventy now. I wonder sometimes how he keeps going. He... he does take things very hard, you see. He's such an idealist. He cannot tolerate failure.'

'They're both alike in *that* respect.'

Again, Lucy was uncomfortable listening to such personal comments. She stayed still, trusting they had forgotten her presence.

'Don't worry about your dad, Lucy love. He's upset at the moment, but he'll pull through. It's just that times are hard, and he hates it when he feels he can't provide for his family. He loves you both so much, you see, and he wants so much for you. It just gets to him when he feels he's letting you down.'

Anne was staring into the flames in the fireplace. 'When he heard that Hitler had invaded Czechoslovakia... after all the negotiating, all the promises... I thought his heart was going to give out.'

'Such treachery is hard to assimilate.'

'I have to be honest, Clementine. I wish he'd resigned then. Or after Munich. I wish he'd let himself give in... rest. But he can't allow himself to accept defeat in that way.'

'It wasn't defeat.'

'He sees it as that. He's determined to make amends now. But his constitution is not...' She showed a vulnerability that wasn't normally evident. 'I'm not sure if he has the strength to see it through. Especially if he's fighting Winston as well as Hitler.'

133

Clementine reached across and touched her hand. 'He needn't fear Winston.'

'He's not always right you know, Clementine. He's a fallible man.'

'We're all fallible. But I would say he's more usually right than wrong.'

Anne's eyes were challenging. 'Debatable. Look at his history.'

Clementine withdrew her hand. 'Oh, well let's not go into that.'

'One has to. Gallipoli, India, Ireland... one of the worst Chancellors of the Exchequer we've ever had...'

Clementine's expression was rueful. 'Yes, well economics was never his forte.'

'If he was wrong about such things, he could be wrong about this.'

'Do you think he is? Really?'

She shook her head. 'I don't know. He's vehement, but I just don't know.'

'That's the problem, Anne.'

'What is?'

'No one will make up their mind. And while the nation dithers, Hitler advances.'

'You sound like him now.'

'Yes, well...'

Awkward pause. Lucy's legs ached.

Then Anne again, conciliatory. 'You must be a remarkable woman, Clementine, to have maintained such a strong marriage to such a... strong man for so long.'

Clementine smiled. 'Well, marriage is a different scenario. Many men can be bulldogs in the work place, and puppy dogs at home.'

A note of amusement. 'Winston a puppy dog – I hardly think so.'

'Sometimes.' With a laconic expression, 'Especially in bed.'

The other looked shocked. 'Oh.'

'Oh yes. I sometimes wish he'd bring some of that fire and brimstone into the boudoir.'

Anne recoiled slightly. 'Really? Er...'

Clementine leaned forward and murmured, 'Between you and me, I've occasionally been tempted to look elsewhere for that side of things.'

Lucy could just hear, and felt yet more awkward. So evidently did Anne. 'Heavens!'

'Perhaps Neville's the other way round.'

'Um, well...'

Clementine laughed openly now, a low amused chuckle. 'I'm embarrassing you.'

He was laughing. 'Come on, Lucy, give me another kiss.'

'No, Henry.'

'Why not?'

'Doesn't stop with a kiss, does it?'

'What are you afraid of? You quite like me.'

'What if I do?'

'Got your sights set higher, have you?'

'I haven't got my sights set anywhere, Henry.'

'That's a pity.'

Clementine waved the matter away. 'Anyway, I doubt whether Neville would have got where he is without a great deal of support behind the scenes.'

Anne recovered from her discomfort. 'Well, I run a good household. But I wish I could support him better in his work. Truth to tell, you know...'

'What?'

'I'm never quite sure what politics is *about*. Are you?'

It was the other's turn to be startled. 'I, er...'

Anne's expression was distant. 'It's supposed to be about great principles such as justice, peace, equality... but in practice it always seems to be about a ha'penny on income tax, and who's going to win the Basingstoke by-election.'

Clementine said drily, 'Well, you know that Winston calls it the impossible profession.'

'Why?'

'In order to get elected you have to promise the voters paradise. Then when you can't deliver it they call you a hypocrite. You can never win.'

Anne gave a wan smile. 'Well yes, that rather nails it.'

'Bloody politicians!' exclaimed her father, not for the first time. 'Swanning about in their smart suits and their official cars, and making speeches about saving the country, and the economy, and Uncle Tom Cobley, and doing bugger all about it!'

'They are human,' responded her mother mildly. 'What do you expect? Magic wands?'

'Well, something. What do we elect them for?'

'Then you'd better stand for Parliament yourself, Fred, and do better.'

Anne was gazing towards the fire. 'He was never meant for politics, you know.'

'Neville?'

'His father, yes. His brother Austen. Both destined for great things. Both made for the top job everyone thought. But in the end both brought down by... well their own personalities perhaps. And yet here is Neville, the quiet one, wearing the mantle they both so longed for.'

'Fulfilment of character – as Winston says.'

Anne looked back at her host. 'What does he want from this evening?'

'Winston? I've told you – I really don't know. But he's not an

136

ogre. You shouldn't worry.'

'I do though. He's up to something. Is he looking for the chinks in Neville's armour?'

Clementine met her gaze. 'He's many things, Anne, but he's not Machiavellian.' A rueful smile. 'I sometimes wish he was more so.'

'More?'

'More fox in the dark than bull at a gate. It would be easier for everyone.'

Before the other could respond, Inches returned with a brass bucket of coals for the fire.

'Dinner won't be long, ma'am.'

'Thank you,' said Clementine. To Anne, 'Dinner will be the test.'

'The test?'

'Food and drink. Fuel for the fire. That's when he gets into his stride.'

Anne's brow furrowed. 'Oh. You mean it gets worse?'

A laugh. 'Don't be apprehensive. The secret is to sit back and enjoy it.'

CHAPTER 21

Inches added more coal to the flames, and deposited the bucket in the hearth. Then he came back to Lucy. 'All right?' he murmured softly.

She nodded, and whispered back. 'I'm not sure what I'm supposed to be doing.'

'Just pretend you're part of the furniture.'

That was easy enough – it was how she felt.

The door opened and the two men came back in. Winston inevitably was talking. '...we have to bring the other parties on board, Neville. I told Attlee, we have to forget our petty domestic squabbles and present a united front against this evil, or history will never forgive us.'

'He's still at it,' Anne murmured to Clementine.

Chamberlain was replying. 'But you know his party won't back such a stance.'

'They must!' proclaimed his host. 'It goes to the fundamental heart of the human character. The eternal conflict between pacifism and aggression.'

Clementine's voice was long-suffering. 'Darling, are you still lecturing us all on the ethics of going to war?'

Her husband's voice lowered. 'I mean no disrespect, but...'

Inches came to Chamberlain proffering the whisky bottle, but was waved away. 'I am a business man by instinct, Winston, but I appreciate that war is not like business.'

'Ah, but you see it is,' retorted Winston.

'Oh, good heavens!' Anne quietly expostulated.

He turned to her again. 'They are both about empire building and defending, Anne. And the same principle applies to both -

expand or expire.'

'We've got to expand the business, Mary. We'll get nowhere just selling bread to folk. We need to give them the stuff they like. You're a great cook – how about fancy cakes and tarts and stuff? How about French pastries and birthday cakes and wedding cakes? There's real profit in those, and they've got nowhere to go for 'em.'

'I dunno, Fred. I'm not sure I'm up to that.'

'Course you are, love. You can learn. You're artistic. You'd love it.'

'There's a corollary,' Chamberlain was saying, as he stood by the fire. 'Expand too fast and you explode.'

Winston acknowledged the comment. 'Ha! Well... let's hope Hitler proves that true.' His expression brightened, and he patted his stomach. 'He should learn by my example. Expand slowly and surreptitiously, and hope that nobody notices.' He turned to Clementine. 'A propos of which, I'm hungry. Is it dinner time yet?'

'It won't be long,' she replied.

He chewed on his half-smoked cigar. 'D'you know, despite the arguments, I'm enjoying this evening!' He beamed round the room, his expression transformed, as so often. 'How is it we four have known each other for so long, yet never come together like this?'

'Yes, how?' echoed Anne.

'Quite so,' said her husband.

Winston took the cigar from his mouth and raised it. 'There is a lesson here...'

'I hope it's not a long one, dear,' said his wife.

He ignored her. '...sit down with your opponent - and forgive me, Neville, but we have been opponents for too long - sit, open a bottle, and break bread, and remarkable things will happen. I'm of the firm opinion that more problems are solved over a dining table than over any other style of table - cabinet, boardroom, or, most of all, courtroom.'

'Hear, hear,' concurred Chamberlain, lighting a cigarette.

'You should organise a roster immediately. Every minister to dine with every other minister - together with their wives - at least once a month. Paid for by the Cabinet Office, and with the firm condition that a minimum of two bottles of wine are consumed with every meal.'

Clementine spoke drily. 'I'm not sure that's wise, dear - it's after all the wine that you've had some of your fiercest disagreements.'

'Ah, well...'

'And had to make your most abject apologies.'

He pulled a sheepish face. 'Yes - well, limit the wine perhaps, but not the whisky.' Holding out his glass to the butler, 'Inches.'

Inches and Clementine exchanged glances. He stepped forwards and poured Churchill a small whisky. As he did so, Chamberlain moved away from the fire, and said, 'I still think he can be negotiated with, you know.'

There was an instant silence in the room. Winston stood, glass in hand, an expression of astonishment on his round features. 'Adolf? Are you serious?'

The other was still, cigarette in hand. 'He is holding back from invading France. From bombing England. He knows he has not yet reached the point of no return. He is waiting.'

Winston's growl lowered several tones. 'Yes - he is waiting for one thing. To regather his forces after the resistance of the gallant Poles.'

'I don't think...'

'He has destroyed Vienna, Prague, and now Warsaw! Who can doubt his next objectives will be Brussels, Paris, and London?'

'He is not a madman. He...'

'He is!' The growl became a roar. 'He is a madman! That is the inexorable truth that you have to understand!'

Chamberlain made a mollifying gesture with his hands. 'Not so mad that he will invite his own destruction, Winston. We and the French are a far different proposition. He knows he faces the largest land force in the world, and the largest maritime force.'

The roar did not diminish. 'He knows he faces half-trained French troops, armed with obsolete equipment, led by senile generals and vacillating politicians!'

'Oh, come...'

'He knows he faces an English navy that was built to fight the last war, not this one. He knows he can take his time because his opponents will not do the one thing they should be doing.'

'What is that?'

'Attack him while he's vulnerable.'

Chamberlain blinked beneath his heavy eyebrows. 'With what? You've just said our forces are weak.'

'So are his! More so than he lets on. It's the very time to catch him off-guard.'

The other sounded despairing. 'Oh, Winston, Winston... This is our problem, you see. I would pacify him, you would provoke him.'

Winston's arm flailed. 'Yes! Yes - this is our problem. A wolf in a cage, you may pacify. A wolf on the prowl, you must shoot!'

Chamberlain appealed to Clementine. 'Adolf is a wolf to be sure, Clementine - your husband is a lion. How does one pacify him?'

She spread her hands in a gesture of futility.

Her husband's voice was yet lower. 'If I'm a lion, Neville, what are you?'

'I don't know. What am I?'

A shake of the head. 'A mythical beast, that one can never capture. One moment in reach, the next gone - vanishing into the forest. A unicorn perhaps.'

'Ah.'

'Suitable then,' said Clementine. 'The two of you together upholding our royal coat of arms.'

'I'll take it as a compliment,' said Chamberlain.

'Dieu et mon droit,' commented Winston.

Chamberlain sat, as if to escape his host's intensity. 'Do you know the Chamberlain family motto, Winston?'

'Tell me.'

'Je tiens ferme. I hold firm.'

'Very appropriate. Uphold it.'

'And that of the Dukes of Marlborough?'

A growl. 'I think you know damn well what it is.'

'I've forgotten. Remind me.'

Churchill turned to his butler. 'Tell the Prime Minister, Inches.'

Inches obliged. 'Fiel Pero Desdichado, sir. Faithful but unfortunate.'

'Ah, yes.' Chamberlain reflected, 'Strange motto.'

'Study the Marlborough family history, and you'll see it's apt,' said Winston.

'But not appropriate where you're concerned.'

The eyebrows rose. 'The faithful, or the unfortunate?'

'Oh, I would never doubt your faith.'

'Thank you.'

'Nor your good fortune, Winston,' added Anne.

'Ah. Well...' He seemed at a loss as to how to respond.

Chamberlain was wiping his watery eyes with a handkerchief. 'I shouldn't tell you this, Winston – it's indiscreet of me – but Baldwin once said of you that when the gods saw how many gifts they had bestowed on you, they decided they must redress the balance and deny you judgement. I have to say, in most instances I strongly disagree with him, but...'

Winston glowered. 'At least I have the gifts. The gods denied him both.'

The other protested, 'Oh, come now...'

'Had Baldwin the judgement to stand up to Hitler – had we

142

drawn the line over Austria... had we done so over Czechoslovakia... over Poland... had we shown our mettle over any one of those bloodstained landmarks on this dismal journey, we would not now be at this desperate place.'

'Your imagery is lurid as ever, Winston, but your logic is flawed. I...' He got no further.

'I am not concerned with logic! I am concerned with survival! I am concerned with winning!' The voice rose. 'I am concerned with the preservation of all that this land has stood for throughout its noble history. If we are not prepared to defend it, then we may as well fling wide our doors to the devil now, and welcome him in with open arms.'

Clementine pleaded, 'Winston, please. Do you have to be so apocalyptic?'

Chamberlain's voice was quiet. 'I am not prepared to do that.'

The lower lip protruded. 'What are you prepared for then, Prime Minister?'

The silence was heavy with tension. Lucy stood stock still, as mesmerised as everyone else.

Chamberlain rose from his seat, and spoke quietly, holding out his glass to Inches. 'I am prepared to risk another small whisky before we have dinner, and to raise my glass again to what – however we achieve it – is the only goal that matters...' Inches poured, and he lifted his glass. 'Peace.'

Winston hesitated. The coal in the fire crackled.

Clementine murmured pointedly, 'Winnie...'

His tone was grudging. 'Yes – well, I'll second that. To peace.'

All the glasses were raised. 'Peace!'

CHAPTER 22

The party had moved through to the dining room. Inches and Lucy were striding back to the kitchen. Inches was talking again on the run.

'He handled that one quite well, the PM. He deflected that assault quite neatly, I thought. But this is just the start. This is the lull before the storm.'

'What do you mean, Mr Inches?' asked Lucy, racing beside him.

'I know. I've seen it all before. When the old man's got a bee in his homburg over something, he's going to pursue it until he's nailed it. He's going to hammer at it until he's got to its entrails.' Inches' hands flapped like a swan's about to take off. 'The coffee and brandy stage, that's the danger point. We'll probably survive dinner all right. He'll keep them entertained, show them the usual fireworks, and as long as nobody tries to out-talk him, everything will go fairly smoothly. But, unless I and the mistress between us can limit his intake of alcohol – which we've never yet found a way of doing – then by the time he gets up from the table he'll be well into his cups, his fiercest passions, and his deepest prejudices.' He pushed open the kitchen door. 'And from there on we're all on a train with no brakes. No buffers. No *rails*, God help us! Oysters, Mrs Landemare?'

She was stirring a large casserole pot on the stove. 'On the side there. Where else would they be?'

He marched over to where sat the wide silver platter, on which lay two dozen oysters on their bed of ice. The two kitchen maids scattered out of his way.

'Mind you,' he added as he handed Lucy a bowl of lemon slices and a small jug of something dark, 'I wouldn't miss the ride for the Crown Jewels.'

Neither would she, she thought, as they made their way equally smartly back towards the dining room.

Dear Mum,

You'll never guess what happened last night. They were short of servants and I was brought in to help with a dinner party for the Prime Minister and his wife. I actually served them at table!! The men were dressed in evening dress and bow ties, and the ladies in the smartest cocktail dresses. I had to wear a maid's outfit, and follow the instructions of the Churchills' butler, Mr Inches. I listened to all the talk. You've never heard so much high-and-mighty discussion about the war and politics and history. It was the most fascinating evening I've ever had. Mr Churchill is surely the most commanding man in the country, though rather argumentative, and the Prime Minister is also wise and very polite. The dinner ended with the most passionate argument I've ever heard in my life. It made our family rows seem like storms in a teacup. I really think I should be keeping a journal about my time here at the Admiralty, and write it all down, but I'm so busy I haven't the time.

All my love to you and Dad.

Lucy.

PS Have you heard from Tommy again? Will he be sent abroad to fight?

As the pair reentered the dining room, the diners were already seated at the table. Candles burnt in the candelabra in the centre, smoke rose in the air, and Winston was in full flow.

'...and it is an era that could well be in its death throes. The institution of the great English house - flourishing in its splendour and its wantonness. Where the art of human intercourse and the luxury of intellectual speculation can be practised around their dinner tables and upon their noble lawns by men and women not yet enslaved by domestic chores and financial cares. It is a glory and an indulgence which this war may well destroy for ever. And the working man, upon whose sweat it all floats, will say, 'and no bad thing either'.'

'And he would have reason,' said Anne.

'Yes, indeed,' replied her host. 'Yet he too will be losing an ideal and a stability he will not know the value of until too late.'

'Not my milieu, but I take your point,' said Chamberlain, seated beside his wife, newly lit cigarette in hand. Was he too a chain smoker? wondered Lucy.

Inches placed the oysters in the centre of the table, then took the lemon bowl and jug from Lucy and placed them alongside.

'So is that why you crossed to the Conservatives again, Winston?' said Anne. 'Not very constant in your allegiances.'

The pale eyes flashed. 'I am constant to the principle of efficacy, not to factions.' He sniffed. 'And at least I never crossed to the Labour faction.'

Inches murmured in his ear. 'Shall I pour the champagne now, sir?'

'Yes, yes – let's jazz up the party.'

The butler went to the large ice bucket at the side, where two bottles of Pol Roger reposed.

'Why not join Labour if you believe in welfare, Winston?' asked Anne with a dry glint.

He gestured his guests towards the oysters. 'The socialist principle, whilst worthy in theory, Anne, fails when it comes to efficacy.' His eyes sparked with mischief. 'I found myself the other day at the House going to the gents with Clement Attlee...'

Clementine sighed. 'Don't tell them that story, dear.'

He waved it away. 'Oh, they're broad-minded. When I went down to the far end of the urinals, Clement said, 'What's the matter, Winston - afraid to pee next to a socialist?' I told him, 'The trouble with you lot is, whenever you see anything big you want to nationalise it.'

There was laughter. Clementine gestured an apology to the other woman, but Anne waved it aside. Lucy took a moment to work out the joke, then wondered at the indelicacy amongst these people.

Anne was saying, 'However, Winston, if you saw the conditions some people endure in Birmingham, you would understand the socialist sentiment.'

'Indeed, I have seen, Anne,' he responded. 'And that is the real war we should be fighting.'

'Quite,' commented Chamberlain.

'But socialism will never accept that throughout history it is invariably the few who have powered the machinery that employs the masses. It is why communism constitutes such a chimera – forgive the alliteration.'

'Tell that to Stalin,' said Chamberlain, as he inspected an oyster dubiously.

Winston was swallowing one. 'Another monster from the devil's imagination.'

'Whom we desperately need.'

'Until he also shows his true colours. A treacherous ally. Why else is he even now jumping on Hitler's bandwagon and plundering Poland?'

His guest squeezed lemon onto his shellfish. 'At least we can hope his colours are different to Adolph's.'

'I doubt it. In practice they both arrive at the same end. Vultures at a feast of slaughtered masses. The axiom that power corrupts has never been so graphically proven.'

A champagne cork popped with a muffled report. Inches started round the table with the bottle. Lucy stood waiting for her next instructions.

'And does that axiom apply to you two men?' asked Anne.

Winston shook his head. 'No. We can be voted from power every five years, Anne. We don't have time to become corrupt. It's the value – and the plague - of our democratic system.'

147

'The plague?' she said.

'If the value is moderation, the plague is endless compromise.'

Chamberlain had swallowed his oyster with apprehension. 'And if compromise is the price of moderation, then it's a fair bargain,' he said.

Winston wiped his mouth with his napkin, and spoke with slow deliberation. 'Yes, Neville – but in these immoderate and uncompromising times, are moderation and compromise appropriate?'

There was silence around the table. Chamberlain gave a resigned sigh, and said, 'Ah Winston, I did say it.'

'What?'

'You are determined to pin me against the wall.'

Winston's chin jutted. 'It is Adolf who has done that, Prime Minister. I just want to help you kick him back from the wall, and into the ditch where he belongs.'

'You're a disgrace, Fred Armitage! Look at you! Drunk as a lord, and filthy all over. Where 'ave you been – sleeping in a ditch?'

'Sorry, luv, I fell over. It was bit muddy.'

'As if we can afford you drinking the housekeeping away. What are you thinking?'

'Well, you can't begrudge me celebrating us getting the shop, luv. This is the start of a new life for us.'

'Well, if this is how the new life is going to pan out, I don't want any of it. Go and clean yourself up before I brain you with one of your rolling pins!'

Chamberlain was speaking. His expression was desolate. 'Yes - well I admit this much to you, Winston. I do feel... the humiliation.'

'Humiliation?' queried Winston.

'After hours, days of haggling, I procured his word and his signature in Munich. Peace for our time, I declared. Yet within weeks he reneged, and now...' He shook his head. 'History will

148

paint me a fool.'

Anne put out a hand and touched him.

Winston responded gruffly. 'Not a fool, Neville, never a fool. An idealist perhaps.'

'Same thing.'

'Well, if you're a foolish idealist then I am too. You and I have both been duped by men who broke their contract with history.'

Chamberlain turned to Clementine in query.

'The abdication,' she murmured. 'His support of Teddy Windsor still rankles.'

'Ah.'

Winston reached for another oyster. 'I was fooled by a man with a terror of power - you were fooled by one with a mania for power. There is little between them, except that one is a charming, spineless creature, the other a charmless, unscrupulous one.'

Chamberlain declined a second helping. 'Yes, but you see I also felt I had a contract with history. I lived... we all lived through the Great War. I felt it my absolute duty to ensure that we never had to tread such a path again.'

'Exactly,' asserted the host. 'So the lessons of that debacle were clear.'

'But how? The responsibility... the burden of leading us into such another catastrophe... it's one I cannot... something from which I...' Chamberlain broke off.

Anne spoke with firmness. 'Would you have done differently before Hitler broke all his promises, Winston? Without the hindsight would you have judged him correctly?'

He turned towards her. 'I have made many mistakes in my life, Anne. I have made reckless charges, I have made wild speculations – as all my enemies have noted...'

Chamberlain grunted cryptically.

'But one thing I am infallible on. I know right from wrong. And when I see the actions of such a man, then there is no fragment of doubt in my mind on which side of the line he stands.'

Chamberlain shook his head again. 'I am mystified. How do you approach such a mentality?'

Winston sat back in his chair. 'You know I'm in the throes of writing a four volume history of these isles.'

'Good heavens, Winston!' said Anne. 'When do you find the time?'

'He never sleeps,' answered Clementine, with a smile at her husband.

'I have a publisher's deadline, and a bank manager's ultimatum,' he said.

'Ah,' said Anne, as the butler and Lucy cleared away the first course. 'Well, we do often wonder how you can support a big place like Chartwell.'

Winston's tone was dry. 'I was born in Blenheim Palace. After that experience it's psychologically difficult to scale down.' She smiled, amused. He went on. 'Anyway, the point is this. Wars are ultimately made, not by aggressive leaders, but by the people who support them. I am struck time and again as I write, how peoples choose the leaders and the fate that they deserve.'

'Deserve?'

'That their temperament invites. There is an atavistic streak in both the Teutonic and the Russian peoples that attracts them to bellicose leaders. There is a temperance in the British nature that draws them to temperate men. It is the result of history, and nothing to be ashamed of.'

'No, it isn't,' Anne responded. 'And it's why the British chose Neville as their leader.'

'Precisely.'

'Your point?'

'The point is, as I said, Anne – when facing intemperate foes, is temperance appropriate?'

Chamberlain answered. 'I am in many ways a temperate man,

Winston. Is it appropriate? I do not believe that excess is ever justified.'

'But how do you judge between excess and adequacy?'

'What is it you are asking?'

Churchill's tone was resolute. 'I am asking – quite simply, do you feel up to fulfilling your contract with history?'

Lucy turned from the serving table to see the Prime Minister's reaction. Again, there was the same tension in the room.

'Are you, Neville?' repeated the host.

Clementine put out a hand. 'Dear...'

'I would not presume, but it is of such vital importance. You asked what is the purpose of this evening? If there is one, it is simply to know your mettle.'

'Mettle?' replied Chamberlain.

'I know your integrity, I know your skills, I know your valour. Mettle is something different. It is about meeting ultimate challenges.'

'And what is this ultimate challenge?'

The lower lip protruded. 'That of persuading this generation of British men and women to make the supreme sacrifice - as did the last?'

Silence. The air quivered. Chamberlain lifted his head. 'It was during the last war, remember Winston, that I was responsible for conscription. I enlisted thousands of young men to go to their deaths in the trenches. Even now, I have the nightmares.'

His host's glass had stopped halfway towards his lips. 'Mm.'

'However, as Prime Minister now, I think I am up to whatever the challenge may be. And to the nightmares that may come.'

CHAPTER 23

There had been silence in the room for several moments. Churchill was contemplating his glass. Then he nodded and drained it. 'More champagne please, Inches.'

Inches had started for the door, but he turned back and fetched the bottle. As he poured Churchill said, 'Inches too fought in the Great War. Didn't you, David?'

'Yes, sir.'

'What would you tell us are the lessons?'

Inches looked discomfited. 'Oh, sir I... I couldn't say.'

'Yes, you could. You must have an opinion.'

'I...'

'What are the lessons? Tell us.'

'Don't bully him, Winnie', said Clementine.

'I couldn't possibly,' said Inches. 'Not in this company.'

'Do you think it could have been fought better?'

'Well, sir, I...'

'What? Be honest.'

'It did seem a terrible waste of young lives. But what else could we do?'

'That's the big question, isn't it, Inches? What else?'

Inches looked even more awkward.

'You don't have to respond, David,' said Clementine. 'Just carry on.'

'Thank you, ma'am.'

Winston relented. 'Very well. We won't embarrass you. But not many get the opportunity to voice their opinion to a Prime Minister. You've missed a chance there, Inches.'

'Thank God,' said Chamberlain with a smile at the butler. 'One of you's enough.'

With a look of relief, Inches replaced the champagne bottle and murmured to Lucy, 'Right, main course. Here we go again.'

The pair repeated their hurried journey back to the kitchen, carrying the used dishes. The oyster platter still contained several uneaten shellfish.

'Did you really fight in the Great War, Mr Inches?' Lucy asked as they went.

'Yes, I did,' he replied. 'But what could I possibly say to the PM? The war to end all wars, that was supposed to be. You could never have imagined such squalor, such carnage. I saw things then that no human being should ever see.' He glared at her. 'And it was the leaders who got us into it. You'd think, wouldn't you, that having been through all that, we'd never contemplate such a thing again? Yet here we are, just twenty years on, back in it once more.' He stopped in the middle of the wide passageway, consumed with his train of thought. 'I'm no intellectual, Lucy, but I do like to read those who are. And I know that, according to that Charles Darwin fellow, we're all supposed to be making progress - through trial and error. Survival of the fittest. Well, that seems a lot more logical to me than that some highly incompetent God is directing operations. But even so, if this shindig turns out like the last one, then we're about to lose most of our fittest before they've even reached manhood. So where's the progress there, eh? I wish the politicians would explain that to me.' He swiveled on his heel and continued his own progress.

'Oh, Fred, the lad's only twenty. Can't you knock some sense into him? Can't you tell him that the army's not the place to be?

'I know, luv, but his mind's made up. Short of locking him in the cellar, what can I do?'

'Oh lord! He'll come home minus a limb or two, mark my words. Or if not, in a coffin.'

Back in the kitchen, Lucy was loaded with two china dishes of vegetables, whilst Inches took hold of the large porcelain tureen that Mrs Landemare had waiting.

'Careful with that, Mr Inches,' she admonished. 'Don't want that all over the carpet.'

'You've handed me larger ones than this, Mrs Landemare,' he replied loftily. 'Have I ever dropped one?'

'There's always a first time.' She muttered to Lucy, 'Especially when he's in such a state of neurotics.'

'Neurotics!' he expostulated. 'I'm not neurotic!'

'No, but you are in a bit of a tizz - admit it. Remember, he's just the Prime Minister, not God.'

'Hmph!' went Inches. 'Well, I hope your Irish stew's good enough for God all the same.' And he strode off to the door.

'Always has to have the last word,' said the cook, as Lucy turned to follow. 'How are you managing, dear?'

'All right, thank you,' said Lucy.

'You're doing fine. I can tell you're not neurotic, certainly.'

'I hope not.'

When the pair got back, the tension seemed to have decreased. Both men were puffing smoke again, and the foursome were sitting back comfortably as Winston rumbled on.

'Ambition is a curious thing. I had an ambition at Chartwell. I wanted to create a waterscape in the true Capability Brown tradition. Lakes, streams, a pool for swimming. Every great vista must have water - it is elemental.'

'Oh, yes!' exclaimed Anne.

'So we dug and we dammed, we channeled and we piped... and the wretched liquid ran this way and that... I hired men and machines, and in the end we won through. We mastered the feckless stuff, and now we have a magical series of lakes and pools that visitors wonder at. And they never know the toil and the cursing that went into its making.'

'No, they don't,' said Clementine with feeling.

'And your analogy for all this?' asked Chamberlain.

Winston blew smoke at the ceiling. 'When public opinion is not properly directed, like water it flows hither and thither, rushing off in wrong directions, leaking away into dark caverns. But when channeled properly it will follow the designs its leaders create for it.'

'Apt.'

'We... you and I – can direct the people of this land towards a wide river of fortitude. Just as Hitler has transformed the German mentality into a black torrent that would sweep all before it.'

'But how?' asked Anne passionately. 'How has he done it? They're a civilised nation – I can't understand it.'

He held up the cigar like a baton. 'There you have it. The human animal so longs for messianic leadership, Anne, that it will follow Satan or Christ with equal conviction.'

'Yes!' she exclaimed. 'They've lost touch with their religious roots.'

'No, no,' he retorted. 'As many Germans as Englishmen pray to God for victory. What does that tell you about religion? God has no part in all this.'

'Oh, how dismal!' she said, and violently straightened the napkin on her lap.

'It's the least we can do, Fred. We can't help the war preparations much, but for heaven's sake, we can at any rate go to church on a Sunday and pray for victory.'

'Pray for victory? What good would that do? If God had any say in the matter, wouldn't he have stopped the war in the first place?'

'The war's of man's making, not God's.'

'Then what's the point of 'im then? If we can't pray to 'im to stop the war, what's the point of praying for 'im to let us win it?'

'Well, the more Christians appeal to him, surely the more he'll let the right side win.'

155

'Can't follow the logic, love. Germans are Christians too, aren't they? Have we got to lose a million men before he'll step in? No, sorry, I've got better things to do than listening to sanctimonious vicars ranting about us all paying the price of our sins. I'm better off cooking loaves to feed the five thousand.'

Inches was placing the tureen in the centre of the table. 'You said to let people help themselves, sir,' he murmured to Churchill, as he took off the lid and dipped a ladle into the dish.

'Yes,' said Winston. Then to the assembly, 'Mrs Landemare's famous Irish stew, everyone. Do help yourselves.'

Clementine lifted the ladle towards Anne, as Inches took the vegetables from Lucy.

Chamberlain was drumming his fingers on the white linen table cloth. His face was set in a carved expression. 'You see, this is the problem between us, Winston.'

'What is?'

'I cannot accept that any leader is all Satan. Hitler lifted the German race out of ruin. There has to be a vein of reason somewhere within him.'

'Then tell me where it lies.'

The other shook his head. 'I... I don't...'

'Show me, amongst the litany of oppression and torture, invasion and slaughter – where lies this redeeming vein?'

'You have such a fatalistic view of human nature, Winston...'

That emphatic tone in the voice. 'I have a historical view of human nature! Study the madness that has infected man throughout the centuries. There is no limit to the depravity that may reign once the collective imagination is harnessed.'

'Whence came all this pessimism, Winston?' said Anne as she ladled casserole onto her plate. 'I thought you were the bullish one here.'

'Well, maybe it's our family histories that mark the difference between Neville and me,' he replied more moderately.

156

'How so?'

'I am bred from a race of warriors. Neville – far more respectably – from a race of merchants. Perhaps that is where our instincts divide.'

Chamberlain took over the ladle from his wife. 'Perhaps, yes. Mine are...'

'For peace at any price,' intervened Winston. 'Mine...'

'War at any price.'

'No!' barked the other. 'War when the price of peace is too great.'

'Can there ever be too great a price for peace?' asked Anne.

He looked at her with a grave expression. 'Oh, yes, Anne. That is the whole conundrum. The danger is in not recognising when that limit is reached, until too late.'

'Well, surely it's too late now. We've already declared war.'

'But not yet fought it. The limit is damnably close.'

Chamberlain handed the ladle across to Clementine. 'How do you recognise that point, Winston? What is the benchmark? I would dearly like to know.'

'Exactly,' said his wife. 'How do you recognise it?'

Winston just grunted, and waved his empty wine glass impatiently to Inches, who was still serving vegetables. The butler handed the task over to Lucy, and went to the drinks table.

'Surely there's no point in discussing it,' Clementine said, as she helped herself to the casserole. 'It's hypothetical now.'

'No, it's not,' replied Winston. 'It's a question I've pondered many times.'

'You've always seemed certain of the answer,' said Chamberlain.

'Certain, no.' Then, as Inches came to him with the wine bottle, 'Ah, now I want you all to try this wine. It's a light Burgundy – just right for this dish.' He went on, as the butler filled his glass. 'It's a

157

matter of instinct, you see. By nature some men are pacifists. To them that point will never arrive - even at the moment of death. Others are by nature the fighters, the war-mongers.'

'As is Adolf,' said Clementine.

'They will force conflict whatever the circumstances. Some would put me amongst those, but they are wrong. I try to judge the median place. And there is one. There is a point where we should say, 'Thus far and no further'.'

Chamberlain helped himself to the vegetables that Lucy was holding in the manner instructed, 'I say again, Winston, how do you judge when that point is reached?'

There was a pause. Winston said, 'I hesitate, Neville.'

'Why? It's a straightforward question.'

'Despite our differences this evening has been a pleasure and a respite. I would not wish to endanger that.'

'Nor would I, of course. But since we've been at odds for so long concerning it...'

Clementine intervened. 'Perhaps I could answer. That point arrives when your adversary has proved beyond question that he is a tyrant, a despot, a being without principle.'

'My wife has it! Adolf proved that of himself when he became Fuhrer by intimidation and corruption. We should have faced the fact half a decade ago.'

Chamberlain was incredulous. 'You're saying we should have gone to war half a decade ago?'

'No. However we should have read the message. Hieroglyphics.'

'And having read it?'

'It was our duty to prepare from that moment on.'

Chamberlain sighed. 'I say again, you cannot persuade a peace loving nation to take the war path on such incomplete evidence.'

Winston's eyes flashed with passion. 'Incomplete evidence? The whole world watching as Hitler's gangsters rampaged the

158

streets of Austria, of Czechoslovakia, of Germany itself, murdering all who bore a Jewish name, bludgeoning all who opposed his advancement.'

'Rumours, hearsay. How do you interfere in another nation's internal affairs?'

'You do not interfere, neither do you tolerate! The world should have made its reaction to such outrages patent. Adolf saw craven acceptance and knew he could proceed without compunction.'

'We had our own crises - riots in the streets, bloody marches on London. Should the world have branded us pariahs also?'

Winston's growl verged on a roar again. 'Come, Prime Minster! Do you equate campaigns for employment and better conditions with calls to fascism and massacre? Let's have some objectivity here!'

Clementine put her restraining hand on his arm. Chamberlain's own voice became equally fierce.

'Objectivity? That's the last word you should be invoking, Winston!'

'Eh?'

'Did you show objectivity when you sent seventy thousand men to their deaths in the Dardanelles?'

'Ah,' exclaimed the host, 'that old fable raises its head again. That strategy was right. It would have shortened the Great War by a year at least.'

'Well, that's...'

'We were defeated by bad weather, poor intelligence, and weak command.'

'You were defeated by your own impetuosity! Your egotism! Which is what I fear here.'

The women leapt into the breach. 'Darling, enough...' exclaimed Anne.

'Gentlemen, gentlemen!, followed Clementine. 'We have enough war outside. Let's not have more in here.'

The men deflated.

'Apologies, ladies,' muttered Winston. 'Inches, where's that wine bottle?'

'You are drunk enough, Winston,' said his wife as if to a child. Inches dithered with the wine.

'Not so drunk I don't know my calamities from my catastrophes,' he retorted. 'The argument is crucial. It will continue.'

Chamberlain's tone was resigned. 'I've no doubt it will.'

'Oh, heavens!' sighed his wife, not for the first time.

Clementine turned to Inches. 'I think, David,' she said in a tactful voice, 'it might be better if you and Lucy waited in the other room for now. We're fine here with the main course for a while. We'll ring for you when we're ready.'

'Yes, ma'am,' said Inches.

'Just leave the wine on the table,' muttered Winston.

Inches obeyed, beckoned to Lucy, and the two left the room.

CHAPTER 24

'Whew! Hotting up,' exclaimed Inches as the pair entered the empty drawing room. He collapsed onto a side chair. 'Dangerous moment there. Good thing we're out of it.'

Lucy's legs were severely tired now. She hadn't realised the strain waitresses were under whilst constantly on their feet.

'Is it all right if I sit down?' she said.

'Of course, dear, of course.' He waved her to a chair. 'Take the weight off your feet. There's a bit to go yet.'

'Is Mr Churchill right?' she asked as she sat. 'Should we have challenged Hitler early on?'

'Well, I dunno, Lucy. Who knows what's right and what's wrong in all this?' His forehead furrowed. 'But I do remember for years now the stories coming out of Germany. Jews hounded from their businesses, rabbis beaten up in the streets, young girls raped before their parents. None of us took it too seriously at the time. Well, you take all reports about foreigners with a pinch of salt, don't you? As people say, they're all savages east of Calais. None of our concern.'

He noticed the whisky bottle nearby on the serving table, got up and went to it. 'Let's have a wee dram. We've earned it.' He poured a small measure into one of the glasses awaiting the washing-up.

Lucy was slightly taken aback to see him drinking from one of his employers' used glasses. He poured another tot into a sherry glass and held it out. 'Go on, lass – you need a pick-me-up too.'

She hesitated. He pushed it at her. 'Go on, it'll do you good.'

She took it and, avoiding the lipstick mark on the rim, sipped the whisky. It burned her throat, but she was glad of the stimulus.

Inches was going on. 'But the old man's got a point. At what stage do you start to say, hang on - this is getting beyond the pale. When do you stand up and say, "Hoy! You there, with the ugly face and the knuckle duster – enough, belt up and sit down!"' He pulled a lugubrious face. 'Trouble is, if you do that, you've got to be damn sure you've got your own knuckle duster ready, haven't you?'

'Bloody foreigners,' said her father, as he fed the bread trays into the ovens. 'Did you know, kids, that in the Great War over thirty countries were involved? Can you imagine it? All because they couldn't agree which little bit of which land belonged to which tin-pot king or dictator. So, instead of sitting round a table and discussing it, they have to go to war, drag half the world in with them, kill God knows how many millions of people, and bankrupt the whole of Europe. And now, if they don't look out, they'll be doing it all over again! Can you imagine if a neighbour claimed he owned a foot of our garden because it used to belong to his house a hundred years ago, and we started shooting at each other over it? Eh? I tell you, something gets into people's heads once they get power. They just want more and more of it. They lose their reason.'

The pair were quiet for a while, each enveloped in their own thoughts. Lucy was wondering seriously how interested her suitor, Daniel Mountview, would be in the arguments she had witnessed. Would it benefit the enemy to know that two of the country's most powerful politicians were in such disarray?

The tinkle of a bell eventually came from the direction of the dining room.

'Here we go,' said Inches, heaving himself out of his chair. 'Time for cheese and dessert. Let's hope things have calmed down in there.'

They returned to the dinner table. As they entered, Clementine was talking. The atmosphere was quiet.

'...it was suspense from our very first meeting. We stood and stared at each other. He at this gangly, awkward nineteen year old...'

162

'This very beautiful nineteen year old,' said Anne.

Clementine threw her a smile, as she waved to Inches to clear away the dishes. '...and me at this edgy young man with the dashing reputation.'

'Aha,' said Winston.

'...and we could neither of us think of a thing to say.'

'True.' He grinned. 'Unusual for me.'

'Then someone whisked me away for a dance, and the moment was gone. I didn't see him again for four years.'

'I didn't miss my opportunity *that* time,' he murmured.

'No,' she said. 'That was a ruthless conspiracy.'

'Conspiracy?' queried Chamberlain.

Clementine turned to him. 'He got his cousin, the duke, to invite us for a week-end at Blenheim Palace. I was wined and dined and dazzled in that glorious place – a young girl of twenty four – what hope did I have?'

Anne laughed. 'None.'

Clementine looked more reflective. 'But I remember thinking as I wandered round the maze of corridors, the vast rooms – all part of a grandiose vision which virtually bankrupted his ancestors – I thought, what does this all represent? Not home and family certainly. Prestige alone probably. Prestige and power.'

Winston nodded. 'Probably, yes. A foolish fantasy. At least Chartwell's a proper home.'

'But even so,' Anne said to his wife, 'you were seduced by it.'

'He proposed to me in a Greek temple, by a lake, in the rain – who could say no?'

Anne looked wistful. 'Ah. It was me who had to propose to Neville. In a café.' She opened her hands. 'There you are.'

There was laughter around the table, even from Chamberlain. Peace seemed to have been made. Lucy collected used plates.

Anne was leaning forward towards her hosts opposite. 'I feel I

163

should say this to you both, since my husband probably wouldn't. I know how frustrated the two of you must have been during Winston's years out of office. For such an ambitious man, it must have been unbearable.'

Clementine shrugged. 'Ah, well...'

Winston was relighting the remains of his latest cigar.

She continued. 'But Neville had good reasons, you know.'

'Well, yes,' said Clementine. 'As he said, the rest of the Cabinet would never have...'

'No, not just that they were all scared of him.' Anne glanced at her husband. 'But also that Hitler was.'

Winston looked up. 'Hitler?'

'You must know that, Winston. Neville told me that Adolf had apoplexies every time your name was mentioned.'

'Really? That's encouraging.'

'He knew you were leading the campaign against him. He knew his history. He saw you as just another Marlborough – thwarting the Sun King at every turn.'

Winston grunted. 'I'm flattered at the comparison.'

'But whilst Neville was trying so hard to negotiate... to find diplomatic ways of avoiding war... you must see that he just didn't dare antagonise the brute further by giving you office. It would have sent all the wrong signals.'

Inches handed Lucy a tray piled with the used dishes, and picked up the tureen, nodding to the door.

Winston was muttering, 'I do understand. I may not altogether sympathise... but I understand.' He puffed to keep the cigar alight. 'Does Neville?'

Chamberlain's eyebrows rose. 'Do I what?'

'Understand my arguments?'

'I understand. But I too find it hard to sympathise.'

'Then we have a problem.'

'Yes.' The door closed on the discussion.

Back in the kitchen, Mrs Landemare had several more tray-loads ready to relay to the dining room. A large treacle tart, a cream covered trifle, a bowl of fruit, a platter of cheeses, a dish of biscuits, and a bowl of home-made chocolates. Enough to feed our family for a week, thought Lucy.

'How are things going in there?' the cook asked, as Inches surveyed the array.

'On a knife edge,' he mumbled. 'Safe for the moment, but anything could happen. You know what it's like, Mrs Landemare.'

'Well, good luck. I might come and listen at the door.'

'I don't advise it. It may be too much for your sensitive ears.'

She chuckled, as he took up one of the trays and nodded to Lucy to do the same. The pair made their way back to the dining room.

'Don't you speak to me like that, William Armitage! I'm entitled to my opinion, and if I think he's right to try and negotiate with Hitler, then who are you to argue? You'll pick a fight with anyone over anything, but this is war we're talking about, where people get killed and countries ruined, not just a bloody nose or two.'

'I know that, luv, I know. I'm not saying we shouldn't negotiate. I'm just saying negotiations haven't got us very far up to now, have they? And if all you do is negotiate, whilst your opponent is openly preparing to knock down your door, then you'll likely get caught with your trousers down, won't you?'

'You be careful using metaphors like that. You've been caught with your trousers down more than once, haven't you?'

'That's below the belt.'

'Exactly. That's what I'm saying.'

'Hey now! Don't change the subject. And not in front of the kids either. You'll be getting a war in here.'

'There you go, you see. Get trapped in a corner, and all you men can do is threaten a war.'

'Oh, give over.'

CHAPTER 25

Back in the dining room, the mood had changed again. Chamberlain had risen from his seat – for what reason Lucy could not discern – and was pacing up and down. The other three were watching him with apprehension.

'I'm agitated now,' he muttered, rubbing his forehead with his fingers.

'Dearest...,' Anne pleaded from the table.

'You see, this is what happens in the Cabinet room. Argument, dissension, distress...'

'At least we *have* argument,' said Winston, wine glass in hand. 'Whoever argues with Hitler gets shot.'

'Don't tempt me, Winston' said Chamberlain acidly.

Clementine spoke to her husband. 'Darling – keep it for Cabinet. For all our sakes.'

Inches and Lucy deposited their trays on the serving table. Winston was waving a placatory hand as he cast an eye over the desserts.

'Neville, I apologise if I have provoked you. That was *not* the purpose of this evening. But better to have had a war of words now, than lose the war of bullets later.'

'But this is why I – and yes, Halifax – still maintain there is a solution that can be negotiated, if only we have the intelligence to find it.' Chamberlain added pointedly, 'To use your own phrase – jaw, jaw, not war, war.'

'Ah.'

'We must stand firm, yes – but we must also seek an accommodation which will yet save us from the abyss.'

'But that's the thing, you see,' said Winston.

'What is?'

'We are not standing firm. So you have little to negotiate with.'

Chamberlain had stopped pacing. 'What? I have declared war! What more can I do?'

'You have not yet declared your intention to *win* the war. That is the point.'

'How can you say that?' demanded Chamberlain angrily. 'We are doing everything within our means.'

Winston expression was dour. 'No, Prime Minister, with respect, we are not.'

'Oh, goodness!' Clementine was despairing.

Inches delayed offering the desserts whilst the altercation developed. Lucy listened, once more enthralled.

'What else can we do that we are not doing?' demanded Chamberlain. 'Well?'

'Do you want a list?'

'No politics, *please* dear,' pleaded Clementine forlornly. 'We did agree.'

'All discussion leads ultimately to politics' he replied. '*Life* is politics!'

Anne spoke quietly. 'Why is it, Winston?'

'Why what?'

'Why is it you always have to win?'

He recoiled, halted in his tracks. 'Win?'

'Yes.'

Eventually he growled, 'Because.'

'Because what?'

'Because if you don't win you are nothing.' He contemplated the wine in his glass. 'I have lost too often. As my father always commented.'

She looked puzzled. 'Your father?'

He mumbled, more at the carpet than to her. 'He never... he never had faith in me.'

Anne looked at Clementine for clarification.

Clementine said, 'It's his greatest regret. That his father never lived to see his successes. Lord Randolph was a bitter man.'

Anne tilted her head slightly. 'That's sad.'

Winston cast off distant memories, and turned again to Chamberlain. 'Do you want a list?'

'Very well,' said Chamberlain quietly. 'Give me your list.'

Winston waved to Inches. 'Let's have some dessert first. And have another glass of wine. It's only fair you're as drunk as I am.'

Inches started round the table, murmuring to the diners as Lucy laid out the dessert plates.

Winston took a draft of the wine, and contemplated the ceiling. 'To be as concise as possible then. The recruitment effort is dire. We must enlist men and women from every inessential industry, from every private business, every dole queue, and every prison. The training programme is woeful. We must seek out every retired veteran, every old soldier, to help instruct these people. Our arms build-up is inadequate. We must convert every plant, every mill and every backyard workshop into a weapons factory.' His voice accelerated. 'We must recruit every industrial engineer and every scientist to help us improve those weapons and invent new ones. We must commandeer every electronics expert to develop the radar system, which is the key to winning the war in the air, and every mathematician to aid in code-breaking, which is the key to winning the war at sea.' He was going at an inexorable pace. 'We must enlist every language student and every foreign sympathiser to our intelligence network, which is the key to winning the war of information. We must bring every pressure to bear on the empire and the dominions to send us more men and resources, which as always are the key to our strength.'

Chamberlain was nodding. 'Yes...'

'I haven't finished. Above all we must beg, beseech, and

168

blackmail President Roosevelt and the American people to supply us with every facility, every spare tank and warship, every assistance at their disposal - because as always America is the *real* key to winning world wars.' He halted finally. 'I could go on.'

'Thank you, Winston,' said Chamberlain, waving Inches away. 'No dessert for me, thank you.' Back to his host, 'I will not take issue with you. We must do all those things.'

'Good.'

'Whilst still showing Hitler that we are capable of turning the other cheek.'

Churchill gave a sigh emanating from deep down in his chest. 'The devil can cite scripture for his purpose.' He closed his eyes for a moment, then turned his head. 'I'll have some treacle tart, Inches. At least we know *that's* well prepared, and guaranteed not to taste bitter.'

The tense silence in the room continued as the butler went round with the servings. Eventually Clementine spoke.

'My abiding memory of my childhood is the war between my parents.' Her handsome face was solemn. 'It probably isn't relevant, but... I remember the atmosphere, the tension – followed by the fierce arguments, the rows and accusations. I can't recollect now what they were about, but I remember thinking, why can't they agree? Why can't they find a way to – as you say, Neville – negotiate between themselves? When I was six they finally parted. But still the war went on. We children became the ammunition – shunted backwards and forwards between them – from this home to that. My father even tried to kidnap us at one stage.' She hesitated. 'I could never decide which parent it was I owed allegiance to. I wanted them both of course, but eventually I realised I had to choose. They could never come to the decision between them... and so I, young though I was, had to decide where my true loyalty lay.'

'Where did it?' asked Anne.

'I concluded that my real affections had never been with my

father. I finally let myself see him for the feckless, self-indulgent character he was. Not evil – just selfish. And, for all her faults, I decided I had to be with my mother. It was, I suppose, the moment I grew up. I don't know what that has to do with all this, but...' She stopped. Her emotion was evident.

'It must have been hard.'

'The hardest moment of all, Neville, was losing my sister. Kitty was older than me by two years. She had been my strength and my salvation through all those trials. She died at seventeen – they said of typhoid – but I was convinced she was worn out because of all we had been through. It was the saddest moment of my life. With death there can be no redemption.'

A moment's pause. 'Quite,' said Chamberlain. 'For all the victims of war there can be no redemption.'

Winston's lip protruded. 'And from all the victims who meet death needlessly, there can be no forgiveness.'

'Needlessly?' The PM's face appeared to be growing leaner and more hawklike by the minute.

'Do you doubt that, if we and France together had called Hitler's bluff at the borders of Czechoslovakia, we would have saved the countless lives of all who died there under the Nazi jackboot? All who are dying now in Poland? All who are about to die here?'

'It would have been a futile gesture. We were even more unprepared then than now.'

'So was he. I can tell you from my own information, Hitler's forces were not nearly as invincible as he wished us to think. It is all a matter of psychology, Neville. Who has the stronger will, the larger moral case.'

Chamberlain growled. 'Oh, it's no use. We go round in circles.'

Anne spoke. 'This is why your presence in a peacetime government could never be tolerated, Winston.'

Clementine exclaimed, 'Oh please! Don't let's start that row again.'

'It has to be said, Clementine,' said Chamberlain. Then to Winston, 'We have to appreciate the nature of the beast, you said earlier. That's true. Germany is a wounded beast. And the reasonable man does not corner such an animal until he explores all other means of calming it.'

'Even as it devours your sheep, and threatens your own children?'

'We have no proof of that! He has never declared his intention to invade us.'

Winston's eyes bulged. 'You expect him to *announce* it?'

'He has specifically stated that is not his ambition.'

'And you in your innocence believe him?'

'I in my wisdom know that to challenge him in the way we are doing is to risk provoking the very reaction we fear!' The mask hardened further. 'Hitler is a monster, I do not deny it. But the fiercer the monster, the more cautiously you have to deal with it. Is that not so?'

A pregnant silence. 'No.'

A series of despairing sighs round the table. The desserts sat untouched.

'You may not deal with monsters. You must slay them.'

His guest shook his head. 'I cannot discuss with you. We are as different to each other as we are to Hitler.'

Winston spoke with slow passion. 'No. No we are not. There is a crucial distinction.'

'Well, at this moment I cannot see it.'

The relentless rumble continued. 'No, you cannot. Because you will not open your eyes. You hide your face, and refuse to see that this is a struggle that will define mankind for the next hundred years. This is the issue by which the destiny of our entire species hangs.'

He waved a sweeping hand at the Nelson portrait hanging above Lucy's head. His voice was an engine growl.

171

'You turn the blind eye – you, and all your timid minions in the House, all those who would try and talk their way out of the labyrinth. Every creature out there who would sell their birthrights for a quiet life – the pacifist intellectuals, the wishful thinkers, the dull masses who wait for leadership and who will perish for want of it – you all resolutely refuse to open your eyes and recognise the terrible truth that stares you in the face. Because you do not want to believe it'

'Which is?'

'Which is that the head of a great nation – like so many who have usurped such positions in the past – is nothing but a criminal, a tyrant, a psychopath. For whatever fathomless reasons the psychoanalysts might find. And as such he has no scruples, and only one ambition. To go on conquering, and murdering, and coercing until he is master of all within his vision. Which means first his own people. Then his neighbours. Then the world.' The engine accelerated. 'Such perverted mentalities do not understand themselves that there will never be limits to the craving that compels them. They cannot hesitate for a moment in their voracious path, for that would be to recognise the depravity of their own ambitions. And because they are so utterly without constraint or conscience in this quest, there is only one way to prevent them. That is for the sane world to become as ruthless as they are.'

'As *insane* as they are,' said Chamberlain.

'Call it what you will. It is they who create the insanity.' He glanced at Anne. 'So to win is all there is, Anne. You cannot negotiate with such a creature, because he will prevaricate and lie and deceive to use time to his own advantage. You cannot face him with your morality, because despotism is his morality. You cannot sign treaties with him, for he will tear them up without compunction. You cannot face him with reason, or logic, or pleas for compassion, because he does not comprehend these concepts. You cannot oppose him with half measures, with unprepared armies, with bluff or with bluster, because he is unequivocal in *his* preparations. And you cannot hesitate for a day in your determination to destroy him, because you can be certain *he* will not hesitate for a second.'

Churchill rose from his seat, the chair almost falling backwards behind him. The voice thundered.

'We... no – *you* have already hesitated far too long, Prime Minister. You have stood by and vacillated whilst he has seized state after state, annihilated city after city, butchered dynasties and sects and whole populations – and the sole reason we are still here ourselves is because there are only so many directions he can spit his venom at once. But the days are running out.' He was striding around the table. 'If we do not rise from our lethargy, if we do not cast off this delusion that the world is at heart a reasonable place, then we will have the monster roaring at our gates, and we will have nothing with which to combat him but our pious protestations of good manners! The ballrooms will have closed for ever. We will have slow-danced our way into oblivion.'

There was total silence in the room. Time hung still about the stuccoed walls. Lucy stood, still as a statue, at her post. Never had she heard such passion. Never had she heard such eloquence. Never had she imagined such an apocalyptic vision of mankind's nature. She was aware of things existing far beyond her previous knowledge.

Inches stirred at her side, and murmured. 'Let's, er... fetch the coffee.'

But before they could move, Chamberlain was leaning back in his seat.

'I surrender.' He wiped his mouth with his napkin. There was a sad dignity about him. 'You're right, Winston. I do have to decide whether I'm up to the challenge. Whether I *want* to take on such a challenge.' He took a deep breath and threw a wan smile to his host. 'You know, in my worst moments I sometimes wonder whether it's not better to let the sea roar in and drown us all, than endure the agony of resisting it.'

'Hah,' came the reply. 'To die, to sleep.... No more.'

A nod. 'A consummation devoutly to be wished.'

Winston raised a hand, and continued the quote. 'Ah - But in that sleep of death what dreams may come...' The hand waved. 'What nightmares. There is no alternative, Neville.'

'Perhaps.'

Lucy did not know the quotation, but she understood the meaning. Winston's head had meanwhile sunk onto his chest. He was contemplating the folds in his starched shirt front, oblivious of the company around him. His voice was now a low rumble.

'I confess... I do confess that I myself am an intemperate being. I have been driven all my life to champion causes and crusades – some worthy, some futile.' His lower lip trembled slightly. 'My irrational energy has been my inspiration and my demon. It has burdened all around me...'

He glanced up at Clementine, his eyes moist. She smiled briefly back at him. Then he raised his tone. 'But this is why I recognise in Hitler a kindred soul. Why I understand him. Why I know he must be stopped.'

There was silence again. Chamberlain nodded. It was enough. No one spoke.

Eventually Clementine turned to Inches. 'I think we'll take coffee in the lounge, David.'

'Yes, ma'am.' He nodded to Lucy, and the pair headed once again for the kitchen.

CHAPTER 26

The remainder of the evening, back in the lounge, was a quiet affair. The party were all in a kind of sopor. The talk was muted, polite, aimless. Inches and Lucy served the coffee and its accompaniments, and at Churchill's command offered port and brandy. Chamberlain declined, Anne and Clementine took small ports, and Winston himself a large cognac.

'Despite all, we 'aven't done so bad, y'know luv. We've come through the worst, we've made a good business, we've brought up two great kids. We 'aven't done so bad.'

'No. We've done as well as most folk.'

'Better than many.'

'Yes, well, it's the luck of the draw, isn't it?'

'No, it's not. It's hard work and canny thinking. You make your own luck.'

'I suppose so.'

'Oh yes. People blame bad luck, and bad governments, and bad weather, and bad everything else. But in the end it's down to theirselves.'

'Yes, well don't get carried away, Fred Armitage. There's a stretch to go yet.'

Chamberlain was putting down his coffee cup. 'I think perhaps it's time we left.' He brushed his moustache, and rose. 'Thank you so much for an absorbing evening. One I wouldn't have missed.'

Clementine rose also, and gestured for Inches to fetch their coats. The butler left the room.

Winston heaved himself up. 'I apologise, Prime Minister,' he said, 'if I was too outspoken tonight. Don't take my drunken outbursts to heart.'

'Oh, but I do. It was your duty to voice your feelings. And indeed... you may be right.' Chamberlain gave a wan smile. 'It is a sad thing for mankind, but you may be right. Time will tell.'

'Yes.'

'Meanwhile we have the budgetary meeting in the morning. So it continues. You can harangue them all as well.' He turned to Clementine. 'Thank you, Clementine, for such a kind invitation.'

'Yes, thank you,' repeated Anne, straightening her dress as she rose. Wryly, 'A memorable evening in many ways.'

Winston took her hand. 'I have lost your last shreds of approval, Anne.'

She smiled with some grace. 'No actually. You have gained a few.'

'Ah. I'm glad.'

She turned to Clementine. 'Thank you so much.'

The two women clasped hands. 'I hope next time will be in happier circumstances,' said Clementine.

'Yes.'

Chamberlain was peering again at Churchill's paintings. 'It's hard to believe the fierce lion can be so delicate,' he said.

Winston grunted. 'Or the gentle unicorn so gracious.'

The other turned back. 'Despite all, I'm glad we have you with us, Winston.'

'Despite all, likewise.'

Inches returned with their coats, holding them expertly in turn for the pair to don. Lucy had forgotten them amongst all the events, and wondered whether they were dry now.

Chamberlain turned to Inches and herself. It was virtually the first time he had acknowledged their presence. 'Thank you for your kind attention tonight.'

Inches nodded acknowledgement, Lucy did an involuntary bob.

'Goodnight, Prime Minister,' said Winston. 'Good night,

Anne.'

Inches held open the door, and they left, the butler following.

Lucy went to collect the coffee cups, and Winston strode to the drinks table to pour himself more brandy.

'Now, pug,' said Clementine, protesting.

He stopped her with a gesture. 'Just a small one. I've earned it.' He poured what looked to Lucy quite a large one.

Clementine pulled a resigned face and handed her empty glass to Lucy as Inches came back from the hall. Her husband was taking a cigar from the box.

'Light please, Inches.' The butler struck a match. 'Well... how do you think it went, David?

'Very well, sir.'

'Over the top as usual, eh?'

'Splendidly so, sir.'

'Well, you've served a Prime Minister now. Something else for your memoirs.'

Inches lifted his chin. 'They tell a lot of lies about him, don't they?'

'Hm. The world is full of lies about us all. The worst of it is, so many of them are true.' Winston waved the cigar. 'The Irish stew was excellent. Tell Mrs Landemare.'

Inches nodded. 'Is there anything else, sir?'

Winston glanced at Clementine.

'No, thank you, David,' she said. 'That's all.'

He picked up the coffee tray. 'I'll finish in the dining room. Lucy will clear up in here. Good night, sir. Madam.'

He went out. Lucy continued collecting the numerous used glasses and ash trays. Winston had turned to his wife.

'Don't say it. Too far again.'

She smiled. 'In a good cause.'

'They all hate me, you know,' he growled, puffing smoke.

177

'Who?'

'All his gang. Most of parliament. They hate me for speaking the truth.'

She came and ritually brushed ash from his lapel. 'Not hate.'

'Oh yes. I'm only in the Cabinet because of public opinion.'

'Well, thank heavens for public opinion,' she said. 'Perhaps the voters aren't such fools after all.'

He reflected. 'Well, they usually get there in the end – if often by the wrong route. I trust they do. Otherwise there isn't much hope for any of us.'

She gazed steadily into his eyes. They were oblivious of the third person in the room. 'Do you really feel you've lost too often?'

'Oh, yes. As a child. And even now.'

She kissed his cheek. 'I admire you so much.'

'Ditto.'

'Time for bed.' She turned, and saw Lucy. 'Ah, Lucy, you must go home to bed too. The maids will clear up the rest.'

'Yes, ma'am.'

Clementine smiled. 'It's back to 'Clementine' now, Lucy. You did well tonight.' She turned to Winston. 'Lucy must have the day off tomorrow, mustn't she?'

'Yes, yes. Thank you for your assistance, Lucy.' He held up a finger. 'Don't believe all the hot air you heard this evening.'

Lucy smiled. 'Good night, sir.' She left the room, and headed gratefully for her bed.

She woke late next morning in her shared hostel room, and lay looking at the ceiling for a long moment. Her room-mate – the third she had known during her year there, since they seemed to come and go like mayflies – had already gone out for the day. Lucy reflected sleepily on the evening's experience. Once again it had stretched the bounds of her knowledge. Once again she wondered at how contingent was the human condition on the dispositions of a few people in stations of influence.

She rose, put on her robe, and went out into the chilly corridor to the chillier communal bathroom. She had the whole day ahead of her, the first complete free day since commencing her employment. Oddly, weary though she was throughout her entire body, she felt a strange disappointment at not attending the Admiralty that day. She missed the huge sense of anticipation and stimulus that the place induced. She missed the infusion of energy that her employer generated wherever he was engaged. The hours stretching ahead offered a bland and dreary prospect in comparison, even though it was a weekend Saturday, when most people expected to be off duty.

She decided to go looking for new lodgings. It was high time she left this place and had a home of her own. She bathed and dressed, and headed downstairs. On the way out she found a letter waiting for her. She recognised the writing on the envelope. It was from her brother Tom. She tore open the flap.

Dear Luce (or should I call you Loose now I hear you have a boyfriend?)

Henry and I have a couple of days leave before we are being sent to join the troops in France. We have decided to come to London this weekend and hit the hot spots for a final fling. We arrive Saturday and will be staying at a small hotel near Kings Cross. We thought we'd go to the famous Windmill Theatre in the evening, and maybe a jazz club after. Why don't you come too? We'll pick you up from your hostel around 6 pm. Wear your most fetching dress!

Your loving brother Tommy.

P.S. Maybe the boyfriend will want to join us?

Lucy smiled to herself. Tonight out in London with the boys. Even a visit to the Windmill with its *risqué* reputation. How could she refuse?

She mulled over whether to ask Daniel to join them, but swiftly decided against it. Bringing her two worlds together in such a way would be fraught with uncertainties, vulnerable to any number of pitfalls. She wasn't certain when she would be seeing him again, but tonight was not the best idea, even if he was available.

She went out to seek a news stand. The weather outside was a brisk October day, with a hazy sun brightening the streets of London. They thronged with people out shopping and sightseeing. The only signs that the nation was at war were the piles of sandbags at street corners, the prevalence of uniforms on the thoroughfares, and the various posters advising of conscription, blackout regulations, emergency instructions, and other warfare matters.

She bought a copy of yesterday's *Evening Standard* at a street vendor's, and took it to a nearby café, where she ordered toast and tea and settled down to scan the accommodation ads. This was the paper to which all London home seekers turned for available housing. After twenty minutes perusal of its adverts she had marked four which offered rooms to let within her modest price range, and within reasonably pleasant areas that had quick transport access to Whitehall.

She made a note of the telephone numbers, finished her breakfast, and went out to find a public telephone. She phoned all four numbers. Two of the rooms were already let, one had a kitchen and bathroom shared with five other inmates, and the fourth offered a self-contained attic room in Euston, with a kitchenette, and access to its own toilet and wash basin - a rare accessory. The rent was twelve shillings a week, more than she wanted to pay, but the accommodation sounded attractive, and the address was within walking distance of buses to Westminster. Also of Euston station, where she could catch a train to Cumberland if ever the chance arose to go home. She made an appointment to view it within the half hour.

It was three floors up in a brick Victorian terraced house in a drab back street behind the huge Euston Station. The landlord was an old boy with a walrus moustache, who seemed to be of an educated background. The interior hall and stairway were clean and hanging with old mirrors and prints, and the room - once she had reached it up the steep climb - was more spacious than the one at the hostel, with a small cooking stove in one corner, and the prized toilet next door. A narrow iron fireplace sat opposite the wrought-iron bedstead, an easy chair sat close by, and a small table with two upright chairs stood to one side. The view from the gabled window showed an intriguing mingle of rooftops and chimneys, and there was a quiet air about the place, broken only by an occasional whistle from the nearby steam trains.

'On your own in London, are you?' enquired the landlord, wheezing from the climb. He was probably in his seventies and, judging from his worn velvet jacket, baggy corduroy trousers, and lack of regional accent, possibly of an academic or artistic background. He had unkempt greying hair, friendly eyes, and narrow wire-rimmed spectacles, through which he peered at her with curiosity.

'Yes,' she said. 'I'm from the Lakes, but I'm working in London.'

'Long way from home,' he said. 'What's your job?'

She hesitated. 'Oh, I'm just a secretary in a government department.'

His bushy eyebrows rose. 'Which department?'

'Um... the Admiralty.'

'Interesting. Must be busy there at the moment.'

'Yes, it is.'

'Are we winning the war at sea?'

'Oh, I just type official lists and orders and so on. I don't have much to do with what's happening with the ships.'

'Eh, well...' He nodded his head. 'I have a son out there. I'd like to know he's safe.'

'On a war ship?' she asked.

'No. Merchant ship. But there's all sorts of rumours about the casualties they're having.'

'I'm sure he'll be all right,' she said. 'I know the navy's doing everything it can to protect them.'

'Is it?' He glowered. 'Not while that old bastard's in charge, I imagine.'

Lucy stared at him. 'Sorry? Who...?'

'Churchill! God knows why he's back. Damned warmonger!'

She was stunned. 'Oh. Don't you approve of him?'

'Lord no! Nor do a lot of people.'

'But surely...'

'He's as bad as Hitler. They should put them both in a bull ring and let them fight it out between them.'

She could find no answer.

'Anyway...' He regained his genial self and waved round the room. 'What do you think?'

She pulled herself together. 'It's nice. I'd like to take it.'

'It's a week's rent in advance. If you want hot water, you have to heat it on the gas stove. You can have coal for the fireplace from the back yard, but I make a small charge. There's two other tenants downstairs, but they're respectable people. And I don't allow visitors after five o'clock.' He peered over the spectacles. 'Got your own sheets, have you?'

'Oh.' She hadn't thought of that. The hostel provided those. 'I'll get some.'

'And a towel.'

'Yes. Could I move in on Monday evening?'

'Sooner the better as far as I'm concerned. What's your name?'

'Lucy. Lucy Armitage.'

He turned. 'Right, Lucy, welcome to my little home. I'll show you out.'

CHAPTER 27

The boys arrived in a taxi cab and picked her up as promised early that evening. It had been over a year since she had seen either of them. They were both in uniform, both with short cropped hair, and both already sporting a lance corporal's single stripe on each arm. Advancement was fast for bright men in those urgent times. Henry wore a neat moustache which gave him a dashing air. She met them in the hallway of the hostel, and stared for a moment in shock. Who were these two grown men, so large, so mature, so confident looking?

They responded likewise.

'Hey, Lucy!' her brother exclaimed. 'Look at you!'

'My, Lucy!' added Henry. 'Who'd have known?'

Lucy responded. 'Hey, boys - same to you!'

She gave them each a hug, inhaling the mingled scent of coarse serge cloth and manliness. Henry's moustache tickled her cheek. Part of the surprise was seeing them in their uniforms, but of course she should have known. These days the streets were frequented with people in the regalia of a myriad different military outfits. Even when off-duty they wore them with a proud arrogance, having long relegated their 'civvy suits' to wardrobes and moth balls.

They took the taxi into Soho, where the Windmill Theatre flaunted its seductive photos and flashed its neon invitations, hooded now in the blackout. For several years now the venue had maintained its scandalous but profitable reputation as the stager of variety shows featuring naked girls. The Lord Chamberlain's office had reluctantly surrendered to the argument that, as long as the girls didn't actually move, they could be described as 'living statues', which therefore showed no more impropriety than did the carved ones in the British Museum. The mostly male audiences of course knew the difference, and flocked to the venue at all hours to enhance their cultural education.

'I don't know if I should be coming to see this,' said Lucy as the cab drew up in the busy street. 'Won't it be all men in the audience?'

'Not at all,' said her brother. 'We know a lot of boys who've been. They say women love the show as much as the men.'

'I just hope we can get in, ' added Henry. 'Every man-jack who's on leave will be there.'

They did indeed have to join a queue of bawdily rumptious people, many in uniform, waiting to gain entry. However the line moved fairly quickly, and within half an hour they were inside the modest auditorium, pushing their way to the nearest seats through the semi-darkness as the continuous show revolved on stage.

For the next two hours Lucy sat between the two men with whom she had shared her formative years, watching the peculiar combination of bawdy comedians, bizarre circus acts, and eccentric tableaux of naked girls unfolding in front of her. It all had a faint air of tattiness, and was as far removed from her own erotic experience as she could have imagined, but the vast majority of the audience responded with the loud appreciation of a population facing perhaps its last moments on earth.

When they eventually emerged into the darkened streets the trio hovered for a moment on the pavement.

'Phew!' muttered Henry. 'Well, it made a change from "All Quiet On The Western Front." '

'More like all frontal in the West End,' said Tom. The other two laughed.

'What did you think, Lucy?' asked Henry, taking hold of her lapels and pulling her coat tighter around her in the chill night air.

'Let's call it an interesting evening,' she replied. She was thinking that it bore no comparison to her theatrical experience in the company of Oscar Wilde, but did not say so. 'Why is it that there are no nude male shows for women to go and see?'

'There are,' said Henry. 'But they're not for women, and they're
184

definitely not passed by the Lord Chamberlain.'

It took her a moment to understand. 'Oh,' she said. And to change the subject added,

'Well, I'm not sure that I want to go on to a jazz club after that. I've had enough noise for one evening.'

'I agree,' said her brother. 'I'm hungry. Let's find a restaurant first.'

Soho abounded in restaurants offering various national cuisines. The first two they tried - a Chinese and an Indian - had no tables free. Half of London it seemed were dining out. They eventually found an Italian place displaying amateur paintings of Florence and Venice, and shelves of straw-bound chianti bottles, where they were given a cramped table in a corner alcove. The kitchen smells however were enticing. She remembered Daniel's words, 'You can always tell a good restaurant by its smell.' They settled into the candlelit space.

A dour old boy, who looked as though he had served a million meals over half a century of gratifying London's taste buds, held out voluminous menus, and said in a thick Neapolitan accent, 'We gotta very nice chef special tonight, signori and signorina. Is a kinda Osso Bucco, but with chicken, not veal.' He kissed his fingers in the traditional manner. 'Excellent!'

'Sold,' said Tom, handing back the menu. 'Can't be bothered to look through all that. It sounds lovely.'

'Me too,' said the others, doing the same.

He took back the menus. 'You wanna starter? We gotta nice prosciutto. All the way from Parma.'

'All the way from Smithfield more likely,' murmured Tom as he studied the wine list.

Lucy felt emboldened. 'Have you got calamari?' she said.

The two boys raised their eyebrows.

'Of course, signorina. Very nice baby calamari.'

'I'll have that as a starter.'

185

Henry cocked his head. 'What the devil is calummary?'

'Calamari,' she said. 'It's squid.'

He sat back. 'Wo! You've learnt a thing or two in London.'

She smiled demurely, and did not reveal how new she was to the dish. 'It's nice. You should try it.'

'Well, I'm game,' said her brother. 'Always up for a new experience.'

The waiter bestowed his first genuine smile and said, 'Very good. And for wine, I recommend a nice Soave with the calamari, and perhaps a light Lambrusco with the chicken, eh?'

'Whatever you say, my friend. We're in your hands.'

The old boy went happily off, pleased at such accommodating customers.

'So...' Henry sat back, looking at her. 'Tell us about this new man in your life.'

She returned his look. 'Are you talking about Churchill or my boyfriend?'

They laughed. 'Let's start with Churchill,' he said. 'He's got to be more interesting. Do you have a great deal to do with him?'

'Yes. I take dictation and do other things for him almost every day.'

'Really?' Both boys leaned forward. Her brother said, 'So what's he like?'

She toyed with a fork on the table. 'He's fascinating, intimidating, infuriating, inspiring, exciting, demanding, frustrating... I could go on.'

'And are the things you do for him important?' Henry's handsome face was a picture of captivation. 'Does he dictate important stuff?'

'Often. Orders for the navy, speeches to Parliament. I typed a letter to President Roosevelt just a few days ago.'

'Good lord!' Two pairs of eyes were riveted. 'Lucy, you're in the middle of it all!'

She gave a demure smile. 'I suppose I am. But of course I can't talk about any of it.'

Tom lowered his voice conspiratorially. 'But you can tell us a bit. We're off to the front soon. Does he think we can win the war?'

She wondered how much she should say. 'Let's just say he's optimistic. He's always optimistic, even when everything's going badly. That's his great strength.' She hesitated. 'In contrast to the Prime Minister, I have to say.'

'Chamberlain?' said Henry. 'Have you met him too?'

She paused again. Well, surely there was no harm in telling them. 'I served him and his wife dinner last night.'

They both laughed. Laughs of disbelief. 'You're having us on,' said her brother.

She enjoyed their astonishment. 'No, really. Winston and his wife, Clementine, invited the Chamberlains to dinner at Admiralty House, and there was a staff shortage so I was called in to help serve the dinner.'

Henry straightened a little. 'I thought they were sworn enemies.'

'They are, politically. But privately, they... well, they seem to have a lot of respect for each other. I mean, they argued quite fiercely about how things should be done but they never actually came to blows. In fact they parted on quite friendly terms.'

'So what were they arguing about? The war effort? How to approach Hitler?'

She realised she had said too much. 'I can't talk about it. I'll get shot. Literally.'

The first course arrived and saved her from further interrogation. There was a diversion as the two men contemplated the unfamiliar dishes.

'It's much nicer than it looks,' said Lucy, spearing a small, spikey object. 'Go on, try it.' She put it into her mouth.

They tentatively followed her example.

187

'Well, it's not bad,' said Tom, chewing quizzically. 'Perhaps we'll be getting more like this where we're going.'

'Do you know your destination yet?' Lucy asked.

'No. But it's likely to be France. Everyone expects that will be Hitler's next target once he's conquered northern Europe.'

'You'll probably find out before we do,' added Henry with a dry smile.

Tom added, 'And you can tell your boss that we'll need better mortars than we're equipped with at the moment.'

Lucy's eyebrows raised. 'Mortars?'

'Short range artillery.'

'Aren't they any good?'

'Well, they're quite reliable, but they haven't been improved much since the Great War. They've too short a range. We'll be outgunned by the Boche.'

She tucked it away in the back of her mind.

Henry lent forward again. 'So tell us about the boyfriend, Luce.'

She felt awkward again. It was all so new. 'He's American. Working at their embassy, decoding messages and so on. He's quite a bit older than me, and he's seen a lot of the world. He's teaching me a lot about life.'

'And about sex?' Henry's eyes were twinkling.

Hers flashed. 'Mind your own business, Henry. Anyway, we've only known each other a little while.'

'But might it be serious?' queried her brother.

She felt unaccountably shy about discussing it. 'Maybe. He's nice, he's attractive. It's early days.'

'Trust the Yanks to bag the best girls,' said Henry.

'Well, maybe they know how to treat them better,' she fired back. 'And not just about sex.'

He put his hands up in surrender. They abandoned the subject - in fact both subjects - and the rest of the meal passed pleasantly enough. She drank a little more than she meant to and relaxed. They were all three aware that they were different people now. Their old life in the Lakes was a distant dream.

When the bill came Lucy insisted on paying her share. 'I'm a salaried woman now,' she said. They didn't argue.

It was raining a light drizzle as they came out of the restaurant. The boys suggested going on to a club, but she refrained. 'I have to be on duty early tomorrow,' she said. 'I daren't come in without a good night's sleep. He'll know immediately if I'm not on the ball.'

She flagged down a taxi, and kissed them both goodbye as it drew up to the curb. 'Be careful,' she said. 'Look after yourselves in France. Write to me, won't you?'

She waved to them from the back window as the cab drove off. Two rather lonely looking figures standing in their gaunt uniforms on the wet pavement.

When she got back to the hostel there was another envelope waiting for her with a note inside. How it had been delivered she wasn't sure but she recognised the handwriting immediately, so delicately etched in comparison to her brother's robust scrawl.

Hi there. Sorry not to have been in touch, but things are pretty hectic here at the embassy. I do so want to see you again soon. How about dinner tomorrow evening? It's Sunday, so there won't be much open, but I could cook us supper at my place. I'm quite a good cook. We could have a pleasant quiet evening, with some music and a nice wine. No pressure. I promise not to take advantage of you, but I really would like the chance to get to know you better. What do you say?

My address is 24a North Audley Street. You can take a 14 bus from your digs. Say six o'clock? Daniel.

(I will assume yes, unless you leave a message at the embassy)

Her heart beat faster again.

CHAPTER 28

The next day was Sunday, but the offices were as busy as ever. 'God may not stop the war, but the war won't stop for God,' was the saying round the staff.

'Lieutenant Commander Thompson wants to see you,' said Grace Hamblin, when a slightly hungover Lucy reported for duty at eight o'clock. 'He's in his office.'

Lucy's brow clouded. 'Has he got anyone with him?'

'Yes.' Grace looked curious. 'The same man from MI5 you saw last time.' Dryly, 'Are you being investigated for espionage, Lucy?'

'I hope not.'

'How did Friday night go? I gather you were roped in to help Inches.'

'Yes.' Lucy wasn't sure how to describe it. 'It was an... interesting evening.'

'I've no doubt it was.' Grace was evidently intrigued. 'The Churchills seem to think it went quite well. Did everyone escape without life-threatening injuries?'

'Oh, yes. Mr Churchill was very forceful to the Prime Minister, but they parted friends.' She did not elaborate on the tempestuous elements of the occasion.

'Good. Well, run along to see Tommy Thompson.'

As she entered Thompson's small office, the two men were in the same position as before – the Commander behind his desk, reading a file, Agent Miles in the armchair at the side.

'Come in, Lucy,' said Thompson with a smile. 'Have a seat.'

She sat in front of the desk.

He put down the file. 'So how was the momentous dinner

party?'

Did everyone know about it? she thought. 'You heard about that, sir?'

'Of course. The whole of the Admiralty has heard about it. Not often one of our staff gets to witness an occasion like that. How did it go?'

'Very well, sir.'

The smile widened. He spoke tolerantly. 'Come now, Lucy, don't tell us that's all you have to say about an extraordinary encounter between the two most powerful men in the land. Were you in attendance for most of it?'

'Yes, sir. A lot of it.'

'And presumably the talk involved the appeasement issue at some stage?'

'Yes.' She refrained from adding that it involved little else.

He tapped his pen on the desk. 'Well, we don't want you to break any confidences, but is it safe to say that there is still considerable amount of space between their two stances? Mr Churchill will probably give me his account of the evening, but I'd like your broad opinion also.'

She presumed it was all right to discuss it with these two. 'They do seem to be quite a long way apart in their, um...'

'Attitudes to Hitler?'

'Yes.'

He nodded thoughtfully, then glanced at the other man.

Miles uncrossed his legs. 'Have you had any more contact with Daniel Mountview?'

Lucy felt another twinge of resentment at his intrusion. However she fished in her handbag and silently held out Daniel's note. He read it, handed it to Thompson, and looked back at Lucy. She was uncomfortable under his scrutiny.

'Do you feel inclined to accept his invitation?' he asked.

'I'm not sure. I... It's rather unusual for a man to ask me to his rooms, isn't it?'

He inclined his head. 'Perhaps. But he's American. They can be more forward than our young men.'

'Do you think I should accept?'

He opened his hands. 'It's entirely up to you. But it might suit our cause if you did.'

'Would you *like* to accept?' said Thompson.

'I wouldn't mind. I do quite like him. But I...'

'But what?'

She met his eyes directly. 'I feel like a traitor myself.'

Thompson acknowledged her dilemma. 'Well, yes – it's a choice between loyalties.'

That didn't help. 'Are you sure I'd be safe?'

'Oh, yes. He's not a rapist or a kidnapper.'

Miles intervened, as though such matters were irrelevant. 'Did the discussion at dinner include Russia's involvement in the war?'

Back to the dinner again. 'Some of it, yes. Mr Churchill seems to think they may change sides.'

He nodded. 'It's what we're banking on. Hitler has his eyes on Russia as well as everywhere else. And of course he's frightened that Stalin may have his eyes on *him.*' A dry smile. 'There's no honour amongst thieves.'

Lucy was puzzled about that whole aspect of the war. 'Has Hitler enough armies to fight Russia as well as the rest of Europe?'

Miles shrugged. 'That's the big question. Does his boundless ambition stretch to such insanity?' He leaned forward. 'This is the thing, Lucy. We very much want to persuade Stalin that it's in his interests to back our side. It could alter the course of the war. And you could help that effort in a small way.'

She gazed back at him. She could think of nothing to say.

He went on. 'The events of Friday night could be of great help to us. The fact of your being recruited to serve at the dinner party, and so overheard much of the conversation, is an astonishing stroke of luck.'

She found her voice. 'How?'

'Russia knows well what is happening with our political situation. Stalin knows that the Prime Minister's days may be numbered, and that either Lord Halifax or Mr Churchill is very likely to be his successor. He is anxious to know what their respective attitudes are towards him.' He paused to let her digest the implications. 'As we told you, we think that Daniel Mountview is feeding information to the Kremlin – with similar but more questionable motives to ours. If we can make him believe Britain really does want Russia as our ally, and that, when we win the war and divide the spoils, she will have rich pickings in east Europe, then it could help to swing the balance.'

Lucy looked from one to the other, not yet quite grasping what was wanted of her. 'Are you quite sure Daniel's a spy?'

'We've tracked his contacts and his methods of communication. There aren't many other explanations.'

'So how can I...?'

Thompson was lighting his pipe. 'You see, Lucy,' he said in between puffs, 'Stalin is a strange character. He's both ruthless and paranoid at the same time. He's morbidly suspicious of everyone around him, and also of everyone abroad who he has dealings with. He's certainly suspicious of Hitler's motives, and equally suspicious of our own leaders. Both sides have been wooing him for a long time, but he never commits. We want to reassure him.' He paused for a moment to see if the implications registered. He took the pipe from his mouth and went on. 'We want Mountview to relay back to his masters the message that Churchill is a great admirer of Russia and of Stalin, and that he wants to do business with them. We want to flatter the tyrant's ego, and make him believe that it's in his interests to be on our side if Hitler does turn against him.' He lowered his voice to a confidential level. 'By going to dinner with your admirer tonight, Lucy, you would have

193

the opportunity to tell him about Friday's experience – he has possibly heard about it already – and then feed him that kind of information.'

'You mean, tell him what I heard them all talking about?'

He gave a dry smile. 'Well, a carefully tailored version of what they talked about. It would have to be subtly done. He would be wise to anything that seemed too obvious. For that reason you should never volunteer information, but always wait for the right opening. Wait until he asks specific questions. And even then, you'd have to appear reluctant and somewhat naïve about the whole business.' He raised an eyebrow. 'You've proved you're a good actress so far. Can you keep it up?'

'I don't know.'

'I'm sure you can. Just be yourself, but give the impression that you're hesitant about discussing such matters too much. Let him wheedle things out of you.'

Miles spoke. 'How far do you think things may go tonight – romantically?' He could have been asking what she intended to buy at the grocer's.

She flushed slightly. 'Um...'

'I don't wish to be indelicate, but it may...' He waved a vague hand.

'I don't know.'

'No, but would you be amenable to... an intimate relationship?'

She understood the inference, but found it impossible to answer.

Thompson sensed her embarrassment. 'Never mind, Lucy, that's entirely up to you. But the more you have this man's confidence, the more likely he is to trust you. And so believe you will be useful to him.' He grinned. 'Those in the espionage business call it the honey trap.'

She had heard the phrase. She never thought she might be involved in one.

'So,' said Miles. 'We'd very much like you to accept his

invitation for tonight.' It sounded more like a command than a request. 'Are you prepared to do that?'

A moment's pause. 'Yes,' she said quietly.

He nodded with satisfaction, and looked at Thompson. 'In that case...'

'Yes,' said Thompson. 'In that case, Lucy, we need to go and see Winston, and get his advice on what you should say to your boyfriend.'

She raised her eyebrows. 'Does he know the... the situation?'

'Of course. He knows it all.'

'Oh.'

'Don't worry. He thinks it's a splendid idea.' He rose. 'Let's go across to Admiralty House. I think he's free now.' Another quick grin. 'Though probably still in bed.'

He was indeed in bed. Lucy was familiar with his frequent habit of rising late, having already done an hour's work on papers or dictation over his breakfast tray. Miles had left and gone back to MI5, but Lucy and Thompson were met by Clementine in the hallway of the Churchill apartment. She was dressed to go out to church.

'Good morning, Tommy, Lucy,' she said. 'He's expecting you. Go through to the bedroom.' She smiled at Lucy. 'Don't let them talk you into doing anything you don't wish to do, my dear.'

Evidently the entire household knew of the plan.

The pair went through to Churchill's back bedroom, which was separate from his wife's. He was sitting up in bed in his pajamas reading a file, an unlit cigar inevitably between his lips. Nelson the cat was on the bed beside his breakfast tray, which contained the remnants of boiled eggs, toast and coffee.

'Ah,' he exclaimed at their entrance, and beckoned them in. 'Come in, come in. Take a seat.' He waved the file. 'Damned Graf Spee! She's creating havoc. Done for half a dozen merchant ships so far. We've got to catch her.'

'Do we know where she is, sir?' asked Thompson.

'Not exactly. Slippery customer.' He took the cigar from his mouth and brandished it in his customary fashion. 'But we'll get her, we'll get her. Got a number of ships after her, and there'll be a devil of a fight, but we'll get her.'

Lucy had seen an aerial photo of the *Graf Spee,* Germany's latest battle cruiser, from the air resembling a giant crocodile.

Winston smiled at her over his glasses. 'Morning, Lucy dear. Have you recovered from our own battle on Friday night?'

'Yes, Winston. I'm fine, thank you.'

'Quite an occasion, eh? One to remember when you're writing your memoirs.'

'Yes, sir.'

'However, don't write them just yet.' He threw down the file, narrowly missing Nelson, and looked at Thompson. 'So, Tommy, are we hatching a little plot here?'

'It looks as if we may be able to, Winston. Lucy is seeing her admirer this evening. He's asked her to dinner at his private address.'

The blue eyes peered at Lucy. 'Has he indeed? Romantic assignation, is it?'

Thompson answered for her. 'It hasn't got quite that far, Winston, but he's evidently attracted to her – or at least pretending attraction – and the relationship may well develop.'

'Of course he's attracted to her. What man wouldn't be attracted to Lucy? So, what is she going to tell him?'

'That's what we need you to advise, Winston. She knows she has to be subtle about imparting information. But what is the precise message we want him to take away with him?'

Winston picked up a match box from the tray and lit the cigar. 'Well now... Stalin's a shrewd bugger. Assuming the information filters through to him, how will it appear? Presumably he'll learn that it's come from one of my staff. Presumably he'll know there was an argumentative meeting between Chamberlain and myself.'

'And your wives, sir.'

'Yes, and our wives. So the discussion must have been of a social, rather than an official nature.' He drew on the cigar, and blew smoke into the air. The smell was pungent to Lucy's nostrils, so early in the morning. The cat jumped down from the bed. 'Let's assume that first of all we mentioned the usefulness of having Russia on our side. Let's say that we talked about our historic links with Russia, and our admiration for her stalwart people and gallant history.' The cigar pointed. 'Though without mentioning the Revolution.' More intense thought. 'What he's really interested in is the Baltic states. Those are his priority. Let's hint that we think Russia could after all have an entitlement to certain territories because of the historic connections – Poland, Romania, Lithuania, Estonia...' He glanced at Lucy. 'Can you remember those names?'

'I think so.'

'And then let's assume that we got onto the subject of Stalin's own character.' His voice became a growl. 'Of course the man is a fiend, but we don't say that. We say that I... no, that my wife believes him to be trustworthy, once he's made up his mind. We say that we both have a grudging admiration for what he has done for the Russian people. And specifically that I admire his logical brain, his formidable determination, his strength of character. I believe he is someone with whom I can do business. Hypocrisy, but you get the general thrust of it, Lucy?'

'Yes, sir.' She hesitated. 'What about the Prime Minister's view? He may ask that.'

'Ah, yes.' He pondered. 'That could be useful. Give credence to the story. Say that Neville Chamberlain disagreed with me on certain points. He was more critical of Stalin. We had quite an argument about it.' He twinkled. 'Nothing like a bit of contretemps to add to the veracity of a fairy story.'

'Anything else, Winston?' asked Thompson.

Churchill pondered. 'Would it be too much to suggest that I

believe Hitler is going to betray Russia? Break the terms of whatever agreement they have?'

Thompson said, 'He already suspects that may be the case, surely?'

'Yes, but we might confirm that I believe Hitler could be planning invasion once he's dealt with Poland?'

'Good.'

'However we don't want to over-egg the pudding.' He blew more smoke into the already fugged air. 'No, I think we can hint at that. We can say that we believe Hitler is amassing more forces than are necessary for the simple occupation of Poland. We have information about his intentions from our spy network. Which in fact is true.'

'That's all sounds authentic, sir.'

Winston's eyes turned to Lucy again. 'What d'you think of all that, Lucy? Think you grasp it? We haven't got much time to school you on it all if you're seeing this chap tonight, so you'll have to be crafty about it.'

She nodded. 'I think I understand, sir.'

'Good, good. You're a clever girl. I'm sure you can do it. Tommy will take you through all that again, so you feel confident about it.' He glanced up at the window, where the blackout curtains had been drawn back. 'Fine day out there. Time I got up. Much to do.' He pushed the breakfast tray to one side. 'Hand me that dressing gown, Lucy dear.'

She passed him the silk gown resting nearby. He pushed back the bed clothes, put it round his shoulders, and heaved himself from the bed. 'Right, off you go. And let me know how it goes tomorrow.'

'Yes, sir.'

The pair turned to leave the room. Then Lucy turned back with afterthought as Winston was picking up the file again.

'By the way, sir...'

He looked up. 'Yes?'

'I don't know if I should say this, but my brother is with the Cumberland artillery regiment. They're probably going to the front soon. He says...' she tailed off.

'He says what?' Impatiently, 'Out with it, girl.'

'He says that he thinks their guns have too short a range.'

Churchill took his unlit cigar from his mouth and stared over his spectacles. 'Which guns?'

'Um... I think he said, the mortars.'

'The Mark Two mortars?'

'I'm not sure exactly. I think so.'

'Hah! He's quite right.' Winston looked at Thompson. 'Hear that, Tommy? From the horse's mouth. I've been hammering at the War Office about it. Let's hammer some more.'

'Yes, Winston.'

Churchill looked back at Lucy. 'Thank you, Lucy. We'll have you running a war department before you know it.'

He went back to his file. The pair left.

CHAPTER 29

'Do you sleep with your boyfriend, Mary?'

They were sitting in the Admiralty dining hall, a lunchtime bowl of tomato soup in front of each.

'Yes, of course,' said Mary, gaily. 'We've been together for more than a year now.'

'What... I mean, do you like it?'

'I wouldn't do it if I didn't like it, would I? I'm a Catholic, but then hormones beat God every time.'

'Have you had anyone else?'

'Two others.'

'Was it... the first time, was it difficult?'

Mary held her gaze. 'You're a virgin?'

'Yes.'

'And you're thinking of going to bed with Mr Errol Flynn from the embassy.'

'Well... he's invited me to dinner at his lodgings tonight. I don't know what might happen.'

'I warned you about that.'

'I know.'

Mary sat back, chewing on a bun. Her bright lipstick glowed. 'Well, here's the thing. I got had the first time when I was eighteen - by a boy who had even less idea of what to do than I had. It was awful. It was very painful, there was blood all over the place, and it was over before I'd had time to say Hail Mary. That's not the sort of experience you want.'

'No.'

'Do you love Daniel?'

'Good heavens, I've only been out with him twice. How could I know? I like him.'

'Well, never mind. At this stage love doesn't matter so much. That can come later. What you need at this stage is someone who knows what he's doing, is kind and thoughtful, and who you find attractive.'

'Yes.'

'If you've agreed to go to his room, then obviously you're ready for whatever might happen. But only decide if you really, really want to. If you're uptight about it, it won't work.' She cocked her head sideways. 'Are you doing this because you want to, or just because you think it's high time you did?'

'A bit of both, I suppose.' She didn't mention the other motive.

'Well, I'll just say this. When it works it's wonderful. It's like nothing else. But it's not always easy to make it work. So don't be put off, if it doesn't go perfectly the first time.'

'Right.'

'And don't be shy of telling him what you want, or don't want.'

'Mhm.'

'And make sure he uses a contraceptive.'

'Yes.'

'Good luck.'

He was living in a Mayfair town house. She took the bus to Park Lane, and walked to the address, occasionally glancing about her, wondering whether she was still being followed. The evening was drawing in, and an autumnal chill prompted her to walk quickly. It was a grey stone Georgian terraced building with a grandiose front door and brass fittings. She rang the anonymous doorbell, and after a few moments he opened the door. He ushered her in, smiling.

'You came. I was afraid you might not.'

She looked around the marble-floored entrance hall. 'This is smart.'

'It's one of several rented by the embassy for their staff. There's a waiting list for rooms here, but I finally managed to get one.' He waved at the wide staircase. 'There are half a dozen of us here, and we all have use of the communal kitchen and a couple of bathrooms.' The lop-sided smile. 'I've booked the kitchen for half an hour later on.'

'Better than what I've found,' she said, gazing at an ornate gold-leafed mirror on the wall.

'You have somewhere new?'

'Yes. I found it yesterday. A room in Euston.'

'Good. Nice place?'

'It's all right. Except the landlord is very anti-Churchill.'

'Ah, well – so is half the country. Come on up. I'm on the first floor.'

It was a large room with a view over the rear garden. It was carpeted, and furnished with a chesterfield style sofa, a small side table already laid for two, a desk, and various other pieces. A single bed stood in the far corner, with a patchwork counterpane. A bookcase with a load of books stood to one side. A coal fire burned in the grate. Classical music played quietly from somewhere. Mozart she thought, but wasn't sure.

'Give me your coat,' he said, and hung it in a cupboard set into the wall. She straightened her simple black dress. It was the same evening dress she had worn to the theatre, but she only had the one.

'Sit down. What will you drink? I'm having a vodka martini, but perhaps that's a bit strong for your taste.'

'Have you some wine?'

'Of course. Red or white?'

She was unused to making the choice. 'Um... white, please.'

He pulled aside one of the heavy brocade curtains, pushed up the sash window, and brought in a bottle standing on the outer window ledge. 'Keeps it cool,' he said as he worked on it with a corkscrew.

She sat in the deep velvet covered sofa. The fire gave a warm glow. A pair of Victorian lamp-stands cast a mellow light. Yes, I could take to this lifestyle, she thought. What a pity it had to come with underhand designs.

He came and sat beside her, proffering the glass.

'Thank you.' She sipped the wine. It had a dry, tangy taste.

'That's a Meursault,' he said. 'My favourite white.'

'Nice.'

He leaned back against the arm of the chesterfield. 'So, how's things?'

'Fine.'

'They still working you hard?'

'I had Saturday off. That's how I was able to go house-hunting. I'm moving in tomorrow.'

'Good. Do you want help with your stuff?'

'I haven't got much. Just a suitcase full.'

She watched him sip his drink. There was a seriousness about his features that she liked. It was hard to imagine him as a spy. He caught her looking, and smiled. 'What are you thinking?'

'How old did you say you were?'

'Twenty seven.'

'You seem older.'

'Do I? Aged by life's experience perhaps.'

'Have you experienced much?'

'Quite a bit, I suppose. My mother never stayed married for long. We moved about a lot. It took me a while to find what I wanted to do.'

'You must be highly qualified to work in the American Embassy.'

'I won a scholarship to Princeton. I have the right sort of mind for the job.'

'But you've never...?'

'Never what?'

'Been married, or had a long relationship.'

'I was with a girl from New York for a few years. It didn't work out in the end.'

A whole past history she knew nothing about. 'Why not?'

'She didn't like my politics.'

'What are your politics?'

'I'm fairly left wing, I suppose. I see inequality as the world's biggest problem after world wars. Maybe it's the inequality that leads to the world wars.'

'And the girlfriend didn't agree?'

'She just got tired of my serious... involvement. She came from a well-to-do family. She wasn't concerned with such matters.'

'So she left you?'

He pulled a dry smile. 'You're asking a lot of questions.'

'I'm just curious.'

'Curious?'

'Why would you be interested in a girl like me? From the wilds of Cumberland.'

'I told you. I like attractive girls. And I like the sound of the wilds of Cumberland. Wordsworth and daffodils and all that.'

'It's not always like that.'

'What is it like?'

'Harsh sometimes. Beautiful sometimes. Isolated from all that goes on here.' She thought back to home. 'A tough life for a lot of people, but it's easier being poor there than in a London slum.'

'Is your family poor?'

'Quite. But they manage. My dad's a baker, so he earns a living.'

'What's he like?'

'Now you're asking a lot of questions.'

'I never really knew my dad, so I'm curious.'

'He's a good dad. He's opinionated and not very demonstrative, but I know he loves us kids. He gives my mum a hard time sometimes, but they love each other. They're very proud of me and my brother.'

'Well, Lucy, who'd've thought it? You and Winston Churchill! Your Mum and me think we're dreaming most of the time, and all our friends and neighbours are agog. I bet he's a right bugger to work for – no?'

'He's very demanding, Dad, but he's fair.'

'Doesn't he have a temper though?'

'Yes, he does sometimes lose it when people can't keep up. But he usually apologises after.'

'Well, I tell you, Lucy love, half of our friends think he's the devil, and half of them think he's a hero. So what do you think?'

'I think he's a bit of both, like most people. But I can say this – he's a sight cleverer than most people. He's got a memory like an elephant, and he looks at things from a much broader perspective than we all do.'

'Broader perspective? What's that mean?'

'It means the big picture, not our little tuppenny buns one. And that's what leaders are supposed to do, isn't it?'

Daniel was speaking. 'I'm sure they are proud. You working for Churchill, and your brother in the army. Where is he, by the way?'

'He's at Catterick. But going to France soon.'

'They must worry about him. Which regiment is he in?'

'He's with the artillery.'

'Well, they'll be in the thick of it.'

A pause. They both watched the fire. Then he got up. 'I'll go downstairs and start cooking. You help yourself to the wine and stay warm.'

'What are we having?'

He grinned. 'American style dinner. Sirloin steak, French fries, fried mushrooms and tomatoes, and then a strawberry cheesecake.'

'Wow! Where do you get such things?'

'Ah – that's the advantage of being at the embassy. Don't tell anyone, but I'm friends with the catering manager.' He went to the door. 'I'll be about fifteen minutes.' He waved at the room. 'Look around.'

CHAPTER 30

Left alone, she wandered round the room. The books in the bookcase were an eclectic collection. English classics, American writers - William Faulkner, John Steinbeck, Jack London – political works – John Adams, Karl Marx, Theodore Roosevelt, some modern novels. There were a few etchings of American scenes on the walls, presumably hung to remind him of home. She stopped by the single bed. Not much room for two, she thought.

She went back to the sofa, and noticed a book lying on the small table in front of it. A bookmark protruded from the pages. She picked it up. '*Memoirs of a Fox-Hunting Man*' by Siegfried Sassoon. She was sitting reading it when he returned twenty minutes later with a loaded dinner tray. He put it down, and lifted two plates onto the side table by the window.

'Have you read that?' he said.

She shook her head.

'You should. Wonderful picture of English country life.'

'Why are you reading it?'

'For that reason. We Yanks are fascinated by all that traditional British lifestyle.'

'We don't all go fox-hunting and pheasant shooting, you know.'

'Not even in Cumberland?'

'Well, I've been to a few meets which are fun, but I've never been on a horse.'

'You should try it. It's a great experience.' He turned back to the table. 'So is my steak and French fries. Come and sit down.'

She sat at the table, beside the thick window curtains. It was just big enough to accommodate two settings.

He was opening another bottle. 'You should drink a red with

this,' he said. 'This is a Burgundy. We'll keep the rest of the white for the dessert.'

She thought, he's trying to get me drunk. Then she thought, I don't care.

'So...' he said, 'are the rumours true?'

'What rumours?'

'That you were brought in to help with the big dinner party?'

She looked at him curiously. 'How did you know about that?'

That attractive crooked smile. 'C'mon, Lucy. Stories like that go around like wildfire. Everyone at the embassy knew about the dinner. Then yesterday we heard that there'd been a bit of a staff crisis, and one of the secretaries had been conscripted.'

'How did you know it was me?'

'Oh... one of the cook's kitchen maids goes out with a mail boy from the Canadian High Commission – the staff there are in regular contact with our staff – and so it spreads.' He poured red wine into her glass. 'You can't keep much secret in our business.'

'That's ironic, considering your business is secrets.'

'Yeh, well...' He sipped critically at his wine. 'Anyway, must have been quite an experience.'

'Yes.'

'Was it just the four?'

'Yes.' She contemplated her full plate, wondering where to start.

'What did you have to do?'

'Just help the Churchills' butler with all the serving and so on. They have quite elaborate dinners.'

'So you could hear all the table talk.'

'A lot of it.'

'My God!' He sawed at his steak. 'Have you any idea what an experience that was? Being able to listen to those two discussing things.'

'Those four.'

'Ah, yes. Did the wives participate much?'

'Quite a lot. They intervened when things got heated.'

He looked up. 'Ah! So there was argument?'

She chewed on a chip. It was thinner, more delicate than she was used to. 'Isn't there always – between politicians?'

'I guess so. What were they arguing about in particular?'

Here we go, she thought. 'Oh, just general politics. I didn't understand a lot of it.' She cut off a piece of steak. It was tender, and quite red inside. 'And anyway I'm sworn to confidentiality.'

'Of course. We wouldn't want Hitler to get hold of *you.* '

She threw him a smile. 'I couldn't tell him much anyway.'

He took another sip of wine, and narrowed his eyes. 'What's he like – your Prime Minister? I mean, up close.'

'He's quite gentle. Very polite. Tough underneath, I imagine.' She too sipped the wine. It had a powerful mellow flavour. 'His wife's more open and direct.'

'Did the wives join in the politics?'

'Not so much. They talked on a more personal level. But I don't think Mrs Chamberlain is a fan of Winston's.'

'And did Winston get animated? He has a reputation.'

'He... he talked a lot, yes. Especially after a few glasses of wine.'

'Drank a lot?'

'Much more than I could drink. He has an amazing constitution. It doesn't seem to affect his thinking.'

'So I hear.' He speared a fried tomato. 'Jesus, I envy you.'

'It was very tiring. I had no idea how hard servants have to work.'

He nodded. 'What do you think of the steak?'

'It's lovely. We rarely get to eat steaks.'

'Courtesy of Uncle Sam.'

209

For the rest of the meal they chatted casually about other things. Just family topics, the war, the future. He didn't refer again to the dinner party. But underneath, Lucy's mind swirled with thoughts on quite different matters.

Half an hour later, they had finished the strawberry cheesecake – another treat for her – and he had brought up coffee from the kitchen. They sat together on the sofa. The Mozart had been replaced by Ella Fitzgerald. The coffee cups and the last of the wine sat in front of them. She felt full, and warm, and relaxed, and slightly drunk. All part of the plot, she thought, but didn't mind. She felt ready for anything that might transpire.

He put his arm round her. 'This is nice,' he said.

'Yes.'

'You're quite a girl.'

'You're quite a guy.'

'Would you mind if I kissed you?'

'Isn't that the plan?'

He laughed out loud. 'I guess so. But I don't want to do anything to spoil what we have.'

'What do we have?'

'A good relationship. So far.' He drew back a little. 'At least I think so. Don't you?'

'Yes.'

'There we go then. So I can risk a kiss.'

It was soft at first, then got deeper. Her body responded. When he slipped a hand inside her dress she didn't resist. Her breasts were not large, so her underwear was light and he bypassed it with ease. His embrace became gradually more intense and intimate, discovering her body. When he knew that she was responding without reserve, he drew back and said, 'I want to undress you. May I?'

She said, 'I've never done this before.'

He drew back further. 'You're a virgin?'

210

She nodded.

He hesitated, a surprised look on his face. 'In that case we won't go all the way. I wouldn't want that responsibility yet.' She didn't know whether she was relieved or disappointed. 'But I still want to undress you.'

Strangely, she wasn't at all self-conscious as he made her stand up, and deftly took off her clothes. He looked at her standing there naked, and said, 'You're beautiful.'

Then he picked her up and carried her to the bed. He laid her on it, and took off his own clothes. She had never seen an erection before. He lay down beside her, close on the narrow bed, and she felt it hard against her stomach. His hands moved smoothly over her skin, exploring. She responded. She wanted him inside her.

'No,' he said. 'Not this time.'

'Why not?'

'It's too important, your first time. You're quite drunk, you're vulnerable. But don't worry – there's plenty we can do without that.'

And for the next hour he showed her. They had three orgasms between them - astonishing for her - then they fell asleep.

Dear Mum,

You asked what has happened with my American boy-friend (I suppose I can call him that after three dates). Well, I like him very much, but I don't suppose it will come to much. He's much more worldly and sophisticated than me. However he takes me to the theatre and to nice restaurants, and he seems to like me, I don't know why. But we get on well. We talk politics and the war, and he tells me about life in America, and I tell him about life in Cumberland. He's been to Princeton University, and he's worked in Washington, and he's part of the American diplomatic service here in London. I have to be careful what I tell him because we're all sworn to secrecy about our work, as I told you, and so is he. But we've lots else to discuss. He's quite romantic, but no, you needn't

211

worry, I can look after myself.

I had a lovely evening with Tommy and Henry. They took me to the Windmill club. Quite an eye opener! I'm glad they're both doing so well, but I hope they don't send them to the front in France too soon. This phoney war as everyone calls it is dragging on and on, but Mr Churchill says that's good because it gives us more time to prepare for when it really starts. He and the Prime Minister are very confident that we will win against Mr Hitler, but that's all I'm allowed to tell you.

Much love to you and Dad. Lucy.

CHAPTER 31

She woke early in the morning. He was asleep close beside her in the narrow bed, one arm across her waist. A thin light filtered in through the thick curtains. She lay still for a long time, recalling the evening. Then she remembered her mission. There had been little chance to achieve it so far. Would he give her an opening before she left? Were they right, that he had ulterior motives for pursuing her? If that was all he was after, how explain the intimacy of last night?

He stirred and woke. He saw her looking at him, and smiled. 'Morning.'

'Morning.'

'Are we late?'

'I don't think so. It's not long past dawn.'

'What time are you due at work?'

'Nine o'clock.'

'Good. So there's no hurry.' His hand moved over her body.

'Hey, don't start again.'

'Why not?'

'It's morning.'

'So? Morning's a good time.'

She had not realised that sex could be such an all-consuming business. She was tempted, but thought, no, I'm getting too involved. She stopped his hand with hers.

'All right.' He pulled aside the bedclothes. The chill October air struck her body. He looked her up and down. This time she did feel self-conscious, and covered herself.

'Stop staring,' she said.

213

'Why? You're lovely. I want to stare.'

She sat up in the bed. 'Then I'm going to get up.'

'I'll still watch.'

She gave him a half smile, rose and quickly went to where her clothes lay on the sofa.

'You know where the bathroom is,' he said. 'You can go there while I get up. Then we'll go out and get some breakfast.'

They walked to a café in Oxford Street that opened early for workers. They sat in a corner booth and ordered breakfast. Poached egg on toast and tea for her, bottled orange juice, muffins and coffee for him. He was critical of both the orange juice and the coffee.

'One day you Brits will learn how to make coffee,' he said.

'One day you Yanks will learn how to make tea,' she responded.

He laughed. 'I guess we're evens then.' His expression softened. 'Last night was good.'

'Was it? Even though you couldn't...?'

'It was beautiful. It's not always 'wham bang, thank you ma'am,' you know.'

She hadn't heard the expression. He took a sip of the despised coffee, and sat back. 'So tell me, what really happened during the famous dinner party?'

Ah, she thought, this is it. 'I've told you.'

'No, you haven't. You just said it was lively. What were they discussing?'

'You know I'm not supposed to talk about it.'

'You don't have to tell me state secrets. Just in general. I'm fascinated.'

'Well, I only heard some of it. I was busy with the dinner. But they argued about how to confront Hitler of course. The Prime Minister was for more negotiation, Winston... Mr Churchill wanted stronger responses. Just as they've always argued apparently.'

214

'By stronger responses...?'

'Well – call up more men, rearm faster, bring in allies.'

'Us, you mean?'

'You, and the Dominions. Anyone who's on our side.'

'Do they think America will join the war?'

She hesitated. 'It's what they're hoping, naturally. Do you think you will?'

He opened his hands. 'Who knows? Roosevelt's in a difficult situation with Congress. The people don't want it. But I guess we'll have to eventually. Depends how well you and France can hold back Adolf on your own.'

'Mr Churchill says he's not as strong as everyone believes.'

'Maybe, but he's still pretty strong. Churchill's right - you need to get your act together smartly. You have one advantage though.'

'What's that?'

'Hitler may overstretch himself. He might be tempted to fight on too many fronts.'

'Which fronts?'

'Well, Russia for starters.'

She feigned innocence. 'But Russia's on his side.'

He shrugged. 'As we said before, that could change anytime. Stalin will go with whoever he thinks will cut him the best deal. But he's as wary of you lot as he is of Hitler.'

'Oh.'

'Didn't they talk about that?'

'Yes, a bit.'

'So what do they think of Stalin?'

'The Prime Minister thinks he's as bad as Hitler. The Churchills...' She tailed off.

'Yes?'

'Well, they don't seem to like him much, but I gather they think

215

he'd make a strong ally.'

'Yes?'

She followed her orders. 'Well, I did hear Clementine talking about his strength of purpose, his intelligence, his forceful character.'

'Really?'

'And Winston admires the way he's led the Russian people, and their history.'

'Ah. He's a great one for history, your boss.'

'Well, I don't know much about Russia's, but he has a lot of respect for their nation.'

'Does he think he could persuade Stalin to change sides?'

She shrugged. 'I don't know. I got the impression that, when the war ends, Russia might be entitled to take back land that she once owned.' Feigning innocence again, 'Where would that be?'

'The old Russian empire. She claims territory in Poland, Romania, the Balkans...'

'Yes, that's right.'

'Churchill talked about that?'

She felt guilt at promoting such untruths. 'He said that Russia had been badly treated by history.'

He nodded thoughtfully. 'That's one way of looking at it.'

'And anyway, as you said, they think Hitler might do it himself.'

'Do what?'

'Cause Stalin to change sides.'

'In what way?'

'You're asking a lot of questions.'

He opened his hands. 'Well, it's in all our interests, isn't it? What might strong-man Adolf do to antagonise strong-man Josef?'

'It seems he may attack Russia himself. He's apparently building up forces in the occupied part of Poland.' She took a bite of toast. 'It seems illogical to me. Why would he do that if Stalin's

216

now on his side?'

'Ah, well – the lure of power, the appeal of conquest. They're birds of a feather.'

'Birds of prey.'

'Exactly.'

She shook her head. 'I don't understand it. You'd think that the leaders of countries should be cleverer than the rest of us, but they don't appear to be.'

'Not always.'

'So how do they get where they are?'

'They're more ambitious than the rest of us. They're more ruthless than the rest of us.'

They talked some more, skirting around the subject. He asked further questions about the dinner party, but she felt she had said enough and feigned ignorance. A sense of disquiet grew within. She could not reconcile the two identities of this man – that of her lover and that of an agent, effectively a traitor to her side in a global conflict.

She looked at her watch. 'I must go,' she said. 'I'm due at work.'

'When will I see you again?' He put his hand over hers, and she remembered his touch on other parts of her.

'As soon as you like.'

'I can't tonight. I'm on late duty. How about tomorrow evening?'

'Yes.'

'Why don't I come and see your new place?'

'No visitors after five.'

He drew back. 'Seriously? That's Dickensian.'

'It's quite a Dickensian place.' It was her turn to show affection. 'In any case it's hardly the place for romantic meetings.'

'Well then, it will have to be my place again.'

She felt a thrill, despite the confusion in her mind.

CHAPTER 32

'So, tell us what happened?'

She was sitting this time in another café. A smarter one in a side street in Chelsea, which served rather better fare than the one she'd breakfasted in. Lieutenant Commander Thompson and Kenneth Miles sat opposite. All had a light lunch in front of them. She had wondered why they wished to meet in such a public place, but Thompson said they wanted a more convivial atmosphere than the cramped office in the Admiralty so she didn't object. It was he who asked the question.

'It was more or less as you forecast. He made me supper at his place, and he asked me about the big dinner.'

'Immediately?'

'No. He was subtle.'

'Were you able to convey the message we wanted?'

She glanced around. They were at a discreet side table, with no other customers close by. 'I think so. I managed to get across most of the points. I don't think he suspected.'

Thompson nodded thoughtfully. Miles was looking at her with his usual inscrutable face. After several seconds he asked, 'Did you go home after the dinner?'

She flushed. She had hoped they wouldn't ask too much about the encounter. 'No,' she said simply.

'So... you had some breakfast talk as well as dinner talk?'

'Yes. We went out for breakfast.'

'Did he ask more at that time?'

'It was then that we discussed it most. He didn't ask much very specific the evening before.'

'Clever,' said Thompson.

'And you didn't volunteer anything until he started questioning?'

'No. I kept quiet about it. In fact I began to wonder if he was going to say anything.'

'Well done,' said Thompson. 'You played the game as well as he did.'

Miles drank some water. 'Are you seeing him again?'

'Tomorrow night.'

'Where?'

'At his place again.'

Miles stared some more. Thompson inclined his head slightly. 'Are you getting romantically attached to this man, Lucy?' he asked gently.

She toyed with the chicken salad on her plate. 'I could be.'

'Is that going to present a problem? Divided loyalties, and so on?'

She looked up. 'You said that he was really on our side. He wants Russia to change sides as much as we do. He's wanting the same outcome we do.'

'Oh, yes. He's not a traitor in that sense. He's not working for Hitler.'

'But he's playing a dangerous game.' Miles's eyes were cold. 'If there *is* no change, and he continues sending stuff, then that would be treasonable.'

She was quiet.

Later she saw Mary in the typing office. Her friend came to her eagerly and whispered, 'So what happened?'

'I spent the night with him.'

Mary mimed clapping hands. 'How was it?'

'We didn't go all the way.'

'Why not?'

219

'When he found out I was a virgin, he wouldn't do it. But we did just about everything else.' Lucy smiled at the recollection. 'He's very thoughtful. And pretty expert.'

'Did he make you... you know?'

'What?'

'Come. Climax.'

Lucy nodded, embarrassed.

'Wonderful!'

'You're such a tart, Mary.'

'Not at all. It's what life's all about. So when are you going to do it properly?'

Ah, that was the question. 'I don't know. Soon, I expect.'

'Good. It's high time. And he's obviously the right man.'

'I hope so.'

She said nothing about the other dimension to the relationship.

That afternoon she was sent to take more dictation from the First Lord.

He was working in his study at Admiralty House. When she entered, he was sitting at his desk with Rufus at his feet, Nelson the cat purring on the desk itself, and the budgerigar fluttering round the room. Lucy was by now used to the presence of his animals.

'Close the door, missie,' he said. 'Don't let the bird out. It's her exercise hour.'

She did so, and came to sit opposite the desk, notepad at the ready. He peered over his spectacles. 'So, I hear the assignation went according to plan?'

'I think so, Winston.'

He nodded thoughtfully. 'You don't think he suspects?'

'I don't think so. I pretended to be a bit stupid about everything.'

The eyes twinkled. 'I'd better be careful. I might lose one of my best secretaries to MI5.'

She smiled. 'I don't think I'm really spy material.'

'Nor is he, one would think. He's an odd fellow, this Mountview chap. Hard to know what game he's playing.' He reflected, stroking Nelson's back. The cat purred.. 'Of course there are many species of secret agent. All sides use all types of infiltrators. We have our own sources within the Russian system. But he is different. Bright, clean American boy – no serious revolutionary background beyond the common adolescent left wing stuff – no obvious evidence that blackmail or coercion is involved. Has he given you any indication of his motives?'

'No, sir. He just seems committed to the communist cause. He worries about the inequality in the world.'

He grunted. 'Well, we all worry about that. It's how you solve it is the problem. I'm just surprised he thinks communism is the way to go, given the examples of it around the planet.'

She said nothing. Such major political issues were beyond her grasp.

'Are you going to continue seeing him?'

'For a while.'

'Uhuh. Getting romantically involved, are you?'

Why did everyone want to know that? 'Not too much, I hope.'

'Good, good. Unwise to do that. Many have come to grief over that little dichotomy.' He threw her a quick smile. 'Right, Lucy dear - let's do a bit of work. I want to write to the Leader of the Opposition.'

Lucy took up her pad. He stared into space, for once not immediately ready with his words.

'Delicate, this,' he muttered. 'Have to be careful what I say. Can't have it leaking out.' He reached a decision, and started dictating. 'To the Right Honourable Clement Attlee, House of Commons. Dear Clement, It would appear that Parliament is divided over various questions pertaining to our conduct of the war, and over the negotiations with some of the contestants and prospective contestants. I'm sure you agree that, in this hour of dire national peril, we must not allow party political matters to cloud such issues. We must agree a way forward by mutual consent, even though it may mean abandoning some of our deeply held convictions on minor topics. It is for the sake of the major challenge confronting us all.' He paused for a moment, still stroking. Nelson stretched sensuously beneath his hand. 'What I am suggesting is that, whoever may be leading our two parties in the near future, we must come together and work as an alliance to achieve victory. If we do not now present a united front against the evil that confronts us, then history will never forgive us. I am sure you understand the implications of what I am saying. Yours sincerely, Winston.'

He stopped, and as usual pondered for a while on the words. Then he turned to Lucy. 'Do you understand those implications, Lucy?'

'I'm not sure, sir.'

'Well, I'm sure you heard some of the debate over dinner the other evening. That debate is mirrored in Parliament and all around the country. It goes to the fundamental heart of the human character. The eternal conflict between pacifism and belligerence. Somehow, if we are to win this war, we have to win the opinion of the British people on the matter also.' He caressed Nelson's ears. 'Clement Attlee, although a socialist and our opponent in Parliament, is a far more intelligent man than some of his colleagues. His character is stalwart. We are going to need him onside when it comes to the crunch.'

'I see,' she said, uncertain what the crunch might be.

He picked up a dead cigar end, rose from his chair, and paced the room, chewing on the stub. This meant that more was coming.

He stopped and peered at her again. 'When are you seeing your fellow again, Lucy?'

'Tomorrow evening, sir.'

The round head nodded. 'I wonder... I'd like to hatch another little conspiracy. Just between you and me. It's a sensitive subject, so we can't have others party to it. A leak would be... let's say, very damaging.'

'What about?'

'Well, I'm sure you're aware of the political situation here, my dear. The Prime Minister is probably not going to remain in office for very much longer. He has been a fine guardian of our national administration for some years, but his time is almost up.' A wry expression. 'All politicians have a limited timespan, no matter how effective they've been.' He pointed the cigar stub. 'Now, between you and me, it's likely that either I or Lord Halifax will succeed him. And it's of very great interest to Josef Stalin as to which it's going to be.'

'Why is that, sir?'

The rasping tone. 'It's like this, Lucy. Lord Halifax is from the same mold as Mr Chamberlain. He is a peacemaker, an appeaser. A clever and distinguished man, but without the... backbone to lead us through this war. He has not the determination – the conviction – that will be required to bring victory. Stalin knows this, and knows that, if Halifax becomes leader, the odds are that Hitler will defeat us. He is therefore likely to remain allied to Germany in such a case.'

'I see.'

'I, on the other hand, *do* have that conviction. I have maintained it during all my years out of office, and I will maintain it throughout my time *in* office. Stalin knows this also.'

'Ah.'

'Therefore, in order to convince the tyrant to come over to our side, he needs to believe that it will be I, and not Halifax, who will succeed to the leadership.' His eyes held hers. 'Now do you see where I'm going?'

'I think so, but how...?'

'How can you help? Well, you can convince your admirer, that from what you've heard around these august halls...' He waved his hand at the surroundings. '...and from the various missives to other government departments that you've typed – that the winds are

223

blowing strongly in my favour. Then the message would hopefully percolate through to the Kremlin, and might just help to tip the balance. D'you see?'

She hardly believed that anything she could do would have such a momentous effect, but she nodded. 'Yes.'

'There is another persuasive factor. Lord Halifax has the backing of the large appeasement faction in the party. However he sits in the House of Lords. That is not an effective location from which to conduct the nation's war effort. So, unless he renounces all his titles and moves over to the Commons, it is unlikely he will have the confidence of all.'

'I see.'

He sat at the desk again, countenance dark. 'Stalin is a monster, Lucy, make no mistake. And one day we may have to slay that one too. But in this hour of dire peril we need the monster fighting on our side.'

Lucy was quiet, contemplating the implications.

He watched her. 'Does this give you a problem?'

'No, sir. Not specifically. It's just...'

'What?'

She looked up. 'What might happen to Daniel... if he's found out?'

'He's already been found out. It's how we use that knowledge that matters.'

'Yes, but... once the war is over, what will happen to him then?'

'I can't tell you, Lucy. That's in the hands of his own people. But obviously, if we do manage to enlist Russia to our cause, then he may well end up a hero.'

'And if we don't?'

'Then he might be branded a traitor.' His expression was sympathetic. 'I understand your dilemma, my dear. Do you care for this man?'

'Quite.'

'Hm.' He stared at the desk top. The budgerigar alighted on his shoulder, and began nibbling at his ear. 'Not now, Queenie, not now.' He brushed it away, and the bird fluttered to the curtain rail. 'I can only say, Lucy, that in times like this, personal considerations must give way to national ones. There is no reason why you shouldn't continue to enjoy your relationship with this man, and it may not affect his fate in any case. On the other hand, it might affect it considerably. As it might do on the outcome of the war. We cannot foresee the outcome of such situations. Fate often rests on the slightest of events.'

Such as the breaking of a typewriter key.

CHAPTER 33

He took her to bed almost as soon as she arrived at his address.

'I've been thinking of you for two days,' he said up in the room, as he took her coat. 'I keep thinking of your face and your body, and all that we've shared. I want to make love to you properly. Can I?'

'Yes,' she said, as she flung off her hat, and let her hair fall to her shoulders.

She kissed him deeply whilst he undid her buttons and stripped the clothes from her. Then they were embracing on the bed and, almost before she had realised it, he was inside her. She was ready, and it wasn't painful as she had feared, simply a fulfilment that she had subconsciously been awaiting for a long time.

His passion now became more measured, and slowly, gently, over many minutes, he brought them both to a climax with an expertise that indicated long practice. It was another, perhaps the greatest, revelation to add to the many she had experienced over this period.

Afterwards, they lay quiet for a long time. Then she said, 'I hope you haven't got me pregnant.'

He turned his head and smiled. 'I used a rubber. Didn't you notice?'

'No.'

'Well, there you go. A testimony to Trojan johnnies – American technical genius.' He raised himself onto his elbow. 'Are you hungry?'

'Very.'

'That's what sex does to you. I thought we'd go out. There's a nice place just around the corner.'

She stroked his cheek with the back of her hand. 'Do we have to go out?'

'Don't worry. We're coming straight back here after.'

'Oh well, in that case...'

They went to a restaurant a few minutes walk away. She had stopped wondering whether they were being followed. She did not even look behind her as they entered.

The place served continental food in a discreet atmosphere made more intimate by the heavy blackout drapes across the windows. This time they both ate roast pheasant, which the waiter assured them had been shot recently in the grounds of some Berkshire estate.

'Are you rich?' she asked, as she looked at the menu prices.

'Not at all,' he said. 'But I have a decent salary, and much of my living costs are met by the embassy. So I can afford to splash out on girl-friends.'

'Girl-friends, plural? How many others have you got?'

He grinned. 'I've told all the others to take a jump, now I've found you.'

'You seem...' she tailed off.

'What?'

'Pretty expert at... everything. Have you had a lot of lovers?'

'Not so many. But Americans start rather earlier than you repressed Brits. High school and college teach a lot more than just arts and sciences.'

'Seemed to me there was quite a lot of art and science involved.'

The teeth shone. 'You're a good pupil.' He chewed on a piece of bread. 'I must say...'

'What?'

'You took to it pretty well. Not many girls can orgasm like that the first time.'

She recoiled slightly at the word. It seemed a brutal description of such an overwhelming event.

He sensed it. 'Nothing to be ashamed of,' he said. 'You're lucky. Many women never manage it at all.'

The waiter brought their dishes, and she thought it was time to change the subject. 'So what is happening at the embassy? Are you nearer to joining in the war?'

He looked solemn. 'That's going to take a while. There's far too much opposition amongst our ignorant citizens. It's going to need a realisation of the danger to the whole world before people come round.' He picked up his knife and fork. 'But we're working on it.'

She cut into her neatly sliced pheasant breast. She was familiar with the meat of game birds. It was available from local farms as an alternative to expensive joints bought at the butcher's. However, the sauce and the garnish that accompanied this dish rendered it a far different experience.

'What about you?' he asked. 'What's happening at the Admiralty?'

'Oh, the usual,' she said casually. 'Endless meetings and reports and letters. My typing speed has gone up by half.'

'What about the politics? We keep hearing about furious rows in Parliament.'

'I don't get to see those, but after a debate my boss often comes back in a black mood.'

'Are the Prime Minister's days numbered, do you think?'

'Probably. I think he's quite ill. And with every report from Poland he's losing the argument.'

'So who will replace him?'

She was very conscious of her discussion with the First Lord. Would it be too obvious if she took the plunge now? 'Well, Lord Halifax has had the majority's support, but they say he's losing it fast. And because he's titled he can't govern well from the House of Lords.' She shrugged. 'I don't know why.'

'So it could well be Churchill?'

She met his eyes candidly. 'It seems so. That's what I hear around the offices.'

He nodded, watching her with deliberation. 'Interesting.'

'Why?'

'He's the one both Hitler and Stalin are most afraid of. He's the one they think could best rally the British and their allies. It could have a big effect on their next moves.'

'In what way?'

He waved his fork. 'Could make up Stalin's mind for him. He'd certainly prefer to have the old bulldog with him than against him.'

'But how could a communist and a...?'

'A democrat?'

'Yes. Ever be allies?'

'Ah well, political philosophies always give way to expediency when it comes to war.' He left the fork hovering over his plate, and looked at her with deliberation. 'And in any case communism has a lot to offer the world, you know.'

'Does it?'

'Oh yes. Have you read Karl Marx?'

'No.'

'You should.' The look intensified. 'Much of the world's problems stem from inequality between classes and causes. For instance, it's always in an employer's interests to pay his workers as little as possible, whilst gaining as much as possible from his business. The resulting surplus profit, as it's called, always goes to the proprietor, or the land owner, or the businessman, whilst the worker sees none of it. Thus the inequality continues to grow.'

'So what's the answer?'

He stuck the fork into a slice of pheasant. 'Well, it's not either capitalism or feudalism. They both compound the process. The larger a business or an estate grows, the richer gets the owner, and the more power he has to keep down wages. Just look at the wealthy families of England and America – your aristocrats, and

229

our Rockefellers, Carnegies, Vanderbilts. Is it fair that they are worth thousands of times more than the people who work for them?'

'But they're the ones who create that work in the first place.'

He leaned back in his chair. 'Ah, I see we have a budding capitalist here. Are you planning to found an industrial empire after the war?'

She smiled. 'Not me. But what's the alternative? They have made us the richest countries in the world.'

'Sure. Doesn't mean they can't spread it around a bit. We've got as many people sleeping rough as you have.'

She had never delved deep into the extremes of political opinion. 'So you think communism is the solution?'

'I think state ownership of the nation's assets is part of the solution. Then governments can see that everyone gets a fair share.'

'But...'

'But what?'

'They say that the peasants in Russia are starving. They don't seem to have a fair share.'

'Ah, you've bought into that propaganda.'

'Isn't it true?'

'They were starving under the Tsars. At least they aren't subject to their tyranny any longer.'

'Yes, but...'

'And it takes decades to turn around a huge economy like Russia's.'

She was quiet for some moments, concentrating on the meal.

'I've shocked you now,' he said.

She shook her head. 'No. Just made me think.'

'Good.'

She risked a probe. 'Do you get much information at the embassy?'

230

'About what?'

'About what's going on in the Kremlin. About what Stalin thinks.'

'You mean, do we have spies there?'

'Yes.'

'Probably not as many as you do, but yes, of course we get intelligence. Everyone has spies everywhere.'

'It seems extraordinary. How do they all pass information?'

'Many different means. Diplomatic messengers, coded letters, secret phone calls.'

'I don't understand...'

'What?'

She desperately needed to pry further. She needed to know his motives. 'If Hitler or Stalin wanted to know what was going on in our government for instance, then who would send that information? Why would anyone working here want to betray the country like that?'

He took a sip of wine, staring at her intently. I've gone too far, she thought.

He said, 'You're naïve. There are always people in every society who are opposed to that society. For a multitude of reasons.'

'Such as?'

'The ones we've talked about. Exploitation of the workers, dissatisfaction with the system. Then there are different ethnic origins, different political or religious beliefs. Or they are coerced by blackmail, even by just plain greed. Money always speaks.'

She was no nearer to discovering whether he himself had such purposes. And she feared that, if he did, she had now asked too much. They did not discuss the matter further. They finished the meal, and he took her to bed again.

CHAPTER 34

The days passed, and turned into weeks. The country still awaited the arrival of Hitler's bombers. The work if anything intensified. Her duties grew evermore demanding and arduous. Her employer's requirements expanded to cover yet more widening ranges, and his staff were stretched to the limits of their capacities. The reports from the various war fronts swelled to dark mountains of cloud looming on the horizon. The efforts of the nation to expand its forces, multiply its armaments, strengthen its defenses, intensified exponentially.

At the same time she continued to see Daniel every two or three days, mostly in the evenings, sometimes just at lunchtime. Their meetings invariably ended up in his narrow bed, and once or twice during the daytime, in hers. Their lovemaking grew more and more fulfilling, their conversations more and more profound and inconclusive. From time to time she reported the progress of the relationship to Tommy Thompson, occasionally in the presence of his MI5 associate. Once or twice the pair suggested further calculated information with which to feed to her lover. The conflict between her emotional feelings for him and her uncertainty over his loyalties threatened to tear her heart in two.

Then one cold morning in November she was commanded by Grace Hamblin, as so often, to go to Admiralty House to take dictation from the First Lord. On her way she passed Mary, going in the other direction, full notepad in hand.

'Watch yourself,' said her friend as they passed. 'He's black this morning.'

Lucy knocked on the study door and entered. Churchill was striding the carpet in one of his boiler suits, half chewed cigar in mouth, pets cowering in their various corners. Inches was pouring whisky into an ice-filled glass. Early even for Winston, thought

232

Lucy. That did not betoken well.

'Ah, Lucy,' said the growling voice, 'take a seat.' He waved her to a chair. 'We've a lot to do this morning.'

She risked a small smile. 'When have we not, Winston?'

'No, but this is different.' He grasped the whisky that Inches held out for him. 'This is escalation on a grand scale. Russia has invaded Finland.'

Lucy's breath stalled. 'Why? On what pretext?'

'Oh...' he waved a dismissive hand. 'Protecting Ukrainians and White Russians living under illegal occupation. Some such nonsense. It scarcely matters. Stalin's blatant motive is land grab, and it's not going to stop there. It's a big setback.' He turned to the butler. 'Thank you, David. See that my best parliamentary attire is ready, will you. I'm going to the House this afternoon.'

'Yes, sir.' Inches threw a meaningful glance at Lucy, and left.

'Right, Lucy, take this letter to the Prime Minister.' She raised her pencil as he sipped at his glass. 'Dear Prime Minister. In advance of this afternoon's emergency debate, may I suggest that, apart from the usual diplomatic protests at the Soviets' dishonorable advance into Scandinavia, Britain must also demand immediate expulsion from the League of Nations. Russia has blatantly violated her non-aggression pact with Finland on spurious legal grounds, and has breached all the conditions of her membership. If the world does not instantly make clear its absolute objection to this transgression, then there is little doubt that Stalin will continue his expansionist efforts in that region. I would also suggest that we directly entreat Norway and Sweden to assist Finland in whatever way they can, both militarily and diplomatically, for fear that they will next fall victim either to Russian or to German aggression. Their ambitions are plainly evident now. Remembering our discussion at dinner the other night, I would submit that our course of action must be clear.'

He chewed some more, paced some more, and then waved his acceptance of the draft. 'Signed as usual. See that it's delivered post

233

haste, then return here.' Lucy rose to leave.

'Oh, by the way, dear...' She stopped. He peered at her over his glasses. 'I'm afraid your boyfriend is in trouble. He's been arrested at his embassy on grounds of espionage. I thought you ought to know.'

The ground shook beneath Lucy's feet.

'I see that has disturbed you.' His tone was kindly. 'I don't know quite how much this man means to you, Lucy, but you did know the score.'

'What...? What will happen to him?' Her voice was a fraction more than a whisper.

'I imagine he'll be sent back to America to stand trial. I don't know the evidence against him, but they wouldn't take such a step unless it was conclusive. This news from Finland won't help his case, I'm afraid. Russia is still very much our enemy. Tommy Thompson will tell you more.' He came to her and put a hand on her shoulder, the first time he had ever touched her person. 'I'm so sorry, my dear. I realise this must be a shock to you. I can only say that your cooperation with us in this matter has been of immense value, notwithstanding today's events. This war is being fought on many different fronts, and you have played your part with great bravery.'

Nothing brave about it, thought Lucy. 'Will I have to give evidence?' she asked.

'I don't know. Possibly. The embassy will no doubt inform us if they wish it.' He returned to his desk. 'If so, then you have nothing to fear. Just be as honest as possible, and we will back you in every event.'

'Yes, sir.' She left before her legs could give way beneath her.

In the outer room she sat for a moment on a sofa to regain her self-possession. Her heart was beating violently and her brain was a tumult of thoughts. Up until this moment she had refused to consider the effects of the possibility, but now the truth of it hit her with awful force. The word 'love' had never passed between Daniel and her, but she realised that in some form it must lie at the core of her feelings. Whether it was simply because he was the first man to take her to bed, or because he was the first man to open her eyes to the vast scope of experience the world had to offer, she wasn't sure, but there was little doubt that her whole being was devastated.

She took her handkerchief from her skirt pocket and wiped her eyes. As she was doing so, the opposite door opened and Clementine entered. She saw Lucy's state instantly, and came across to sit beside her.

'What is it, my dear?' She put a hand over Lucy's. 'Has the old bully been too hard on you?'

'No, no, Clementine. It's not him. It's just that... they've arrested Daniel... my boyfriend.'

'Ah.' Clementine straightened a little. 'Yes, well... perhaps it was to be expected. I gather he was playing both sides, as they say.'

'Yes, but...' Lucy tried to assemble her thoughts. 'He's not a traitor. He was trying to bring influence to Stalin. He was trying...' She tailed off. She wasn't sure in fact what he was trying to do.

Clementine smiled sympathetically, and patted her hand. 'Unfortunately in times like these one cannot decide for oneself how to play the game. One has to go by the rules. And it would seem that he has broken those pretty conclusively.'

The dam burst, and the tears came flooding. The small handkerchief was scarcely able to accommodate them. Clementine waited until she had regained control, and then said, 'Do you really love this man, Lucy?'

Lucy gave a small nod. 'I think so. I thought perhaps I just found him attractive, but maybe...'

'That's very hard, my dear.' She looked towards the window. 'This war is creating so many strains in unexpected areas. It is a tragedy that will dog us all for years to come.' She turned back. 'Why don't you take an hour or two off duty. I'm sure we have enough girls to handle everything.'

'I can't. I have to type a letter to the Prime Minister. It's urgent.'

235

'Ah. Well, of course everything's urgent these days.' Clementine rose. 'You'd better do that then, Lucy. And then take things gently. Don't be too hard on yourself. I know that Winston valued your part in this little saga immensely. It's all part of the huge jigsaw that we are putting together here.'

Lucy put away the handkerchief, and rose herself. 'Yes. Thank you.'

Clementine smiled, and went on towards the study.

Lucy managed to get through the morning by immersing herself in the work. Then at lunchtime she joined Mary in the dining hall, more for the want of company than sustenance. Her friend knew vaguely that something serious had occurred.

'What is it?' she asked. 'What's happened?'

Lucy told her in a sentence. She probably wasn't supposed to, but she was past caring.

Mary sat back, eyes wide. 'Arrested? What for?'

'Passing information to Russia. He's been doing it for months.'

'My God! And you didn't know?'

Lucy hesitated. Her vow of confidentiality still pertained. 'Well, let's say I suspected. In fact I was sort of feeding him with information myself. Stuff that our side wanted Stalin to believe.'

The eyes widened further. 'You were in on it? You were acting as an agent?'

'Shhh.' Lucy glanced around. 'I'm not supposed to say anything. I'll be shot. But yes – because of our relationship, in a very small way I was conscripted to tell him certain stories.'

Mary was convulsed with excitement. 'Wow! Bedtime intrigues. It's like a John Buchan story.'

'Hardly. It made things quite difficult between us.'

'Do you love him?'

'I think perhaps I do. So you can imagine...' She broke off as the tears threatened again.

Mary reached across the table with a sympathetic hand. 'What do you think will happen to him?'

'I don't know. They're probably sending him back to the States.'

'Oh, Lucy. I'm so sorry. That's awful for you.'

At that moment Commander Thompson appeared beside the table. He took in the scene.

'Oh, dear. This all looks very tragic. What's happening?'

Lucy put away her handkerchief for the second time. 'Nothing, sir. I was just upset about something.'

'Perhaps I can guess what.' He threw a glance at Mary. 'Not giving away too much, are you, Lucy?'

Mary jumped into the breach. 'She was just telling me she's broken up with her boyfriend, sir. I'm not sure why, but she's upset.'

He nodded. 'Well, on that subject I need to have a chat with you, Lucy. When you've finished lunch, pop along to my office will you?'

'Yes, sir.' She pulled herself together, 'I won't be long.'

He gave her what may have been a warning look, and left.

Fifteen minutes later she entered his office. He was alone with his pipe.

'Sit down, Lucy. You've heard the news, I gather.'

She nodded.

'I'm sorry. It must be hard for you. You've grown quite close to this man?'

'Yes.'

'Mm. Occupational hazard, I'm afraid.'

'What's going to happen, sir?'

'He will probably be sent back to America to stand trial there. However there are still various investigations ongoing on this side of the pond. The authorities at his embassy are aware of your part

237

in the story, and they wish to interview you about it.'

She couldn't avoid an intake of breath.

He went on. 'They wanted you to go to the embassy, but we said no, it should be done on neutral territory. The embassy of course is technically American ground. We've provisionally arranged for you to meet them at the British Commonwealth offices in Whitehall.' He drew on his pipe, and threw her an encouraging look. 'Now you don't actually need to comply with this unofficial request, Lucy, but we think it's best that you do. I know it may be painful for you, but far less painful than an official demand for a witness appearance. They will be on your side. They will want to know a lot of detail about your relationship with Mountview, but the questions will be sympathetic. I, or someone else from our side, will be there to support you. We'll make sure they don't harass you too much.' He sat back, sucking on the pipe. 'What do you say?'

'Will Daniel be there?'

'Oh, no. He's under strict detention at their embassy.'

'Will I...? Will I be able to see him?'

He was thoughtful. 'I'm not sure. Officially, I would have thought not. But maybe we can pull some strings.' His glance was questioning. 'Are you sure you want to see him? Is that a good idea in the circumstances?'

'Yes, sir. I would like to.'

He nodded. 'I'll see what I can do. But it would have to be after you've talked to them. And they may still withhold permission.'

CHAPTER 35

Dear Mum and Dad,

I hope you are both well. I felt I wanted to write as I'm feeling rather lonely and miserable at the moment. I've broken up with my American boyfriend and it's left me very sad. I suppose it could never have worked for long as I knew he would have to go back to America at some stage. But I tried not to think about that, and it's been lovely while it lasted. Anyway he has now been ordered back, so we've had to say goodbye to each other. Ah well...

Luckily I'm still as busy as ever so it takes my mind off it. You've probably heard the news that Russia has invaded Finland. Things seem to get worse and worse in Europe, and Mr Churchill is as hugely occupied as ever. He hardly ever seems to sleep, except for the occasional catnap. How he keeps going at such a pace I don't know.

I gather the boys have finally embarked for France. Well, we've been expecting it. I pray they'll be all right. At least they've managed to stay in the same regiment together, and as they're with the artillery at least they won't be in the very front line.

Anyway I must go. More typing to do!

Love Lucy.

P.S. I wish I had some of Dad's bread here. The stuff you can buy in London is horrid.

Two days later she went with Tommy Thompson to the imposing British Commonwealth offices. They were shown into a meeting room where three men were already seated on one side of the large central table. Two were clean cut men in their thirties, the one between them was considerably older, a heavy set bear of a man in a pale grey suit, with a wide jaw and a contrived amiable

239

countenance. He gestured to the chairs opposite, and introduced himself in a deep American voice that appeared to come from somewhere near his navel.

'Thanks for coming. I'm Senior Foreign Service Officer Jim Statham, and these are Officers Don Atcherson and Michael Curtis.'

Thompson introduced himself and Lucy, and they sat.

Statham leaned back and smiled a friendly smile. Lucy somehow found it more unsettling than if he had no expression at all.

'Okay, Lucy – may I call you that?'

She nodded.

'We gather that you've been having a relationship with the man attached to our embassy called Daniel Mountview.'

'Yes.'

'As you know, Lucy, he's been arrested on charges of providing intelligence to the enemy. Now I realise that this may be awkward for you, and I don't want to pry too much into your personal affairs, but we do need to know the extent of your conversations on political matters.'

'I understand.'

'Lieutenant Commander Thompson and I have talked at length on the telephone. He has informed us that you've been assisting in an unofficial capacity to feed... let's call it, targeted information to this guy, which might help the allied cause in the war.'

'Yes.'

'Okay. Well, I'm going to ask you some specific questions.' He pushed a jug of water across the table. 'Help yourself to water when you feel like it.'

'Thank you.'

Thompson interrupted. 'Can we agree that, if Lucy cooperates with you in this matter, she will be allowed a visit to Mountview afterwards?'

Statham threw him a glance. 'Well, that's not in my hands, but I'll put in a word for her. I don't see why they wouldn't allow it.'

It was the best she could hope for.

The reassuring smile widened as he turned back to her. 'So how did you meet this feller, and how long have you known him?'

'He introduced himself to me one day, six or seven weeks ago in the dining hall.'

'Introduced?'

'Well... he struck up a conversation. Then a couple of days later he was there again, and he invited me to join him at his lunch table. It went on from there.'

'So, to be clear, he approached you – not the other way around?'

'Yes.'

'How did the relationship develop to a more, uh... intimate one?'

'He asked me out to dinner, and then a few days later to the theatre, and eventually... well, we realised we were attracted to each other.'

'You think his attraction was genuine?'

Lucy met his gaze directly. 'Well, he'd be a very good actor if it wasn't.'

He opened his hands in graceful assent. 'So you saw a lot of this man over the last couple of months?'

'Quite a lot.'

'You dined together, you went out together, you spent whole nights together?'

'Yes.'

'So you talked intimately about a lot of things?'

She nodded.

'And somewhere, quite early during this time, you were approached by Commander Thompson here, who explained that there were concerns about Mountview's contacts with Russia.'

'Yes.'

Thompson added, 'In the company of MI5, who had contacted me in the first place.'

'Sure. At our instigation. Now...'

Before he could continue, Lucy said, 'How did you know the Admiralty would be the place to...'

'Look for a way to get to him?'

'Yes.'

His expression was frank. 'We'd been keeping an eye on the guy for some time. We knew he'd approached a couple of the other girls there. He knew that the secretaries by virtue of their job had access to a lot of information, and he reckoned they'd be easy meat to try and seduce.' He noticed Lucy's reaction to the term. 'Sorry, I didn't mean to imply that you were easy meat, Lucy. I'm sure you had a genuine relationship with the feller. I'm just saying that it's likely he targeted you in the first place with other objectives in mind.'

The pain stabbed at Lucy's heart.

'So anyway,' he went on, 'the Commander here then suggested to you various scenarios that you could slip into your conversations with Mountview, which, if relayed back to the Kremlin might help Britain's cause in the war?'

'Yes.'

'Some advised by Winston Churchill himself,' added Thompson.

One of the younger Americans leaned forward. It was the first time either had spoken. 'You're a personal secretary to the navy minister?'

Lucy replied, 'Well, I'm one of a pool of three or four secretaries who he uses to type all his letters and memos. He does dictate a great deal.'

'Stuff to do with the war at sea? Stuff to do with his business in Parliament?'

'Yes, everything. Notes to other ministers and departments,

letters to foreign governments...'

'Including ours?'

'Yes.'

'So you get to know a lot of what's going on with him?'

'I suppose so.'

The man leaned back, with a quick glance at Statham.

Statham took it up again. 'And we gather that you were also present at a historic dinner party between your boss and the Prime Minister, and their two wives.'

'Yes. They were short staffed, so I was brought in to help with serving the dinner.'

'That must have been quite an occasion.'

She allowed herself a dry smile. 'It was rather animated.'

'The discussion on that occasion covered the war effort, and Britain's approaches to Hitler and Stalin, and so forth?'

'Yes, all of those things.'

'And did Daniel Mountview know about that evening?'

'Yes.'

'Did he show interest in what happened?'

'Yes.'

'Specifically...?'

'He wanted to know what the arguments were about. How Mr Churchill differed from the Prime Minister, and so on. But I couldn't tell him too much for fear of appearing to break my confidentiality.'

'Sure.' He folded his arms. The smile had faded, the look more concentrated. 'So now, here's the thing, Lucy. I'd like you to describe as closely as you can the actual content of what you told this man – whether at your employer's suggestion, or off your own bat. We already know quite a lot of what he's sent back to his Russian contacts, and we need to establish what else there was, and how and where he got such information, true or otherwise. You see

243

what I'm saying?'

'Yes.'

'So...' He gestured for her to take the floor.

'Well... it started with the question of whether America might join us in the war. He was interested in whether our government thought it likely. I'd been advised by Mr Churchill to suggest that we didn't think there was much chance, because your people and the politicians were against it.'

'Why did he advise that?'

'He thought that, if it got to Hitler, it would lull him into a false sense of security. Make it less urgent for him to attack quickly.'

'Go on.'

'Then later, everything became concentrated on whether Russia might be persuaded to change sides, and join us against Germany.'

'What messages did you give your boyfriend about that?'

'I had to tell him that Mr Churchill was an admirer of Stalin. That he thought he had been a strong leader of the Russian people, and that we could do business with him. And, as an incentive, that he felt Russia might have the right to take back old Russian territories after the war.'

'You mean in Poland and the Baltic states?'

'Yes. And also that we suspected that Hitler mistrusted Stalin, and might well turn against him.'

The trace of a smile again. 'Sure. There's never much trust between psychos. Did you mention any evidence for that?'

'Only that we thought Germany was bringing more soldiers up to Poland's border with Russia than seemed necessary.'

'Okay. All good stuff. Go on.'

She had to search her memory. 'Well, Mr Churchill also suggested to me privately that it was likely he was going to be the next Prime Minister, and everyone felt he would win the war for us.'

'Because...?

'Because therefore it would be best for Russia to be on the winning side.'

She sensed Thompson's eyebrows rising at her side.

'Anything else?'

'Not much. We talked a lot about his political beliefs. Why he thought communism was the way to solve the inequality and injustice in the world, and so on.' She glanced at the other two, who were still watching her intently. 'I suppose that's why he felt he needed to give Russia information.'

Statham unfolded his arms. 'Well, whether he was helping solve injustice or not, I couldn't say, but he certainly wasn't helping your side's war effort.'

She felt compelled to comment. 'Wasn't he? Wasn't he right to try and influence Stalin over changing sides?'

'It hasn't had much effect so far, has it, missie? Maybe Stalin will do so, but I guess that depends more on what Hitler does than what tidbits Daniel Mountview might have told him.' His chin lifted. 'Stalin is currently the enemy, and you don't pass information to the enemy.'

'Even though...'

'Even though nothing.' His thick fingers drummed on the table. 'It ain't up to the individual citizen to decide how to conduct international relations in war time.'

She sipped her water, and was silent.

'Well done,' said Thompson as they walked back to the Admiralty. 'You handled that splendidly.'

'Did I?' She walked fast. 'Didn't help Daniel's cause much though, did it?'

He lengthened his stride to keep up. 'That's out of your hands. You did best by being honest.'

She threw him a glance. 'Do you think all that stuff I fed him

245

got through. Would it have made any difference?'

'Who knows, Lucy. It might have. It will have been another small drop in the vast mass of information that governments and leaders acquire, and which helps them make decisions.' He gave a small chuckle as he strode. 'It could even be the one tiny contribution that in the final analysis tipped the scales. You never know - history may one day record that Lucy Armitage, baker's daughter from Cumberland, won the war for us against Nazi Germany.'

She didn't smile. It was small compensation for the pain in her heart.

CHAPTER 36

She was granted access to visit Daniel two days later, in the afternoon. She was told to go alone to the American Embassy in Grosvenor Square. It was a monstrous neo-Georgian building occupying much of one side of the graceful garden square. When she arrived at the entrance desk, she was given an identity badge, deprived of her handbag, and conducted to Senior Officer Jim Statham's office on one of the upper floors. Its wide windows overlooked the big old trees of the square, now losing the last of their autumn leaves.

Statham was alone in the room as she entered, and he ushered her to a chair with the same ingratiating grin.

'Okay, Lucy. So here's what's going to happen. One of my assistants will take you down to see Daniel Mountview, who's being held in the basement. You can have half an hour with him, with my guy in attendance. You can talk to him, but you aren't to make physical contact of any kind, and of course you can't discuss any of the charges or evidence against him. Neither can you tell him anything more of your work at the Admiralty. Do you understand?'

'Yes.'

'I should tell you that he's in a pretty depressed state. I don't know what sort of reception you'll get.'

'Does he know about my... involvement in giving him information?'

'He knows a bit, yeh. His meetings with you were obviously covered in our interrogation, and he soon started to guess that you weren't exactly, let's say, an innocent party – any more than he was.'

'So how much have you told him?'

247

'Just that your people were using you to feed him stuff they wanted him to pass on. We didn't go into detail.'

'What will happen to him?'

'He's being shipped back to the States as soon as we've got a suitable boat going back, or maybe plane. Probably within the next coupla days. Then he'll face trial in the US courts.'

'On charges of espionage?'

'Maybe on charges of treason, depending on whether it's considered it was us, or an ally at war, he was betraying. I dunno, I'm not a criminal lawyer. But he's looking at a good few years in prison.' His expression was sympathetic. 'Are you really fond of him, Lucy?'

She nodded, not trusting herself to speak.

'I'm sorry about that. I guess it's an occupational hazard in cases like this.' That expression again. 'For what it's worth, I don't think he's a bad man. He's highly intelligent, he was doing a good job here, and I believe he was morally driven. He's just deluded.'

'Yes,' she whispered.

'Okay.' He lifted the in-house phone on the desk, and pressed a button. 'She's ready now, Don.' He replaced it. 'Thanks for your cooperation on this, Lucy. I know it's been tough on you.'

She nodded. She was beginning to like him better.

'I gotta say, you did well over this whole business.'

'Thank you.'

'If you ever want a job in the States, let me know. We could use bright girls like you, with contacts in London.'

She smiled. 'I don't think so, Mr Statham. I've had enough of diplomatic intrigues.'

'Yeh, well...'

There was a tap on the door, and one of the younger men who had been present at the earlier interview entered.

'Half an hour, Don,' said Statham. 'And give 'em a bit of space,

248

yeh?'

Don took her to the lift, and they descended to the depths of the building.

He was in a windowless room that housed a table and single chair, narrow bed, wash basin, and little else. He rose from the table as she entered. He was dressed in casual clothes. His face was dull-eyed and impassive.

Her escort stood beside the door as she stood undecided on the other side of the table. Then Daniel turned the chair around, and gestured to it, while he sat on the bed facing her.

'I'm surprised you came,' he said, as she sat. His voice was a little hoarse, as if he was recovering from a cold.

'Why wouldn't I?' she said.

He shrugged. 'Presumably you know why I'm here.'

'Yes.'

'Did you know all along?'

'Only what they told me. I didn't know how much was true.'

'When did they tell you?'

'Quite early on.'

He smiled ruefully, and gave a little sigh. 'And there was I thinking I was playing you. And all the time it was the other way around.'

'Were you just playing me?'

His blue eyes were sincere. 'No, Lucy. Maybe the first date or so... but then it wasn't playing. It was for real.'

'Even though you used all the things I told you?'

'Even though. That was just part of my job. Everything else was sincere.'

'Your job?'

'Well... my assignation.'

'You were being directly instructed from Russia?'

'Indirectly.'

249

The man by the door coughed. She took note of the censure.

'Why, Daniel? Why?'

He was silent for several moments, staring at the floor. 'I thought... I just thought I could make a small difference. America's doing so little in this goddam catastrophe so far, and it seemed to me we should be using our influence more. Unofficially if not officially.'

'But by informing the enemy!'

'I was hoping they wouldn't be the enemy for long. You confirmed that. And I still think...'

'What?'

'Communism has much to offer. Remember what I told you about Karl Marx? This world's in a mess, and no one else is doing anything about it.'

'Well, Stalin is just making it a worse mess. You know he's invaded Finland?'

He nodded slowly. 'I know. It's not working out as I'd hoped – so far. But we still need him on our side. And he won't be there for ever. Russia will have a great future once that man's gone.'

'I like your optimism. But is that really enough to make you turn traitor?'

He lifted his head and gazed at her directly. 'Why did you keep seeing me, if you thought I was a traitor?'

She glanced at the man by the door. He was studiously examining the floor. 'Because I was in love with you,' she murmured simply.

'Because I was your first real lover?'

'No. Because I loved who you were. Underneath.'

He held her eyes. 'Well, if it's any consolation, I loved you too.'

'Really?'

'Yes.'

'A naïve baker's daughter from Cumberland?'

'Not so naïve. You made a fool out of me.'

'I think I've made fools of us both.'

He put his hands together as in prayer. 'You're a great girl, Lucy. You knock spots off all the others I've known.'

She blinked back the tears. He reached one hand out towards her.

'Uh, uh,' came from the door. He retracted it.

'Have you any idea what will happen to you?' she asked.

He shook his head. 'My defence is that I was just trying to help the war effort, so I may get a lighter sentence. But I'll probably go to jail.'

She attempted flippancy. 'Oh well, at least they won't shoot you.'

He responded, 'If America had already joined the war, they probably would've.'

There was a prolonged silence.

'What will you do now?' he asked eventually.

'Carry on. Everything's intensifying at the Admiralty.'

'Churchill obviously thinks a lot of you.'

'No more than the other girls. We're all in what he calls his Secret Circle.'

'But he trusts you with a lot of stuff. As well as serving at crucial dinners.'

'I just happened to be there at the time. Fate.'

'And you just happened to be in the dining hall when I was. Fate.'

Her eyes flashed. 'You were on the hunt for someone like me. That wasn't fate.'

'No. On the hunt, yes. But not expecting to capture the pick of the bunch.'

She took out her handkerchief and dabbed at her tears. She seemed to be using it a lot recently. 'Well, you could never convert me to communism, so perhaps it's for the best.'

'Ah well, we'll just have to see which ideology wins in the end.'

'Yes.' She got up. 'A pity we have to go to war to decide it.'

'Thank you for coming,' he said. 'It would have been terrible if I'd never seen you again.' His own eyes looked moist. 'Have a good life, Lucy.'

'Goodbye.'

The officer by the door averted his eyes as she went past him.

A watery sun was shining as she left the big building. She decided to walk the mile or so back to the Admiralty through Green Park.

London was brazenly displaying its glories in the clear air, the huge trees and green spaces of the park tranquil, oblivious to the foolish brawls of mankind. She felt a strange calm now. The direction of her life was no longer in her hands. She simply had to follow where the world's great tumults took her, and, whatever the outcome, she was content to accept it.

She lengthened her stride, and smiling through her tears, headed for Whitehall.

CHAPTER 37

The months passed. The war rumbled on across the waters, but with little effect within the country, except for increased rationing on various commodities. The armaments and ammunition factories worked at full throttle, the reports of atrocities in the invaded lands of Europe continued to escalate, the diplomatic wranglings filled the airways, Parliament argued and debated the issues with ever more vociferous passion, and the young men and women of Britain trained intensely for the business of lethal combat.

Winston Churchill remained as immersed and as interfering as ever in all aspects, becoming seemingly sharper and more energised with each task. His small team of secretaries worked frantically to keep up with his prodigious output.

Lucy went about her business, grateful that the intensity prevented her from dwelling too much on the ache in her heart. The longing for Daniel continued, drifting in the background like a passing surf wave. Thrilling, but she knew never to return. And, like waves, there would be others to come.

She was given a few days break at Christmas, and went home to her family, where she relaxed and recuperated in the familiar surroundings, whilst at the same time realising that she had outgrown them, and would probably never be able to settle back there in the future. Her father and mother, so thrilled to have her back, seemed to have aged in the intervening months, and her brother Tommy, returned on leave and with two stripes on his arm, was now a mature soldier who also was permanently altered by his experiences in the military camps. She saw Henry too, briefly. But he was a similarly changed person. Serious, grim, detached. Any romantic connection was far from both their thoughts.

Then it was, one weekday in May, back in London, that Lucy was summoned as usual to Winston's study to take dictation from him. The news on the wireless that morning had been calamitous. The armies of the Third Reich had invaded the Low Countries with an immense force, sweeping aside all opposition, and were now spreading into northern France in contravention of every agreement and treaty previously agreed to. The phoney war was over.

She found Churchill seated at his desk, the customary pile of papers scattered across it, the telephone to his ear, Rufus in full attention. He waved her in as he spoke.

'...yes, yes, but what do the other parties say? Are they all now willing to drop their opposition and their petty prejudices, no matter who leads, and come together for the sake of national unity? It is vital that they do, David, so you are key to this. You must cajole, bully, and blackmail every man-jack of them to that end. I trust in your valiant efforts.'

He put down the phone. 'The Chief Whip,' he growled at Lucy, although she had guessed as much. He heaved himself from his chair, picked up his inevitable glass of iced whisky, and began his preamble up and down the room. As always it presaged a major piece of dictation.

'This is the moment, Lucy dear. This is the moment when destiny finally calls me to account.'

She waited, pencil and pad at the ready. But they were not yet called upon.

He went on. 'The monster Hitler is invading France. The Prime Minister is going to resign. I am going to a meeting this afternoon, where it will be decided who is to take his place. It is not yet certain, but if it is me then I will immediately address Parliament. The speech will be a vital one. It has to bring together all parties and all factions. It has to prepare our government and our people for the ordeal to come. It must inspire them to yet greater efforts in this titanic struggle. We must have our words ready. They cannot be left to chance or improvisation.' He picked up a cigar stub and continued to prowl, chewing. Lucy and Rufus waited. Eventually he stopped, and signed for her to write.

'I say to the House, as I said to ministers who have joined this government, I have nothing to offer but blood, toil, tears, and sweat. We have before us an ordeal of the most grievous kind. We have before us many, many months of struggle and suffering. You ask, what is our policy? I say it is to wage war by land, sea, and air. War with all our might, and with all the strength God has given us. And to wage war against a tyrant... No – against a monstrous tyranny has never been surpassed in the dark and lamentable catalogue of human crime. That is our policy.' He paced again, cigar waving, iced glass clinking. 'You ask, what is our aim? I can answer in one word. It is victory. Victory at all costs. Victory in spite of all terrors. Victory, however long and hard the road may be. For without victory there is no survival. Let that be realized. No survival for the British Empire, no survival for all that the British Empire has stood for, no survival for the... the urge, the impulse of the ages, that humanity... No, not humanity... that mankind shall move forward toward his goal. I take up my task in buoyancy and hope. I feel sure that our cause will not be suffered to fail among men. I feel entitled at this juncture, at this time, to claim the aid of all and to say, come then, let us go forward together with our united strength.'

The flow stopped, he stood silent, glass in one hand, stub in the other, pondering. Then he nodded.

'Yes. I will do a preamble, explaining the immediate administrative measures I must take, but that will do as my appeal. That will be my exhortation. What do you think, Lucy?'

'I think it's magnificent, sir.'

'Hm. Well, if it doesn't do the trick, there is little hope for any of us. Go and type it up.'

As she went to the door his voice stopped her.

'Lucy.'

'Yes, Winston?'

'If I do find myself in Downing Street, may I hope that you will accompany me as part of my team?'

'Of course.'

'Good, good. Need all the help I can muster.'

'As long as I won't have to wait at table.'

His deep chuckle. 'I think I can promise there won't be many dinner parties there. Not for a long time.'

She smiled at him, and left.

Her head was erect on her long neck, her eyes lined a little now, but bright. As she traversed the wide corridors she had the erect, self-possessed walk that was the norm amongst the inhabitants there, so different from the countryman's trudge around the undulating wilds of the Cumberland countryside. The hills and the lakes would always be there, slumbering in her subconscious. But now she had experience of public affairs, political affairs, and love affairs. She was a woman of the world, and whether the end might come through bombs, bullets, or a broken heart, she had at least properly lived. She was her own person. And she could feel the inspiration of his words deep within her own being. The certainty of rightness.

Milton Keynes UK
Ingram Content Group UK Ltd.
UKHW020937081124
450926UK00012BB/596

9 781738 423125